# Nicholas

by Michael J. Scott

# NICHOLAS

By
Michael J. Scott

PUBLISHED BY:
ICHABOD

Nicholas
Copyright © 2015 by Michael J. Scott

ISBN-13: 978-1516857203
ISBN-10:1516857208

To Sarah, David, and Rachel,
for all the cloud-factories you showed me.

"I am the resurrection and the life; he who believes in Me will live even if he dies, and everyone who lives and believes in Me will never die. Do you believe this?" – John 11:25-26

 **One**

Gunfire rattled my ears, sending me scurrying for cover. My camera banged against my chest and fell away, dangling precipitously over the edge of the building. For a moment, I thought the strap would break and send it careening into the rubble below. That would mean a broken lens, at best. I reached for it and lost my hold on the ledge. I started to tip over.

A hand snagged my shirt from behind, yanking me backward to the deck. The camera flew with me, catching the bridge of my nose as I hit the floor. I saw stars.

A face appeared above me. Lance Corporal Grissom. He must've pulled me back. "Thanks," I muttered.

"What are you? Crazy?"

A trickle of blood ran down my cheek from where the camera had gashed my face. I wiped it away, thinking, *I must be.*

"Keep your head down. They'll shoot at anything that moves."

I grabbed the camera and lifted it. "So will I." The retort sounded ridiculous as soon as I uttered it.

Grissom sneered. "Yeah, but your shooting don't kill. Theirs does. Try to remember that." He turned away from me and raised his M16 over the barricade, squeezing off a spate of rounds at the mujahedeen pinned down in a house across the street.

I'd been embedded within the ranks of this unit for almost six months now, collecting photos and anecdotes to send to the paper back home. Despite the near constant danger, this was the closest to death I'd come yet. I could just hear the gossip about my demise back home.

*"He died filming the combat?"*

*"No. He died tripping over his own feet."*

*"Well, ain't that just like Davis?"*

*Not today,* I told myself. *Not for a long time to come.* I turned over to my knees and crept back to the edge, hoping the shot I'd been angling for was still available. I peered over the side even as I lifted the camera to my eyes, seeking the squad of soldiers diligently setting up the mortar round that would take out the house. A sudden *whump!* blew air across my face. Inadvertently, my thumb depressed the button. I ducked back down, studying the photo.

Incredible. I'd actually caught the blurry mortar as it left its launcher. Might not be the best shot for the paper, but it was a one a million regardless. Behind me, a sudden explosion deafened all else. And then, impossibly, the gunfire stopped.

A cheer broke out from the ranks beside me. I caught Grissom raising his defiant fist toward the now obliterated structure, a rebel yell tearing from his throat. I snapped another photo, and then several more of the smoking ruin that had been their target.

Grissom turned to me, "You got it?"

I showed him the photos. He swore. "God must be looking out for you."

I grinned. "That's just skill, Lance Corporal. God's got nothing to do with it."

"Don't tell Him that. He might not keep you around."

I waved him off and he rejoined his companions. The squad congratulated each other and hurried off the roof to inspect the remains of the snipers' nest. I watched them depart, then lay back against the surface of the roof, just grateful to be alive.

Less than a week later, I was back in New York. Greeted with cheers like a returning hero, I walked—no strutted—into my editor's office feeling like the planets had finally aligned for me. My status as the star reporter for the Uptown Free Press was guaranteed, and my career never looked brighter.

I couldn't have been more wrong.

"The paper's been sold."

"What?" I looked up, uncertain I'd heard him right. Marshall Severn was known to have a caustic sense of humor, one that leached into his editorials about city politics on a regular basis. But as I regarded him now, I saw nothing in the dull resignation of his face that confirmed this feeble theory. Heavy bags hung beneath his eyes, making him look perpetually exhausted. It wasn't far from the truth.

"Deal went through last Thursday, just before you got back." He rose and stood before his espresso machine, offering me a cup as well. Usually, I'd decline, arguing that I was quitting.

Today felt like I might need one after all.

"We haven't announced it yet," he continued, pouring the shots, "but it's a done deal. I wanted you to know before you heard it through the grapevine. Rumor mill's been spinning like a top."

He handed me the demitasse cup.

"So what's it mean?"

"Good news is, you still have a job. Rest of the staff is getting cut about thirty percent."

I closed my eyes and swore, trying to guess who'd be gone by the end of the year. "Just in time for Christmas."

"Yeah. It gets better. New owners want to take the paper in a different direction. They want us to write positive news stories."

I'd thrown back the shot of espresso and almost choked when he said this. "They do know this is New York, right?"

He grimaced like he tasted bile. "That's just what I said. They wouldn't listen. They want to renew the news business. Change the way things get done. Change everything. Change the city, if you can believe that. I said, 'We don't make the news. We just tell it like it is.' You know what they said to me? They said, and I quote, 'No more blood on page one.' As if everything that goes wrong in this town is somehow our fault."

"How they gonna sell papers?" Every newsman knows, if it bleeds, it leads.

Marshall shook his head. "Let's just say they're kinda new to the news business."

"Ya think?"

He shrugged and gave me a hopeless smile. I stood and paced to the window, staring down at the hard concrete of the street below. "I give us six months and we're under."

"We're going down anyway. Whole business is in the toilet."

I thought of the thirty percent, and started wondering whether or not they got the raw end of the deal. "Is it too late to get fired?"

"No. But it is too late for the good severance package."

I handed back the cup and frowned. "What are we gonna do?"

Marshall opened his desk drawer. "Funny you should ask."

The assignment Marshall handed me was unlike anything I'd ever done before, and I'd written up some pretty strange assignments in my time. In fact, my recent stint in Afghanistan was the most normal thing I'd done in years.

I've written about the lives of basketball superstars and the janitorial staff in the same article, just to show they're both human. I've investigated city politics and the sanitation practices of upscale restaurants, not that there's much difference between the two. Both are more for show than for cleanliness.

I've never been afraid to get my hands dirty. And like I'd told Grissom, God had nothing to do with it. Couldn't imagine the Big Guy sticking His hands down in the filth I dealt with. I meant that literally.

There was the time Marshall sent me into the sewers to explore life as a subterranean urban dweller. I took that to mean investigating the bums, what we euphemistically called "the homeless people" in polite company. I spent six weeks living under ground with the rats and other forms of subhuman life, and by the time I was done I had enough material to write up a major exposé on the city's homeless problem. Presciently, that prepared me for my next assignment: touring the inner workings of the mayor's office. I think he—the mayor—intended it as a political ploy, an answer to my story on the homeless—a way to show the city what he was doing about the problem. Of course, writing a report on the mayor's financial double-dealings hadn't helped buff his image any. He dropped twenty points in the polls after that, and lost the election.

I'm sorta convinced that sending me to Kabul was the former mayor's idea—some strings he'd pulled with the previous owners in the hopes I'd get shot over there. All I know is that Marshall barely cracked a smile when I joked about it. I told myself he was just worried for me. The old softy.

But this! This assignment took the cake. Given the recent staff cuts—ostensibly to save money—I was both surprised and put off by the trip. Surely, the money could be better spent elsewhere. Not that they'd exactly splurged on my travel arrangements, or accommodations, for that matter.

I stared out the window of the Bombardier Dash 8 turboprop at the web of snow and granite that formed the ground far below. Jagged breaks of rock rose to craggy peaks above the irregular inlets of the north fjords, with tiny fishing villages and hamlets tucked against the shorelines far below. We flew above a particularly long channel dotted by small islands, and approached the airport from the southwest.

As we neared the landing strip, I saw blocks of slate gray roofs of homes around narrow streets that made me think of the housing tract where I grew up. I hadn't been in New York long enough to rent an apartment, and now here I was on a plane over northern Europe, heading to an airstrip in Hammerfest, Norway.

We touched down, and in moments I deboarded into the terminal and went inside to the baggage claim. The entire airport looked like it was little more than a large cinderblock with windows. I shook my head. Such a small city couldn't command anything larger.

Certainly not this far north.

After retrieving my luggage and picking up a map (in case my

GPS went out. It happens) and an English-Norwegian dictionary, I rented a car and set off on my "adventure."

Finding a monastery this far out proved to be a bit of a challenge, and it was nearing dark by the time I finally pulled to the side of the road beside a lonely sign that read, "*Kloster* 5 Kilometer *Fremover*."

I knew from looking for the past five hours that the *Kloster* was just what I wanted. For a moment, I wondered if "*Fremover*" wasn't a town until I consulted my dictionary, and realized it meant "Forward." The monastery was five kilometers ahead.

I turned down the narrow road and drove the remaining miles to my destination.

Arriving at the *Kloster av St. Nikolas*, I felt utterly underwhelmed by what I saw. Five large buildings with red tile roofs and whitewashed walls stood three and four stories within a copse of barren trees, looking much like some of the wineries I grew up around in my native Finger Lakes region of upstate New York. A stone wall rose alongside the road, with an arch over a narrow path barely large enough for my car. Despite the cold, I unrolled the windows on either side and pulled in the mirrors before squeezing the car through the passage. The path before me wound uphill in a generally straight direction until it spilled out onto a stone surface I took to be a parking lot. I shut off the car and was rolling up the windows when a door opened in what I assumed was the main building. A barrel-chested man in a thick monk's robe plodded out to see me through the blanket of snow. He clutched a flashlight in one hand and with the other held onto a rope that had been tethered to an eye-bolt in the wall.

"*God kveld*," he said when he reached my car. "*Kan jeg hjelpe deg?*"

"Uh," I fumbled for the dictionary before giving up the attempt. "I'm sorry. Uh, *sn-snakke engelsk?*" I hoped I pronounced that right.

He grinned. "Yah. Better than you speak Norwegian."

"I'm looking for the Abbot."

"Ah! The reporter, yah?"

I nodded and stuck out my hand. "Brett Davis. Uptown Free Press."

He shook my palm. "I am Brother Don. Welcome to Norway."

"Thanks." I felt tired from the flight and more than a little cranky. Still, I tried to keep the edge from my voice. I climbed out of the car and retrieved my luggage from the trunk, demurring when he offered to carry it for me. "It's okay. I've got it. Learned a long time ago to pack light." I followed him to the building, grateful to be getting out of the cold. As we neared the door, I asked, "What's with the rope?"

"The winds and snow blow sometimes so fiercely that you cannot see even your hand in front of your face. The rope keeps us tethered to civilization."

I stared doubtfully at what he called civilization. "It's not snowing now."

He gave me another grin. "It is best not to get into the habit of letting go of the rope."

"Good tip."

When we entered the room, I was immediately struck by the warmth and by how clean the building smelled. Not a sterile, hospital kind of clean—but an earthy, organic clean that suggested hospitality and food. My stomach rumbled. I took off my coat, grateful to be relieved of its weight. Brother Don hung it from a hook for me.

"I can have your bag taken to your room," he said. "Dinner has already been served, but if you haven't eaten, I'm sure we can provide something. The Abbot is entertaining one of our members at the moment, but he has asked to see you as soon as you arrived."

"I see."

Brother Don's face grew serious. "I must insist, however, that you keep your voice down. The man is quite sick and ah, well, needs his rest."

"Oh. Sure. It's not anything catching, is it?"

"No. Nothing more than you or I will face ourselves some day. He's dying, you see."

"I'm sorry to hear that."

"It's a journey we all must take. Well, most of us anyway."

I frowned at this and wondered what he meant, but the man

10

moved past me, leading the way down the hall toward a staircase. He brought me up to the second floor and to a room at the end of a narrow corridor. He gently rapped twice, and then depressed the latch, holding the door open for me. With a glance in his direction for reassurance, I entered the room. Brother Don closed the door behind me.

The room couldn't have been much larger than twelve foot square, with a narrow bed against one wall and a pair of hard back wooden chairs set against opposite walls. An oil lamp glistened on a bedside table. In the bed, a gaunt, wizened old man lay with blankets pulled up to his chin, propped up by several pillows. His eyes were closed, and he was breathing shallowly.

Despite the cleanliness of the monastery, I smelled death in this room—a sickly sweet smell seeping from the man's pores.

Gingerly, I approached the bed, wondering whether or not I should wake him, at least let him know I was here, if not find out why I was here. Marshall sent me to interview the Abbot, but how was I supposed to do that if he wasn't awake and talking?

The door opened behind me, and another monk came through. He wasn't nearly as stocky as Brother Don, and he sported a carefully trimmed silver beard and equally silver hair that contrasted with Don's clean-shaven face and head. I pegged him around fifty. In his hands he carried a teapot and a pair of cups.

"He's sleeping?" He moved to stand beside me, studying the man in bed. "Good. Though I doubt he'd be pleased if I didn't wake him and tell him you're here. He's been so looking forward to your arrival."

"Has he?"

"Hmm. The strings we had to pull to fulfill a dying man's wish. You have no idea. But a promise is a promise. Would you like to sit?"

He set the pitcher and cups down on the nightstand and nodded toward the chairs. I brought them both over to the side of the bed and sat across from him.

"Well. Shall we get started?"

I pulled out my notebook and recorder, propping it on the nightstand beside the water, and nodded that I was ready.

After an awkward silence, the monk said, "Did you want to start with a question?"

I glanced from him to the sleeping form on the bed. "Shouldn't we wake him?"

He waved him off and grinned. "Nah. Let him sleep. I'll face his wrath later."

I furrowed my brow."I'm sorry. I thought I was here to interview the Abbot."

"Yes."

I motioned to the old man with my pen. A chuckled erupted from the monk. "Apologies! This is Brother Oleg. I am the Abbot. You may call me Nicholas. Or Nick, if you prefer."

I grinned. "Like the monastery."

"Exactly."

"I was told I'd be interviewing a man named Christopher."

He waved a hand. "A common error. Christopher is my title. It means 'Christ-bearer.' But I've long given up any interest in titles."

"I see. So he wanted me to interview *you*."

"Yes. His last request. Insisted on it, in fact. I reminded him the last time we did this, it didn't go over so well. But he was adamant, and who am I to refuse such an appeal?"

"I naturally assumed he was Abbot because he was older."

The Abbot snorted. "Things work differently around here."

"My mistake. Why don't we start with your childhood?"

"My childhood." The Abbot looked at his hands. "Have you ever seen the Mediterranean?"

I nodded.

"Mostly what I remember about my childhood is the smell of the sea. The warmth of the sun on my face. And my mother's smile. It was all so very long ago. I treasure this memory, more than almost anything since—save when I came to know my Lord and received my calling. Before we continue, there are some things you must understand. The tale I'm about to relate is one you will not believe. Not in your wildest imagination could it possibly be true. It is the singular reason I do not grant interviews such as this—or seek them out, except on the insistence of my young friend here."

He tapped the old man's arm. He was doubtless being ironic.

"I am therefore going to ask that you wait until the tale is done before passing judgment. You are a war correspondent. Is that correct?"

"True. I was recently in Afghanistan."

He nodded. "A difficult part of the world. In this capacity, you must have learned to hold your questions and let things play out—simply recording your observations. Would that be fair?"

"Reasonable."

"Then for me you must do the same. The story I give you is a story of war, and of woe, and ultimately, of triumph as well. Will you do that?"

"Certainly." He had my curiosity piqued. I had to see where he was going with this.

"Very well," he nodded. "Then let's begin. I was born in the village of Patara. My parents were neither poor nor wealthy. Well-off, I suppose you would call it today, though for our little village, he was the richest man they knew. My father owned a tiny fleet of ships, and made his living plying trade with merchants and others."

"Any siblings?" I interrupted.

He smiled and shook his head. "I was an only child. My mother, Nona, often said I was an answered prayer. They'd been childless for such a long time. I was named for my uncle— himself the local bishop and founder of the New Zion monastery.

My parents raised me in the faith, and it was the only thing that sustained me when they died. I still remember that terrible day. I was only fifteen years old..."

 **Two**

Nicky sat up abruptly, his breath caught in his throat, a sheen of sweat over his olive skin. He listened for a moment to the sounds emanating from the outside. Birds chirped in trees rustled by the wind. The waves of the Great Sea crashed against the sandy beach a half mile away. And distantly, he could hear the sounds of the market as merchants and customers haggled over prices. His room was set nearest the door to the family home, though in truth he could have had any room he'd wished but for the one in which his parents slept. Despite countless prayers, his parents had never been able to grant him any siblings, which meant the *domus* they lived in remained largely empty, except for those times when Mother or Father would open their home to strangers, travelers seeking lodging, or the occasional itinerant preacher.

But no guests inhabited their *domus* of late. Except for the plague. That was the only company they kept these days.

Nicky swung his legs over the side of the bed and listened more carefully. It was still early, but something had woken him. Quiet as a shadow, he rose and shuffled to the door, then opened it slowly and peered into the room.

A solitary figure sat in the atrium, the pale light from the *compluvium* reflecting off the man's bald head. Even from where Nicky stood, he could tell the man was praying. It wasn't so surprising. Many people came and prayed at the *domus* these days. Begging God for mercy. For healing. For answers. Sometimes, they thought they heard from the Lord. Most times, their prayers went unanswered, almost as if unheard. Still, they kept praying, as this man did now.

Nicky watched him a moment, leaning against the portal, his hands resting on the smooth surface of the column.

No, not praying. Weeping.

Nicky slipped into the atrium and cautiously approached. As he came around the side, he recognized him. "Uncle?"

His uncle lifted his head, smiling sadly back at him. "Nicky. I didn't want to wake you."

Nicky swallowed. "Uncle, what's wrong? Why do you weep so?"

His uncle nodded toward his parents' room. "Your father and mother—" he began.

"Has God healed them?"

His uncle flinched. "He's called them home."

Nicky frowned. "No. That cannot be." His uncle smiled sadly. "But—we prayed. We asked God for healing. We—" Uncle Nicholas reached out for him, clutching at his hand. Nicky pulled back. "No! They're not dead! They're not!"

He flew past the man, ignoring his calls, and raced to the door to his parent's bedroom. He grabbed the latch, and his hand froze there, as if it had a mind of its own.

Did he really want to see what lay on the other side of this door?

His uncle came up behind him, gently laid his hands on Nicky's shoulders. "Don't see this, Nicky," he whispered, and then let go.

Nicky's hand trembled. His vision blurred with tears. He wanted to ask 'Why,' but already knew the question was pointless. The Lord in His indefinable wisdom and mercy had decreed it so, and who was he to question the will of God?

"H-how?" He swallowed against the lump in his throat. "How did they—"

"In their sleep. Holding hands!"

Nicky turned and flung himself into his uncle's arms, letting his grief wash out his eyes and run down his cheeks, wracking his body with sobs. The two of them stayed there a while, clinging to one another.

And clinging to faith.

"What will you do?"

Nicky dried his eyes with the back of his hand, and pulled

away to look at his uncle. The question unnerved him. *What shall I do?*

His father's servants were in the bedroom now, gently washing and wrapping their bodies for burial, ever mindful of the death that stalked them in doing so. Already, a steady stream of mourners had come to pay their respects, and Nicky had dutifully stood by as they swept by him, their faces and words blending into one another till he could no longer tell them apart. The priest of Patara had scheduled the funeral for the next day, apologizing profusely for the delay, but there were so many other families who'd lost loved ones to the plague. Uncle Nicholas had taken care of everything, conferring with Epiphanius, the steward of his father's house, and sparing Nicky many of the unpleasant details. But now he stood before Nicky, and the question he asked had nothing to do with the funeral.

Uncle Nicholas must have taken Nicky's silence for confusion. "All that Theo and Nona worked so hard for is now yours. His ships. The house. The money."

"I want none of it," Nicky whispered, finding his voice. "I'd give it all away if I could have them back again."

"As would I, were it mine to give. But that is not for us to say or decide. What we must do is decide what to do with what is left to us."

"And what should I do?" He searched his uncle's eyes.

"It is not my decision. Seek the Lord. Ask Him what you

19

should do."

"I would rather have your counsel. The Lord has not seen fit to answer my prayers of late."

"Nicky," Uncle chided, "do not add to their tragedy by wavering in unbelief now. Theo and Nona raised you better than this."

"I want to believe." His lip trembled, though no new tears would come. He'd cried himself dry. "But how can I in the face of this?"

"It is a severe test of faith, to lose your parents when you are so young. And those whom the Lord chastens so severely, He does so out of His great love. And those whom He loves so greatly, He also intends for great things."

"So your counsel is that I should do great things for God?"

The hint of a sad smile flickered on his uncle's lips. "No. My counsel is that God intends to do great things through you. Yield yourself to Him. Give yourself wholly unto the work of the kingdom, and in such a way you will honor your father and mother with riches that are far greater than any they've left you in this world."

Nicky let his arms fall. He turned and surveyed the house, taking in the rich ochre of the columns supporting the roof, the verdant greens of the frescoes on the walls. The scenes depicted the pastures behind the *domus*, where his father's field hands— no, where *his* field hands—worked the fields, growing food for

his family and for the poor of Patara. What would become of
them now? Could he, Nicky, really carry on his father's legacy?

A new thought entered his mind, then. If all God wanted was
his father's legacy to continue as it was, then would not the Lord
have been better served by keeping his father alive and at his
task? He shook his head. No, if what Uncle Nicholas said was true,
then God intended more for Nicky than this.

Long before he could walk or understand, his parents had
dedicated him to God. Perhaps the Lord intended to claim his
soul now.

A sense of peace filled him then, and he knew now that he
was right. "Uncle," he said, "I would come and live with you at the
monastery. I would become a devoted brother as you are. But my
parent's generosity and kindness cannot be left to wither and
die. Too many in this community have depended on them."

"The poor—" his uncle began.

"Not just the poor," he interrupted, "but those in my father's
employ as well. Whole livelihoods are built upon my father's
prosperity beyond his simple generosity. My father always
taught me the wealthy bear great responsibility. They not only
open their hand and give generously to the poor, but they also
support those in their employ, and even the community and the
magistrates depend upon their wealth for taxes." He heaved a
breath. "I cannot simply walk away from that responsibility."

Uncle nodded. "A conundrum."

Nicky blinked. It wasn't a conundrum. Not really. His eyes flickered upward, catching Uncle's patient gaze. "Would you be so kind as to call Epiphanius to come see me at his earliest convenience?"

Epiphanius came to him in the atrium later that evening, apologizing for the delay. Nicky waved it off. "It is no matter. Did you bring what I asked?"

Epiphanius readily handed over several scrolls. "The deeds and record of your father's accounts, including the list of those who still owe him money."

He unfurled the scrolls, laying them out on the low table so Nicky could see. Nicky glanced up at the sky, visible through the *compluvium*, and wished the man had come sooner. The sun was setting, and banded streaks of gold and magenta were fading into slate blue. It'd be too dark to see in less than an hour.

"Let's start with debts," Nicky said. "How much harm would come to the household if these remain unpaid?"

"Harm, sir?"

Nicky almost flinched. Epiphanius had never called him by his formal title. He only used that for Nicky's father. He cleared his. "Would we be unable to pay wages, or buy food or other supplies?"

Epiphanius cocked his head a moment, then shook it firmly. "No. We could absorb the loss."

"Good. Cancel them."

"Sir?"

"The debts. Cancel them all. No one should owe a debt to a dead man. It is impossible to repay."

"As you say, sir." Epiphanius began making the notations.

"And now the fields, and the house. Are they sufficient? Can they sustain the current outlays without the ships?"

"I don't quite understand—"

"I want to know whether or not the ships must be used to support the household, or if instead there is sufficient income from our fields to sustain our staff."

"It would suffice."

"Excellent. Last question: is there someone among our staff that you trust? Someone with ability, who could do as you do?"

Epiphanius's jaw slackened, as if he'd forgotten how to use it.

Nicky folded his hands and rested them on his knees. "I mean to relieve you of your position."

Epiphanius's face lost color. "Sir, your father was always satisfied with my service."

"Indeed. He spoke highly of you. Said he knew of none better, in fact. That's why I'm doing this."

"H-have I disappointed you? Offended you in some way?"

"Quite the contrary." Nicky reached across and took the

man's hand, conscious of the callouses and strength Epiphanius bore. Still, the man's hand trembled in his grasp. Nicky suspected he was skirting the edge of cruelty. "You have always been dear to my parents and to me. Therefore you are no longer steward of my father's house." He reached his other hand down and offered Epiphanius the deed. "You are now its owner."

Epiphanius put his hand over his heart, the look of shock on his face utterly priceless. Nicky couldn't resist a smile. The steward shook his head. "Nicky, you cannot give me this."

"I can and I have. I only ask that you retain everyone in their current employ, for at least a year, and then conduct the business of this house as you will. You are a rich man, now. Remember the poor."

"But what about you?"

"I will be joining my uncle at New Zion, and when I am ready, taking vows. My father and mother have done a great and mighty thing, caring for the people of this town. I entrust that work now to your care, in hopes you will carry on the tradition."

"Gladly. Most gladly I shall!" he exclaimed. Nicky nodded and gathered the remaining papers together. Epiphanius caught his hand. "And what of your father's ships?"

"I have my own plans for them. I will see you at the funeral on the morrow, and then I shall take my leave of you."

"You will always be welcome here."

"Thank you, but I don't think I shall be coming back."

24

That evening, Nicky shut the door to his room and set the oil lamp he carried on a small table. The first task was done. Tomorrow would be the funeral, and then he would finish divesting himself of his father's wealth.

*Well,* he amended, setting the scrolls on the table beside the lamp, *of his father's ships, at least.*

He unfurled the ledger of his father's accounts, staring at the figure written in the last place, in Epiphanius's careful scrawl. The sum was substantial, even after Epiphanius had adjusted the tally to account for the forgiven debts. He wondered if Uriah the banker even had such a sum on hand. The Jew lent money out at interest to those in need, and paid less interest than he received to those who, like Nicky's father, entrusted their money to his care. Nicky recalled that his mother often expressed distaste for the whole business, but Theophanes insisted that usury wasn't as bad as it was made out to be, and that the Jew provided a valuable service to the community.

Nicky could only imagine the difficulty that would ensue if he cashed in his father's note all at once. Doubtless Uriah would feel compelled to call in his other debts to shore up his depleted accounts, and that would create hardship for those least able to afford it.

No, the wise thing to do was proceed slowly, perhaps by thirds or even fourths, withdrawing the money in stages so as to give the banker time to recoup his losses without rupturing the delicate balance of credit.

He rolled up the scroll and put it away, and was about to blow out the lamp when his gaze fell upon the tiny wooden ship his father had carved for him when Nicky was only six. It was a gift to remind Nicky of the strength of the vessels that carried Theophanes on those rare occasions when he went to sea himself, so that Nicky wouldn't worry. He'd always treasured this toy above all other things.

He picked it up now, gently running his finger over the tiny lines of the carefully whittled gunwales and the slender mast in the center. If only a ship like this had been able to carry his father and mother through the sickness. He put it down quickly. It slipped off the table and fell to the floor, where the mast broke off.

Nicky felt his heart clutch, and he bent down, carefully picking the pieces off the floor. Perhaps he could repair it...

An angry snarl curled his lip. It was just a stupid toy! Of what use was it? He hurled it out the window. It sailed over the sill and vanished into the brush on the other side.

The words of Saint Paul flickered in his mind then, and he spoke them aloud. "When I was a child. I spoke as a child, thought like a child, reasoned like a child. When I became a man, I did away with childish things."

His parents were dead. And now so was the child Nicky used to be. Toys were useless and benefited no one. He had more pressing matters to address.

A heaviness pressed down upon him, and he crawled onto his mat and blew out his lamp.

Sleep was a long time coming.

I held up my hand, impatient to interrupt but regretting it all the same. "I'm sorry. I just have a quick question, if I may."

The Abbot's eyes crinkled, and he gave me a bemused smile. He pulled back into his chair and folded his hands, waiting.

"It's about the timeline." Really, it was about a lot of things he'd said, but the timing of all this concerned me at present. I'd never heard of Patara and wondered where it was, and why life there sounded so idyllic, so Greek, and, well, ancient.

"And what about the timeline?" The Abbot seemed to know what troubled me, but was waiting for me to say so.

I cleared my throat. "How old are you?"

"It depends."

"On?"

"On how you reckon time. Or when you choose to start counting."

"Most people start from the day of their birth."

"Not to be impertinent, but again, I could ask which one. You could mean to ask when I was born from my mother, or more importantly, when I was born from my Father."

I sighed. The allusion wasn't lost on me. Not completely anyway. I had done enough time in Sunday School to recognize the idea of being 'born again.' What concerned me then was the fact that this man was choosing to be so evasive.

It could only mean one thing: he didn't want talk about it. At least, not yet anyway. I could press the issue, and risk being shown the door. Or I could let him share what he would in his own time.

I'm experienced enough as a reporter to know the answer to that question, and restraining my over-developed curiosity is a critical job skill—almost as critical as the curiosity itself.

"Fine then. I withdraw the question."

"I did ask you to refrain from asking."

"So you did. My apologies. Please, continue."

He opened his mouth to speak, but we were interrupted by a moan from the bed. Brother Oleg opened his eyes. Nick immediately turned and gave him his full attention, checking his temperature with the back of his hand and taking his pulse.

"Welcome back," Nick said.

"Yah? Did I die?"

"No," he laughed softly. "Not yet anyway."

𝔑𝔦𝔠𝔥𝔬𝔩𝔞𝔰        Michael J. Scott

Oleg nodded. "I thought I would remember if I had."

"I'm sure you would."

Oleg's eyes flickered to me, then back again. "Who's this?"

"The reporter you asked for. His name is Davis."

"Brett Davis." I offered him my hand. "Uptown Free Press."

Oleg's hand moved slowly to take my own, but his mind seemed as sharp as ever. He glared reprovingly at the Abbot. "And you didn't wake me?"

"I thought you should sleep."

"Yah, you rascal!" He shook my hand. "How much have I missed?"

"Not much," I said. "The Abbot was telling me about his childhood."

"Hasn't he gotten to the story of the three maidens?"

I eyed the Abbot, wondering who the three maidens were and how they might figure into his tale. Certain automatic suspicions seemed curiously out of place at the moment.

"Hush now," the Abbot chided. "You'll spoil it."

"Well then? What are you waiting for? Get on with it." Brother Oleg winked at me. "This is my favorite part."

29

# Three

Nicky's uncle sent for him early the next morning, when the sun's rays had barely brightened the eastern sky. Nicky met him in the door and brought him in to break their fast together. He offered his uncle salted bread, milk, and some eggs. Uncle smiled, accepting the offer, and then pointed out the obvious. "We don't eat so well at the monastery."

Nicky paused, the bread partway to his mouth. His uncle waved him on. "Go ahead. You're not at New Zion yet."

Nicky chewed thoughtfully. "This will take some getting used to."

"Mmm. You always have had a hearty appetite."

Nicky smiled at his uncle's girth. "I can see it runs in the family."

Uncle smiled. "Your mother says this is why I visit so often. I told her, 'If God did not mean me to be fat, He would not have let my brother marry such a good cook.'" Then he laughed, a great, mirthful sound erupting from his chest. "Ah, forgive me, Nicky. I should not laugh on this day."

Nicky put his hands in his lap and stared at the food on his plate. "Today we put my parents in the ground. And here I am

eating their bread and drinking the milk of their labor." He
pushed the plate away.

Uncle frowned. "Is this grief? Or is it guilt?"

"I don't know. But you are right. We should not laugh on this
day." He rose from the table and went outside. His uncle followed
after him.

"Come with me, Nicky. I want to show you something."

Uncle led him out through the front gate and along a wide
street through the town, giving polite greetings to those
shopkeepers and merchants who knew them well, and letting
Nicky receive the condolences that were mentioned with such
grave earnestness.

At long last, Uncle took him down a side street to a stretch of
ramshackle apartments in a two-story *insula* Nicky did not
recognize. Here, he drew him to a stop and had him wait beside
the wall. Just around the corner, a young maiden was feeding the
chickens that squawked and scurried in the tiny yard behind one
of the apartments.

"Listen," Uncle said. "What do you hear?"

"I assume you don't mean the chickens."

Uncle snorted and shook his head.

"She is singing," Nicky replied, and hazarded a glance around
the corner. The woman had a nice voice, and while not
remarkably beautiful like the high-born ladies of the magistrate's
court, was still pretty in her own way.

31

"Yes. Singing." Uncle raised his eyebrows. "What do you think? Is she happy or sad?"

"I do not know. Happy, I suppose."

"Mmm. And what if I told you that she lost her own mother not two days ago? Would you still think her happy? Don't answer yet. Her father is poor. He has managed to stave off the creditors, but it is only a matter of time before they are forced to leave the *insula*. This girl is the eldest of three. She ought to be the first to marry, and indeed, has a willing suitor. But her father cannot offer him a dowry. The money that was meant to be her wedding gift was instead spent on the medicine for her mother, who died anyway. If the girl cannot provide a dowry, she is liable to lose her beau to another. Moreover, her father spent so much time caring for his ailing wife that his business has suffered, and he has no ready means to recover. There is a real possibility that he will lose everything—and might even be sold as a slave himself. Worse, his daughters may be sold as prostitutes to pay his debt. So tell me this: why does she sing? What right does she have to be happy at all?"

Nicky frowned. "I suppose I don't know."

"You don't know? Really. Look around you. The sun is shining. The sky is blue. The air is warm. There is food in your belly and clothes on your back. All these blessings are yours and ten thousand beside. I could as well ask what right you have to be sad. Your father and mother loved you, Nicky. And they loved the Lord as well. You shall see them again. They are not dead. They only sleep, and only for a time. One day you, too, will join them in glory."

"I know this," he protested.

"I know that you do." His uncle ran a hand through Nicky's hair and rested it on his shoulder. "But what you do not yet realize is that grief and joy are but two sides of the same coin. And we oft experience them both together. This is why there is laughter in sorrow, and why moments of pure joy sometimes reduce us to tears. They are both reminders that we are meant for more than this world. Both are moments when the veil of heaven lifts, and time seems to stop, and we stand on the other side." He blew a breath out through his nose. "You must learn to find the one in the other, to sing even in sorrow, and to laugh until you cry. Can you do this?"

Nicky looked down. "I think so." The maiden went back inside, her song muffled by the thin walls of the house.

"Good." Uncle touched Nicky's arm, tugging him back toward home.

Nicky held back. "What's to become of them?"

"Their fate is in God's hands, as is our own. But fret not. He knows how to care for His children. And not even a sparrow falls to the ground without His intense concern."

All through the funeral service, Nicky found his thoughts returning to the maiden. Uncle Nicholas gave the prayer, and together they walked with the bier that bore his parents' bodies into the tombs. Nicky stood to one side as they were carefully laid within the graves carved into the rock, and their bodies strewn with flowers. Uncle spoke of The Christ raising Lazarus from the dead, and reminded them of the Lord's words to Martha, "I am the resurrection and the life; he who believes in Me will live even if he dies, and everyone who lives and believes in Me will never die. Do you believe this?"

When he said these words, he looked right at Nicky, as if the Lord Himself were asking. Nicky stared hard at the shrouded forms of his parents, weighing the obvious fact of their death against the nebulous hope of resurrection. Did he really believe this? Would his parents rise again? In Martha's case, when Jesus had told her, "Your brother shall rise again," she'd simply replied with the rote answer, "Yes, Lord, I know that he will rise again in the resurrection on the last day." It *was* the right answer, but Jesus hadn't been satisfied. He wanted more from her. He wanted her to *believe* the truth, not just *acknowledge* it.

What did He want of Nicky?

*If I pray hard enough, will my parents rise again—right then and there like Lazarus of old?*

He clenched and unclenched his fists. Did he dare ask? Did he dare declare, like Christ, *'Theophanes, Nona! Come forth!'*

He hesitated, and in that hesitation, found his answer. Calling the dead to life again surely required a vast faith, and Nicky simply did not possess such. Not then, in the face of his pain.

But Jesus wept at the death of Lazarus, and yet the dead man still came out of his grave after four days behind the stone. Jesus' faith did not depend on His feeling no pain. He believed because He knew Who He was.

And who was Nicholas of Patara, son of Theophanes and Nona?

No one at all.

But his uncle still stood there, still watching him carefully. The question Jesus asked still hung in the air, as if waiting an answer. And all Nicky could do then was give a curt nod. Less than even the verbal acknowledgement of Martha.

He sank to his knees, and fresh tears rolled down his cheeks.

That night, he lay on his bed for the last time, staring up at the ceiling. After the funeral, he'd gone down to the docks and sought out Captain Marcus, who'd been in his father's shipping service these many years. The captain was gracious in meeting him, and apologetic for not coming to the funeral. Nicky waved it off with his hand, proffering the man a scroll. When he left, the captain stood speechless, now the sole owner of the ships on which he'd long served.

The next morning, Nicky would go to New Zion to live with his uncle. He would become a novitiate, and learn the ways of the holy order.

*But will it give me enough faith to raise the dead?*

He studied the silent ceiling, the unuttered prayer caught on his lips, as if he lacked the courage to put his thoughts into words.

*The Spirit also helps our weakness; for we do not know how to pray as we should, but the Spirit Himself intercedes for us with groanings too deep for words.*

He blinked, recognizing the words of St. Paul to the Romans. But he didn't remember consciously thinking the passage. Rather, it just sort of popped in there, like it belonged to the voice of another, bypassing his ears and speaking directly to his mind.

Was this the Holy Spirit speaking to him now? Telling him that He understood Nicky's heart? His unuttered prayer?

"I would ask of You," he said aloud, startled by the sound of his own voice. "I would pray like the demoniac's father, 'I do believe. Help my unbelief!'"

*Let us then approach God's throne of grace with confidence, so that we may receive mercy and find grace to help us in our time of need.*

He swallowed hard. "Confidence before God. Is that what I lack? Is this why my parents are still dead? Would You have raised them, had I asked You?"

*You have not because you ask not.*

"So it's my fault."

There was no answer. Nothing to either confirm or deny his conclusion. He dropped the back of his hand across his forehead, and looked at the wall. A pallid glow from the moon outside cast inconstant shadows across the wall.

*That's how I feel,* he thought. *Like I'm trying to see, with nothing but shadows from the moon to guide me.*

"If I asked You now," he whispered, "would You raise them today?"

*You ask and do not receive, because you ask with wrong motives.*

"But if my motives were right?"

*All things are possible to him who believes.*

He frowned. Was that a yes? Or only the promise of a yes? He closed his eyes, unable to resolve the quandary to his satisfaction, and after a few minutes, fell asleep.

Uncle Nicholas showed up just after sunrise, and Nicky was

still wiping sleep from his eyes when he opened the door to let him in.

"Are you ready?" Uncle asked.

Nicky nodded. He'd packed a few clothes in a sack and had it ready by the door. He looked around a moment, realizing there was nothing left to do, and picked up his sack. Together, they left the house behind.

The path Uncle led him on he knew well. He'd been on it many times before. It led along the cliff where they could watch the ships come in and out of the harbor, and then up the side of the mountain to the monastery, bathed in the light of the morning sun.

The monastery itself was little more than a chapel set on the hillside, with a large common room for the monks to share their meals, a field out back where they could grow their own food, taking such comfort as they could in the simple task of working the earth, and the dormitory on the side, where the monks and the Abbot slept and kept to their prayers.

"Our life here is simple," Uncle said. "We start with personal prayers and reading the scriptures at midnight, then again at sunrise. Afterward, we take our meal, and then we work the fields in the morning. When the sun is hot, we gather in the chapel for worship, prayers, and the public reading of the Word. After this, we attend to our ministry to the poor. Then Vespers. Supper is served at sunset, then we part for evening prayers and bed. After our first sleep, we rise again at midnight, and the day resumes."

"Every day?"

"No, of course not! Sunday is a day of rest. After worship, we spend our time in quiet contemplation." He opened the gate and led Nicky through. "I've arranged for you to begin your tutelage under Brother Francis. You will start in the kitchen until your hands are used to hard work, then you'll join Brother Dominic in the fields."

Nicky eyed him with a sly smile. "I know how to work, Uncle."

The Abbot smiled. "One more thing: in here, you shall address me as Brother Nicholas, and shall speak of me as The Abbot when naming me to your brothers. I'll not have you speaking of me as 'my uncle' amongst the brothers. It might create resentments or fear of favoritism."

"I understand. And what will I be called?"

"Late for work if you don't hurry. Brother Francis is expecting you. Now go!" He tousled Nicky's hair, and then sent him scampering off to the kitchens.

I frowned and tapped my pen against my lower lip. The Abbot's eyebrows arched. "Something wrong?"

"No. It's nothing. I don't want to interrupt."

"Please."

"Just a quick question, then. What sort of order is the New Zion Monastery?"

"Was."

"Pardon?"

"Was," he repeated. "New Zion ceased long ago."

"Oh. When?"

"Many years after I was gone. But as to the order itself, New Zion was independent."

"I see. So it wasn't Dominican, Franciscan, Benedictine, Jesuit?" I was quickly running out of known monastic orders.

"None of these."

"Is that common?"

"Oh, it certainly used to be. Monasteries began in Egypt during the second century. Saint Anthony was hardly the first monk to choose a hermetical life, but he's credited as the father of monasticism. And yet he predates the rules of Saint Basil the Great by a generation. And, of course, long before the medieval orders of St. Benedict or the Dominican friars."

"Yah, don't get him started," said Brother Oleg. "He can go on for hours about the history of monastic orders alone. And you," he turned to the Abbot, "get to the good part already. Some of us haven't got much longer to live."

"As you will," the Abbot replied. "I'll try to speed things up, but there are certain things he should know."

"Like your famous temper?" Oleg chided.

He opened his mouth as if to object, but then relaxed that into a smile. "Yes. Like that as well."

"Temper?" I asked.

"I'm getting to it."

# Four

Nicky's new life in the monastery proved more challenging than he'd first assumed. The Abbot was gentle, but firm, as Nicky had always known him to be. In a way it was almost disappointing, discovering that his uncle was entirely consistent in his manner and bearing behind the walls of the monastery as he'd been behind the walls of Nicky's former home. The difference now, of course, was that Nicky was beholden to him in a way he'd never been at home. Brother Nicholas had always deferred to Nona and Theophanes in their decisions raising Nicky, including giving the lad a much longer leash than he now experienced.

After a few weeks, Nicky started to chafe under the rules. The schedule constrained him, and despite his best efforts, he found that his temper flared at unexpected moments, usually when Brother Francis directed him to wash the dishes each day after meals.

"I know already!" he'd spat back the first time his temper flared when the monk instructed him that morning. "I wash dishes after every meal."

Brother Francis raised an eyebrow at the outburst, watching

as Nicky nearly tossed the dishes into the stone sink. One of the plates struck the bottom at an odd angle and shattered.

Nicky stared at the fragments, swallowing. Finally, he announced, "One of the plates broke."

"Is that what happened?" Francis intoned.

"Yes."

"All by itself? A pity. It must've been a truly magical plate."

Nicky said nothing. He pulled the fragments out of the sink and put them in the trash to be taken and buried later.

But before the day was even hot, the Abbot asked to see him. When he met his uncle in the common room, the pieces of the broken plate lay arrayed before him. Nicky's throat constricted when he saw the plate, and his eyes dropped.

"Brother Francis informs me you've made an amazing, though tragic discovery," the Abbot began. "He tells me you've learned some of our dishes are enchanted, and that they leap into the sink all by themselves. Undoubtedly, this makes washing them easier, but sadly, this one did not survive its attempted vault. Is that what happened?"

Nicky shuffled his feet. "No, unc—Brother Nicholas."

"Something else, then?"

He nodded. "I broke it."

"Hmm. So you were being clumsy. An accident, then?"

Nicky squirmed. "I was careless."

"Hmm. Indeed. And with what were you careless?"

"The plate," he blurted. A patient look from the Abbot told him his answer was inadequate. "And my temper."

"Temper. *He who is slow to anger is better than the mighty, And he who rules his spirit, than he who captures a city.* Do you know this scripture?"

"Is it from the Psalms?"

"Proverbs. I want you to memorize this passage. Brother Francis will help you find it in the scrolls."

Nicky frowned, and then shook his head.

"Something?"

"Could Brother Philip help me?"

"You object to Brother Francis?"

"It's just that he's so—he's always telling me what to do!"

"That is his job."

"But I already know what to do. He doesn't have to constantly remind me."

"Oh, but he does."

"Why?"

"Because I have instructed him to."

Nicky's mouth hung open. "Why? I am no fool!"

Brother Nicholas folded his hands. "Temper." Nicky closed his mouth, shamed by his outburst. The Abbot spoke carefully, measuring Nicky with his eyes. "I've asked Brother Francis to instruct you daily in your responsibilities because I want you to get used to listening. Your head is too full of your own thoughts.

There is so little room for the voice of God."

"I *do* hear God," he protested.

"As I'm sure you do. But do you listen? Do you hear and obey?" He turned and started walking with Nicky toward the front of the monastery. "You told me, the day your parents died, that you wished to join me here in this life, knowing full well that to do so means you must abandon all worldly possessions. As our Lord said, *'Sell your possessions and give to the poor, and you will have treasure in heaven. Then, come, follow Me.'* And yet, you have not yet divested yourself fully of your father's estate."

They came to a stop by the front gate. Nicky glanced doubtfully at it, and then back at his uncle. "Nicky," the man continued, "the money is yours to do with as you see fit. As it always has been. You are free to keep it, to become a man of business, a man of means like you father, if that is who God is calling you to be. But the one thing you cannot do is hold onto your wealth and pursue a life of poverty and contemplation at the same time. You must choose."

"Are you telling me to go?"

"No. I am telling you to choose. *You cannot serve both God and money.*"

"I choose God, of course."

"There is no 'of course,' when it comes to choosing God. You must count the cost of discipleship, or you will find that you lay hold of the plow and try to walk a straight line while looking backward at all you've left behind. Such a man is not fit for the kingdom of God."

Nicky stared hard at the gate. "I don't want to go," he mumbled.

"That is not the same thing as wanting to stay."

He met his uncle's eyes, and knew that moment it was his uncle, not the Abbot, looking back at him. "There's nothing for me out there. You talk about my money, but it means nothing to me. I didn't tell Uriah to close out my father's accounts because I knew what would happen if he did."

"And what is that?"

"Uriah doesn't have the money. At least, not with him. He's taken my father's wealth and loaned it out to people in this community. He pays my father interest for this privilege, and charges his customers even more for theirs. That's how he makes his living."

"Usury."

"He is a Jew. He is not subject to the laws of the Church. My father said he performs a necessary service, one that benefits the community. And Uriah also knows that if he abuses his customers, my father would have withdrawn his wealth and ruined him for it."

"I see."

"And that is why I haven't divested myself. If I demanded the money, then Uriah would have to call in his debts to pay it. It would mean ruining all those who owe him."

The Abbot pursed his lips and turned away from the gate. Nicky felt a surge of relief when he did so. "Do you mean then to give him the money? You could, you know."

"I could," he agreed, "but that would hardly obey our Lord's command. He told us to sell all we have and give to the poor. Most would agree that Uriah does not qualify as poor."

"Except in spirit, perhaps."

"True. I did give away the house, the lands, and all my father's ships. All that's left is the gold."

"Hmm. So how do you intend to quit yourself of it?"

"I don't really know. I thought to call it in a little bit at a time, but even if I did so, I have no idea what to do with it." He turned abruptly. "I could give it to the monastery!"

The Abbot held up a cautious hand. "No. I would not accept it. We survive on what we earn with our own hands, and the generous donations of the community. Word gets out that we've a wealthy benefactor supplying our need, and the community itself would stop giving."

"What difference does it make if you have the money?"

His uncle frowned. "All the difference in the world. Do you really think we need the money? Our Lord owns the cattle on a thousand hills. He can take the few loaves and fish of a small child and multiply them to feed the masses. The earth is the Lord's, and the fullness thereof. The world, and all it contains. No,

Brother Nicholas, we do not need the money, for our Lord knows what we need before we ask Him, and He supplies everything we need to live. But what the Lord wants from us is a generous heart and an open hand. He seeks that we should give even as He gives, and thus become a bit more like Him. You would take that blessing away from the people in this community? Deny them the privilege of knowing the heart of God? Giving your money to us would be a disaster."

"Then who should I give it to? And how?" he wailed.

The Abbot put a finger out and touched Nicky's nose. "That is why you need to listen. Seek the voice of God. Ask Him what He means you to do with the money. And then? Simply obey."

With that, he left him standing there by the gate.

Nicky found himself distracted through the rest of the day. He mumbled an apology to Brother Francis when he met him again that evening after supper. The monk only grunted when Nicky said the words, as if he didn't believe them genuine. But Nicky held his tongue as he washed up, nodding and agreeing, "Yes Brother Francis," whenever he received an instruction. In truth, his mind was elsewhere, puzzling over the Abbot's instructions.

*How can I obey when I don't know what He wants of me?*

He'd asked the Lord several times already to give him insight, but instead of clarity, he rather found his thoughts returning to the maiden the Abbot had showed him before his parents' funeral. When he lay his head down that night for prayers, instead of holy thoughts coming to mind, he heard her singing in his mind, the lilting tones from her voice carrying his imagination far away.

And something stirred within him, an impulse toward her, a yearning to know more of this young maiden facing such misfortune. The more he thought of her, the more beautiful she seemed. Her hair didn't simply sparkle in the morning light, it fairly shone with a radiance all its own. Her face, far from being creased with worry and lined in sweat, rather glistened with the smooth sheen of a pearl. She didn't simply walk as she fed the chickens, she swirled and danced.

*Dear God,* he thought, *how can this be? I'm to become a monk, and yet my thoughts turn toward her. Is this what You have in mind? Did all this happen so that I would see this girl in her proper light, where before I'd not have given her a passing glance?*

*And what does this mean for my future? Or hers?*

"You fell in love with her," Once more, I interrupted the narrative. Brother Oleg gave me a knowing wink, but Nick shook his head.

"Not as you think."

"Yah, you did," said Oleg.

"No."

"Yah."

"No.

"Yah. You did. You know you did."

"You'll confuse him."

"Too late," I offered.

"You were young and you fell in love. Admit it."

The Abbot rolled his eyes. "I was young. And I did fall in love, but not the way you think."

"At that age, it is exactly the way we think," Oleg returned. "Love is love."

"She was betrothed to another."

He raised his eyebrows. "And if she hadn't been?"

The Abbot hesitated, and Oleg raised a shaky finger. "There, you see? You did love her."

"All right then. Yes. I do love her. As I loved her sisters, each in their turn. And many, many since then."

My pen faltered. This was getting interesting, and my nose for scandal twitched. I wondered just what sort of monastic order this was.

"Tell me about the girl," I said. "Did you pursue her?"

The Abbot's eyes flickered toward me. He patted Oleg's hand.

"You see? He is confused already. I did pursue her, but not in the way that you think. Remember, she was betrothed to another."

"So your love was unrequited?"

"No," he shook his head. "It was elevated."

Nicky wrote a letter to Uriah the next day, asking for a third of his father's wealth to be withdrawn in a month. That Sunday following worship services, he found a young lad to carry the letter to the Jew, with the promise that Uriah pay him a denarius from his father's account upon receipt of the letter.

When the boy returned later that afternoon, he carried with him a sack of gold bearing a seal around the drawstrings. Nicky took the gold in hand, eyeing the break in the wax. He met the young boy's eyes.

"It's all there," the lad protested. "I tripped on a rock and the seal cracked when I fell upon it. That's all. I didn't take nothing from it."

"Is that really what happened?" Nicky asked.

"On my honor, sir."

"And you didn't have a look inside?"

The boy opened and closed his mouth.

"So you did."

He hung his head.

51

"Is that the truth of how the seal came to be broken, then?"

Slowly, the lad nodded his head. "But I didn't take none of it! I swear! I was only curious. I-I'd never seen so much gold in one place."

Nicky bent down, opened the bag, and dumped its contents on the ground. The gold coins glistened and rang when they struck each other, landing in the dust. "So now you see it all. How does it look to you? Pretty, isn't it?"

He reached down and lifted a single coin, passing it over to the boy. "Here are your wages, as we agreed."

"Thank you, sir!"

"And this," he picked up a second piece, "is for being honest."

The boy's fingers hesitated at the coin. "I-I wasn't. I broke the seal."

Nicky smiled. "You discovered that you carried a bag holding more gold than you are likely to see in your life, and rather than running off with it to make your fortune in this world, you brought it here instead. What is that, if not honesty?"

The boy's hand dropped. His face clouded. "My papa would call it foolish."

"I prefer to call it innocent curiosity. And do not judge innocence too harshly. It is worth more than all the treasure you see here. Once it is lost, it can never be recovered."

After a moment, the boy nodded. Nicky pressed the coin into his palm. "Take it. You've earned your reward. There's sure to be more where that came from."

With that, he sent the lad off and began scooping the gold back into the sack.

"That is a noble treasure you've given him," said Brother Francis. Nicky glanced up as the monk came around the corner.

"You saw?"

"Aye, I did. And heard, too. The Abbot informed me of your... circumstance... and asked that I keep an eye on you." He offered Nicholas a hand up. "You took a risk trusting that child."

Nicky shrugged. "The gold isn't mine. It belongs to God. I simply trusted Him to watch out for it."

"Hmm. What would have been the greater loss? The gold? Or that lad's innocence? You tempted him. You realize that, don't you?"

Nicky hesitated, suddenly keenly aware of the truth in the monk's words. "I didn't mean it that way. I only wanted to recover the gold."

"You could have gone to the Jew yourself."

"That would have meant leaving the monastery."

"This is no prison. You are free to come and go as you will."

He pressed his lips together. "I didn't want to go, because I didn't want any of the other brothers asking questions. I didn't want them knowing what I'd done."

"Why?"

"Do not let your left hand know what your right hand is

doing. And let your giving be in secret."

"And your heavenly Father, Who sees what is done in secret, will reward you."

"Yes."

The monk folded his hands. "'Tis a curious problem you created. Perhaps it would've been better to rid yourself of the gold before coming here."

"The Abbot knows my reasons not to."

"I see."

"But you are right. I tempted the boy. I intended to buy his services a few times more, but now I see that I should do this myself."

"And yet you have made a promise to the boy."

He sighed. "Are all moral dilemmas this difficult?"

Brother Francis chuckled and tousled Nicky's head. "Of course. That's what makes them dilemmas. They are like the rocks sunk beneath the waves. Only by moving slowly, deliberately, can we learn to avoid them without foundering our ship."

Nicky nodded. "I suppose I can still have him bring me the gold from Uriah, but I shall have to do the rest on my own."

"And the rest is?"

He eyed the older man slyly. "I'd rather not say. I think I know whom the Lord wants to receive this, but I want to keep it a secret."

54

Brother Francis chuckled. "This is a small community. Word gets around."

He broke into a grin. "Surely you don't listen to gossip!"

The man's jaw dropped, and then broke into a grin. "I think we must have some dishes to do." Together, they returned to the kitchen.

# Five

That evening, following prayers, Nicky stole out at night, crossing through the yard and quietly opening and shutting the gate. The town was dark, though the streets glowed with light from the half-moon riding in the sky.

A cool breeze blew, penetrating his cloak and making him shiver. As he reached the crest of the hill, he paused and looked down to the sea. The ships were gone, their new Captain moving on to make his fortune even bigger than what he'd been given. Nicky offered up a prayer on his behalf, asking the Lord to grant him a prosperous voyage and a safe return. "And help him to learn to be generous, too," he said, "even as You are teaching me the same. I pray his lessons are learned easier than mine. I know he is a wiser man than I."

The water reflected the moon's light in broken rivulets that glistened below the craggy cliff like an explosion of stars. Even from where he stood, he could hear the rush of the waves as they caressed the shore and lapped against the docks where the villagers waited the safe return of their husbands and fathers and sons. He felt the wind teasing at his shoulders, as if the Lord's Spirit were gently reminding him to move on.

His eyes seeing better in the dark now, he turned and hurried into the town, seeking that same street where his uncle had brought him just a few weeks earlier. As he turned up the alley, he listened to the sounds of families talking to one another from the windows that overlooked the street. Several had gone up to their roofs to sleep in the cool of the evening, and if they dared peer over the edges of their apartments, they'd have seen his solitary form scurrying resolutely up the street.

When he reached the corner he stopped. Glancing around the corner, he spied the *insula* where the maiden had danced and sang despite her sorrow, and felt a twinge of panic clutch at his chest.

*What if I am seen? What if they learn it's me?*

He swallowed, and for a moment pictured the maiden coming to the door, her beautiful eyes shining in the moonlight, speaking his name.

*No!* He shook his head. *This is not for me. I have given myself to God.*

"She loves another," he said. "The Lord loves her as well, and wants her to marry this man. That is why He's led me here. I," he pushed himself away from the wall, "am only the conduit for His blessing. Yes. That is my purpose here. Nothing more."

He rounded the corner, and then fell back again. The lamps were still lit in the home, giving it a warm glow.

What should he do? Should he knock on the door? And tell

them what, that gold was found in the street and it must belong to them? No. That was ridiculous on its face. Could he leave it for them on the doorstep. Surely, that was the better plan. Why, he might even knock and run off before they answered. That would preserve his anonymity, and ensure they received the blessing.

Unless they did not open the door all the way. Or worse, if some vagabond came during the night and wandered off with the prize.

He looked up to the heavens. "Well, Father? What would you have me do?"

The answer came quite easily and simply, and when it did, he felt a surge of relief. It was easy, deliciously simple.

He slipped away from the wall, casually walking toward the *insula*, hefting the bag of gold in his hand. As he passed by the open window, he tossed it inside, and kept walking. A sudden crash and a cry announced that the gold had landed on something fragile. He winced, and hurried away. At the end of the street he dodged around the corner, then dropped to his knees and poked his head around.

A man breathlessly dodged into the street, looking both ways, his hands on his hips. His breath trailed into the sky like a tiny trail of smoke. A cry from behind him made him turn around.

"Papa! Papa, look!"

The maiden rushed into the street, cupping her hands in

front of her. "Is it real?"

Her face seemed lit from the moon. Nicky felt a warm pang in his heart. *She is beautiful, Father, and I pray she finds her happiness.*

"This cannot be," the man said.

"Gold!"

"Shh! Someone will hear. Come, get inside. Quickly now!"

Together, they vanished inside the *insula*. Nicky pulled his head back and sat against the wall. The sky seemed brighter now, and clearer, as if heaven itself had turned out to watch the performance.

The glow in his heart faded. He was being prideful. "I am an unworthy servant, Father," he said to the sky, "for I have only done what my Lord has asked of me." He gathered his robes about himself and stood. He looked up one last time and added, "But I hope You are honored nonetheless. Thank You for the privilege of serving You."

I raised my hand, impatient to interrupt. "Don't you think you were being a little hard on yourself?"

The Abbot shrugged. "Not at the time."

"What about now? In retrospect?"

"In retrospect I've learned that generous deeds should not be checked by cold counsel. That's from *The Lord of the Rings* movies. The third one."

I nodded. "Thought it sounded familiar. I didn't think you guys watched movies up here."

He smiled cryptically. "On occasion. There was a time when all we had were books, and novels were frowned upon. But then I discovered Dickens." His eyebrows raised when he said the name. "Quite a writer. Quite the man. Very enjoyable fellow. And since movies are now our world's way of telling stories to each other, we sometimes allow them." He raised a stern finger. "We screen them carefully, of course. Stories are important. So much can be communicated through them that would otherwise never be believed. Jesus, you know, was a master storyteller."

"Parables, right?"

"Yes. Parables. But I digress. You wanted to know if I thought I was being too hard on myself." He rubbed his chin, scratching the beard that grew there. "At the time, I still believed my heart to be desperately wicked and full of deceit. And I'm sure parts of it were. Still are, I suppose. It's so easy for selfish motives to cloud out the light of our better natures. What I'd yet to learn was just how utterly self-indulgent all such soul-searching really is. Some of it is good. But too much of it? Well. Brother Francis and my uncle, to their credit, wanted to train me in the ways of right and wrong, and more importantly to teach me to think before I acted—"

"And to look before you leap," Brother Oleg commented dryly from the bed.

Nicholas burst out laughing. "Ah, once more you are getting ahead of the story. Shame on you!"

I shook my head. "I'm utterly lost."

"There," he said to the old man. "You see what you've done? He's referencing the time I flew. Again, it's something you'll understand when we get to it." He said this last part with a glare at the old man.

"Flew?"

"It's not what you think, and far less than what's been made of it."

"I suppose that's what I get for interrupting."

"Yes. Where were we?"

"You tossed a sack of gold through an open window."

"Ah. So I did. Well, remember the man had three daughters..."

The second attempt to help the old man began smoothly enough. Once more, Nicky recruited the lad to bring back the gold from Uriah. The boy received three coins as before—Nicky didn't think it wise to tempt the lad by giving him less, and giving him more would only enrich him unwisely. Nicky's father had told him on a number of occasions that true wealth had to be earned slowly, or the newly rich would lack the discipline to handle the money correctly, and it ruin them.

"Money is like fire," Theophanes had counseled. "Enough can warm you, cook your food, and light your way. Too much can burn your house down, and even destroy your neighbor as well."

"Yes, Papa," he'd answered.

With the sack of gold in hand, a month since he'd last gone out, he once more let himself out of the gate at night and crept under a half moon toward town. The first daughter was recently wed—the celebration and the good fortune coming unexpected and unawares to the family had been the subject of much gossip and speculation in the neighborhood. Nicky listened carefully for any indication that those in the village suspected it came from him, but he heard nothing. Both Uriah and the boy kept his secret well, and neither The Abbot nor Brother Francis gave any hint that they knew who was behind the gift.

Satisfied that his generous deed remained a secret, Nicky once more stole through the night to the *insula*. He thought to perform the deed as before, tossing the gold through the window, but this time the shutters were drawn shut. He shuffled up beneath them and studied them from the outside. Within he could see the light of the lamps still burning on the second floor, and hear the muffled conversation of the man and his two remaining girls. But he had no way of delivering the gift.

*What shall I do?*

He stood there a full minute, shifting his feet indecisively. He could always come back another night, but there was no guarantee that the window would not still be closed, and with each passing day the face of the moon shone more and more brightly, thus increasing his risk of discovery.

He reached up to try the latch on the window when he heard a harsh whisper from within. "Papa, there's someone outside."

Nicky froze, every nerve on fire.

"Where?" said the man.

"Below the window. I could almost see his face."

"A burglar? Or mayhap our mysterious benefactor?"

"Oh Papa, do you think it could be?" the other child fairly squealed.

"Hush now. I will go see."

That was all it took. Nicky dropped the sack of gold on the street outside their window and fairly flung himself away toward the corner. Behind him he heard the man. "Stop!" Then again, "Stop! Why do you run?"

Nicky paused at the corner, his sudden halt slowing the man to a crawl. "Don't run," the man said. "I mean you no harm."

He was still looking toward Nicky, and had almost passed by the gold entirely. Nicky pointed. "By the window!"

The man turned, spying the bag of gold on the ground. As soon as he reached for it, Nicky bolted, running headlong down the side street, and then weaving between buildings and putting as much distance between himself and the man as he could. He tripped over a rock and fell to his knees, frightening a cat, which let out an awful shriek. His knee screamed with pain. He could feel the blood dripping down his shin. Scrambling to his feet, he stumbled blindly up the alleyway until he found himself on the path by the cliff's edge. Only then did he slow and retrace his steps back to New Zion.

When he got back to his room, his leg was throbbing in pain. He lit a lamp and washed the gravel out of the wound, binding the gash with strips of cloth. Then, he lay back on his bunk, and without bothering to pray, fell fast asleep.

He was late to morning prayers the next day, saying only that he had injured his knee when he was questioned about it by The Abbot. His uncle wisely avoided pressing the issue.

The next week the whole town was abuzz with tales of the mysterious benefactor. Villagers openly wondered whether or not the mysterious gift giver would visit them that night—some even complaining that it was unfair that they should be overlooked. Were not their own needs just as desperate as that of this man, now twice blessed with gold for his own daughters? The plague had decimated the town, and surely God would appoint someone to ease the suffering of more than one of them.

Nicky, upon overhearing these gripes, went at once to The Abbot. "Am I doing right?" he asked when his uncle admitted him.

"About what?"

Nicky took a breath. "About what neither of us will admit I'm doing, but which we both know is happening?"

"Oh. That." The man chuckled at Nicky's obfuscation. "Why do you think you're not doing right?"

"I overheard some men complaining how unfair it was that they had not been similarly blessed."

His uncle made some tea and offered Nicky a cup. "They are correct. It is unfair."

"So it is wrong."

"Not in the least."

"How can something unfair be right?"

His uncle took a seat across from him. "Are you familiar with Jesus' parable of the rich man and the workers?"

"I think so."

"Early in the morning, a man hired some men to work in his field for a denarius. A little later in the morning, he went out and hired some more. Then again in the afternoon. And then at last toward the end of the work day. When it came time to settle their accounts, the man started paying out a day's wages to the men, beginning with those hired last. When he got down to those hired earlier in the day, each of them supposed they would be given more. But they also received a day's wages. The men began to grumble and complain about how unfair it was. The landowner said to them, 'Did you not agree to work for me for a day's wages? Is that not what I have paid you? Then what right do you have to complain? Am I not permitted to be generous with my own money? I have decided to be generous with those hired at the end of the day.

"Do you see, Nicholas?"

"I think so."

"The only answer to your question is: are you doing as the Spirit has directed you? If so, then you have not done wrong. No one has the right to demand generosity, for if you merit a gift, it is no longer a gift, but what is due you."

"I see."

But the Abbot wasn't finished. "Can you imagine what would occur if you were to give so generously to each and every needy person in this community?"

He shrugged. "Everyone would be blessed."

"Would they? Or would they rather instead cease from their labors, and merely await for the generosity of their benefactor? And consider when this reputation for generosity got out? Patara would become a magnet for every worthless, lazy fellow for miles around who resents the necessity of labor. Soon our streets would be clogged with the indigent and the criminal. Working for your bread is a blessing, Nicky. As much as some resent the need for labor, we do not produce virtue by rewarding idleness."

"But aren't I just as idle?"

The Abbot frowned. "How so?"

"I did not earn my wealth. Even though I may be divesting myself of it all, the simple fact is that none of what I possess has come to me through my own efforts. It was my father's labor that enriched me, not my own."

"That may be," the Abbot replied, "but you are far from idle. You work here in the kitchens, assisting Brother Francis. And you are generously serving the poor by helping this man and his daughters, even as you assisted Epiphanius and Captain Marcus. The mere possession of wealth—even inherited—is no vice. It is idleness itself that is the problem."

"I understand."

"So I ask you again: are you doing as the Spirit has asked you?"

Nicky heaved a breath. "Yes."

"Then it is not wrong. However, perhaps it would be best for all if you were to finish your work quickly, and end the fascination to the town that it brings."

"Yes sir. Thank you, sir."

 **Six**

The third time he went out was less than a week later. The gibbous moon shone ever more brightly on the path, but the air felt colder, and he shoved his hands inside his sleeves as he walked, watching his breath curl away from his face to dissipate beneath the glare of the stars.

He would easily be seen tonight, if the man was keeping watch at his window. Nicky had considered waiting for the new moon, but Uncle's insistence that he finish his business quickly pushed him out the gate that much sooner.

The path now familiar to him, he let his mind wander toward thoughts of what his life would be once this business was complete. Surely, a life of quiet contemplation and service to his Lord would be fully rewarding, and yet he couldn't shake a nagging discontentment, as if he were meant for something more. As he reached the street of the man's *insula*, he shook it off. These feelings were brought on by the excitement of his clandestine activities, nothing more. They were foolish emotions of a childhood fantasy—Nicholas the mysterious benefactor—and he would do well to put them aside as the haughty thoughts that they were.

As he neared the apartment, though, his heartbeat nonetheless sped up. There were voices in the courtyard. No, he thought as he crept closer, not voices. A single voice. That of the father.

He was praying.

Nicky didn't want to listen, but couldn't help himself. The man made no attempt to keep his words to himself.

"Righteous Father," he prayed, "You have been so good, so kind to this unworthy servant. I am filled with relief, with gratitude for all that Your angel has done for us. Two of my daughters are secure in their future—and I know, with all the faith that is in my heart—that You will provide for my last child as well. It need not be through this means. You have shown Yourself more than able to surprise me with Your kindness. Forgive me for ever doubting Your good will." He paused to choke back his tears. "Foolish man that I am, I am just so grateful. I ask only this—and if it is too much just say the word—but I ask only for the chance to repay this kindness this man—mayhap this angel—has shown my children. I would gladly give my daughter to him if he should ask for her hand. Anything would be a worthy price. Anything, anything. Just say the word."

And so on he went in his prayer. Nicky bit his lip. How was he to get close enough now to deliver this last bit of gold? Should he come back the next night and try again?

He leaned back against the wall by the street, looking up

toward the moon. *What would You have me do?* he prayed.

That's when he spied the ladder leaning against the wall of the apartment beside the man's. It was just a short leap from one rooftop to the other, and though most people slept out on their roofs during the heat of the summer, tonight felt brisk. Surely everyone would be inside, asleep by their fires.

That was it, then. The way to deliver this last gift. What a delight it would be, too, for the man to go inside and find the gift he'd prayed for waiting for him beside his own warm fire.

Nicky grabbed hold of the rungs and started to climb. At the top of the wall, he eased himself over the side and crept alongside the ledge toward the gap between the two buildings. The courtyard was below him on the left, where the man still lifted his prayers to the heavens, unmindful of the virtual shadow Nicholas had become on the rooftop behind him.

Nicky took a few steps back, and ran for the edge, ready to leap full onto the roof of the *insula*. As he neared the edge, he caught himself just before he jumped and skidded to a halt, ducking low behind the parapet, his heart thudding in his chest.

One of the daughters—the youngest, he thought—had come outside. "Papa?" she was saying, "when are you coming in?"

"Johanna," the man answered. "Soon. When the Lord and I have finished our talk."

"Does the Lord say whether or not His saint will come tonight?"

"I know not," he answered. "I have not asked Him."

*Saint?* Nicky thought. *Surely not!*

"I hope he comes soon," she said.

Nicky backed up, and made ready to try again.

"I'm sure the Lord will take care of matters," her father replied.

Nicky ran for the edge and leaped, sailing over the short gap and landing on the far side.

Johanna gasped. "Papa? Did you hear that?"

"I heard something."

Nicky lay flat on his stomach, daring not to move.

"What do you think it was?"

"I don't know. A bird, perhaps?"

Nicky raised his eyes. In front of him, not ten feet away, was the opening to the fire in the room below. A steady stream of smoke drifted upward toward the moon. It was his best chance.

"It sounded much larger than a bird," the girl said from below.

Nicky crawled forward on his belly toward the opening.

"Hush now, little one. Go inside."

"But I want to see!"

He reached the edge, and fumbled for the bag of gold tucked within his shirt.

"Go inside now," her father insisted. "I will check this out."

Nicky drew out the gold and hastily tossed it through the

71

opening. Too late, he realized it might land in the fire.

A cry from below drew his attention. "Papa! Papa, come quick!"

Nicky scrambled backward, fleeing toward the ledge.

"Do you see?" she said. "It landed in the sock you were drying over the fire."

Nicky flung himself over the edge. He hit the far wall and felt a jarring impact in his bones. His knee smacked painfully against the brick. Gasping, he struggled to draw himself onto the roof, his hands clutching at the ledge. A chip of stone broke free beneath his fingers, and he slipped backward, a cry escaping his lips.

Just then, a ladder smacked against the wall beside him. Nicky pushed up, but his toes found scant purchase on the smooth surface of the wall. He sagged back against the brick and felt himself slip downward.

"Hang on," the man panted as he climbed up beside Nicky. "There now, friend. I've got you."

Strong arms reached around Nicky's waist, tugging him toward the ladder. "Careful now."

"Misjudged the landing," he said hoarsely.

"And what you thinking? Flying around on the rooftops like that, eh? You could have broken your neck."

When they touched ground, Nicky tried to hide his face. "It was the only way." He gasped again when he tried to put weight on his knee.

"Here now. Better let me have a look at that." The man gently lay Nicky against the wall and lifted his robe over his knee. "You've gone and made a bloody mess of your leg. Johanna! Bring oil and wine." He turned back around and studied Nicky's face. "Only way, you said? Only way to what?"

Nicky swallowed. "Let my giving be in secret."

The man snorted. "Some secret. The whole town is buzzing about it. And what will they say when I tell them my benefactor is flying about on the rooftops like an angel of God?"

"Please, sir. I beg you: say nothing."

"Should not generosity be rewarded?"

"Nay. Let it be rewarded in heaven alone."

Johanna showed up at his side, bearing the oil and wine. She met Nicky's gaze with dark, round eyes in a perfectly oval face, hair as black as a raven's, and far from being a child, was rather a woman grown. She couldn't have been more than two years younger than he. Nicky felt a sudden flush in his cheeks.

The man poured first the wine, and then the oil onto Nicky's wound. Nicky gasped in pain as the alcohol seeped into the cuts on his skin.

"Hmm," the man grunted as he wound a strip of cloth over his knee, "and what possessed you to notice us? Do I know you? Are you in debt to me in some way?"

"No sir."

"Then perhaps you were entranced by my daughters'

beauty?"

"No. I mean, yes, your daughters are quite... quite beautiful," he grinned stupidly. Johanna blushed. "But that is not why," he added hastily.

"Then tell me."

"Your eldest—"

"Mary."

"Yes. She was singing."

"She does that. No one has ever paid her for it."

"I had—my parents died recently. I was awash in grief. My uncle brought me here. And he showed me your daughter, and told me of all you have suffered. Your wife's long illness and her passing. How you've lost your business. How you've become so poor that you risk eviction, and that you might even have to have sold out your own daughters to men to pay your debt." As he spoke, the man lowered his head in shame. Nicky continued, his words tumbling out in a torrent. "And yet she was singing! Her heart was full of joy despite all that pain, despite that she might never marry her beau, and be sold instead to someone else. Still singing. It made me realize there can be joy in pain. Laughter in grief. And that if we are alive just to enjoy the sun on our faces, we are blessed.

"So when I chose to abandon all worldly possessions, and dispense with the gold I had inherited, I could think of no better family to give it to than to the one that taught me to smile again."

The man and his daughter were silent a long while. When the man spoke again, his voice was low and full of wonder. "You are from the monastery."

Nicky nodded.

"Your parents were that wealthy couple that died from the plague this summer. They were much loved. Theophanes and Nona, yes? He owned the ships and the vineyard. You are Nicholas. Their son. I am Antonius."

Nicky shook his hand. "I belong to God, now."

"You do Him and your parents credit."

"Please," he winced. "Do not speak of this. To anyone."

After a moment, Antonius nodded. "Your secret is safe with us. Would you like to come inside and refresh yourself?"

"No," he shook his head. "Thank you. I must return to the monastery before they notice I'm missing."

"Can you walk?"

He pushed himself to his feet, gingerly putting weight on his knee. "I think I can manage."

Abruptly, Antonius pulled him into an embrace. "God bless what you have done, Nicholas of Patara. You have saved my family. I will never forget you."

When he released him, Johanna stepped forward, still clutching, Nicky saw, the tiny bag of gold he'd left for her in her father's sock. "I have no beau," she said. "No suitors asking for my hand. But I pray that when I do, that I meet someone just as kind and as beautiful as you." With that, she pressed her lips to his own, leaving him stunned, wide-eyed and breathless.

Together, she and her father went back into the apartment and shut the door.

Nicholas limped back to the monastery, and by the time he arrived, the morning birds had begun their singing, heralding the day. He lay on his bed a long time, missing morning prayers, and as he finally drifted off to sleep, his mind was on that kiss.

"Did he ever tell your secret?" I asked. Brother Oleg had fallen asleep again, and was snoring gently on the bed. The Abbot reached out a tender hand and gently moved a lock of hair out of the man's face.

"Sadly, he did."

"Why sadly?"

His shoulders sagged. "A broken promise is never a good thing. I don't think he meant to do it. He kept his word for years. But gradually, through things he said or didn't say—and more by the attentions he and Johanna showered upon me, word crept out. First, it was his other two daughters and their husbands. Asking me to bless their children. Inviting me to feast with them, and so forth. It raised suspicions. Then others came. I began to doubt their intentions, whether or not they thought I kept a secret stash of gold somewhere, and would equally bless them if they were kind toward me. It turned people away from Christ, and onto me. I assure you, that was the last thing I wanted, and it is something that has plagued me ever since. You have no idea how much it pains me even today. Eventually, it compelled me to leave New Zion behind."

"You're kidding."

"No. I could no longer serve in secret. Uncle sat me down one day and said, 'Nicky, I fear it is time for you to go.' He didn't explain why. He didn't have to. I knew."

"That must've been hard."

He nodded and sipped his tea, then made a face. "Ah. Cold. Would you like some fresh?"

I felt my stomach rumble, and realized I still hadn't eaten. "Actually—"

"Say no more," he held up his hand. "I can see that you're hungry. What say we let Oleg sleep for a bit? We can go down to the kitchen and find you some supper."

I folded my notepad and turned off the recorder. "Thank you. That'd be nice."

"Of course, we'll have to sneak past Brother Don. He guards the pantry like Cerebus at the doors of Tartarus."

I raised my eyebrows at the image. "I think Brother Don offered me something when I arrived."

"Did he? Excellent! I've always enjoyed his cooking. One of

the best chefs we've ever had up here. Did you know he once ran a restaurant in New York City?"

"You're kidding."

He grinned and led the way. "He was the Souse Chef, I believe. Some place on Fifth Avenue."

"Wow. He left all that to come here?"

"People come to us for many different reasons. All are welcome, but very few decide to take vows. I'm sure it was quite difficult for him to do so, but I imagine it would be even harder now if he had to leave, as it was for me."

We turned and headed downstairs to the kitchen. "In some ways," he added, "leaving New Zion was the second hardest thing I'd ever had to do at the time. Well, perhaps the third. The second was coming to New Zion in the first place. But burying my parents..."

"Oh, first. Absolutely," I agreed. "I had that unfortunate privilege two years ago. My mother. Lung cancer."

"And your father?"

"Killed in combat when I was very young. We got a flag and a picture to remember him by. Truth is, it's all I know of him. For years, it was just me and Mom."

"Mmm," he gripped my shoulder. "Time makes orphans of us all." He opened the door to the kitchen, waking Brother Don who'd been asleep on a chair, his head propped on his elbow.

"Up, you old scoundrel! Sleeping on the job, eh?" the Abbot

chided.

"And who are you calling old?" Don yawned. "I wondered when you'd wander down here." He looked at me and nodded toward the Abbot. "This man been keeping you from supper?"

"Not at all," I answered. "Didn't even notice how hungry I was till he said something about it."

He motioned us over to a small table with chairs and plates already set up. An oil lamp glowed invitingly in the center of the table, it's tiny flame flickering like a distant star. As we sat, he appeared beside us with a pot in one hand and a large spoon in the other. "Are you fond of *Ribbe?*" He wore an apron with a picture of a talking Spanish gourd wearing a Christmas hat and sporting a gold tooth that said, *'Hey look! I'm an elf!'* I resisted asking him about it.

"Don't know," I replied. "I've never had it before."

"Then it's high time you did. Today we're serving it with potatoes, sauerkraut, and baked apples with prunes."

"*Ribbe?*" said the Abbot. "Aren't we a little early for the season?"

He smiled. "Seemed appropriate. I also have some *medisterpoelse*, and a fine *juleøl*."

As he served the food onto my plate I asked, "What exactly am I eating here, in English?" I doubted this was standard fare at that Fifth Avenue restaurant he came from.

Don shrugged. "Potatoes. Sauerkraut. Baked Apples and—"

"Yeah. How about the parts I don't understand?" I laughed.

"*Ribbe* is ribs. *Medisterpoelse* is minced pork sausage. And *juleøl* is a dark, traditional Christmas beer."

"Beer? I'll go for that."

"It's an allowance we make for the culture. And hardly unheard of. The practice of faith is somewhat different here in Europe than in America, as it is different all over the world."

"I'm not complaining." To Don I said, "Why Christmas beer?"

A sly grin toyed with the corner of his mouth. "As I said, seemed appropriate." He gave me a wink and moved off.

I looked to the Abbot. "What's he talking about?"

He sipped his beer. "Don relishes serving here. The whole Christmas motif brings him such joy. He'd celebrate year round if I let him."

"Why not?"

"There's more to the liturgical calendar than just the birth of our Lord. We must remember that Christmas is only the prelude to Good Friday."

"I suppose that makes sense."

"Besides," he put his mug down, "the other Brothers would soon grow tired of it. Worse, they'd grow tired of Advent. As the saying goes, 'Absence makes the heart grow fonder.'"

He seemed to grow quiet after that, with the same faraway look in his eyes he'd had while telling me his story to this point. I wondered if he was back there now.

"Do you miss it?"

"Hmm?"

"New Zion. You said your uncle asked you to leave."

"No. I miss the town—my childhood home, sometimes. I miss it the way anyone misses the place where they grew up. But it's not really the place that we miss. It's our innocence. Our youth. The feeling of being a child, with someone else to watch over you, and days filled with eternal sunshine. That's what we miss. But I would not go back there now. So much has happened. So much good was done after I left—and so much I've seen. As the old Gospel hymn puts it, 'I started out travelin' for the Lord many years ago. I've had a lot of heartache, I've met a lot of grief and woe. But when I would stumble, then I would humble down, and there I would say I wouldn't take nothing for my journey now.'"

"Tell me about it," I said.

He smiled and tapped the table. "You left your notepad and recorder upstairs."

I shrugged. "I've got a good memory."

"Well," he savored his beer. "I had no idea where I would go. But as it turns out, my uncle did."

#  Seven

"You want me to go on a pilgrimage?"

"Indeed," the Abbot replied. "I think it would be good for you."

"But why?"

"Nicky," his uncle said, "rumors have filled our town. We can hardly serve without someone expecting a handout from the rich benefactor who flies across housetops dropping gold coins down chimneys."

"I hardly flew," Nicky muttered. "More like fell. And Antonius promised me he would say nothing!"

"A promise like that is very hard to keep. Especially when you've been blessed not once, but three times."

"It was what I felt I had to do." He crossed his arms and thrust himself down in the chair opposite his uncle. The old man pursed his lips, as if sensing a bit of the young man's temper once more rising to the fore.

"I am not questioning your actions, nor your motives. Nor am I blaming you for what has happened. You moved and acted as led by the Spirit, and that is a good thing. Always. The only good thing to do, in fact. But that it has unintended consequences

82

cannot be avoided. Our Lord Himself encountered this many times. How often in the Gospels do we read of Him performing an act of charity, or a miracle, and then giving a stern warning to the recipient not to say anything. And yet He was disobeyed. Quite frequently. Do you know what happened when that occurred?"

Nicky unfolded his arms and put his hands in his lap, as if suddenly interested in his thumbs. "He had to withdraw," he finally said.

"Precisely. Fame is a danger to be avoided. In this case, it is causing a serious distraction."

Nicky held his breath a moment, then released it, considering his uncle's proposal. Several years before, the Abbot had made the pilgrimage himself. When he returned, he founded New Zion. "I suppose it would be exciting to see the Holy Land."

"Indeed. To walk in the footsteps of Jesus? It is not to be missed."

"When?"

"There is a ship come from Alexandria that has put into port just yesterday. They will be leaving in two days, bearing cargo for Tyre. From there they will make for Ptolemais, and then on to Caesarea. From there, you will journey overland to Jerusalem."

"Alexandria? Not Qennios's ship? *The Hatmehit?*"

"It may be."

"Father didn't have good words for that man. Said he was reckless. Didn't like the name of his ship, either. Giving attention to discredited Egyptian gods."

"Your father had very high standards. I'm sure the captain will be fine."

Nicky nodded thoughtfully, working figures with his fingers. "Three days at sea, then, assuming good weather and a strong tailwind." He suddenly sucked in a breath. "Of course, this time of year, the sea is fickle."

"Isn't it always?"

"Sometimes more, sometimes less. Depends on the season."

"Well. I may not have had the privilege of sailing with your father, but I'm sure the captain knows what he's doing."

"Let's hope so."

"Nicky," the Abbot chided. "I know you are nervous."

"I'm not nervous. I've been at sea many times. I know what's out there. How easy it is to founder a ship." He almost mumbled this last part.

"It will be fine. You'll see. The Lord is fully capable of watching out for His own."

Nicky nodded. His uncle was right, of course, but that didn't remove the foreboding that weighed on his spirit. He glanced around a moment, taking in the familiar contours of the room, the scrolls piled on the shelves behind his uncle's table, the daylight streaming through the open windows. How could he possibly leave this all behind?

Uncle Nicholas stood and walked around the table. "You've

grown a lot in these last few years. It seems like only yesterday that Epiphanius came running up the path, breathless to tell me of your imminent birth. And now here you are: a man grown and about to explore the world on your own."

Nicky shrugged. When his uncle frowned he said, "It's just... I wonder if I'll ever see any of you again. Or this place. This town. It's all I've ever known."

"We are only sojourners on this land. Strangers and aliens, looking for a better city, Whose architect and builder is God."

"I know."

"Go to the Holy Land. Walk where Jesus walked. Commune with the saints. And, in time, when the Spirit directs you—go where He sends. In my heart, I feel that a wide, world of adventure in the kingdom of Christ awaits you."

Nicky stood and embraced his uncle, but in his heart, he felt only dread.

"Dread?" I asked. "Why dread?"

He shrugged. "I've often been given to what you would call premonitions."

"Clairvoyance?"

He clucked his tongue and shook his head. "Nothing quite like that. There've been a few times where the Lord has used me to reveal His purposes to others, and many times where His Spirit has whispered His intentions in the depths of my soul. I suspect this is nothing more than the sensitivity that comes from the Holy Spirit, something available to any who believe. Would that we all could prophesy, as Saint Paul said."

"So God was revealing the future."

"After a fashion. Amos 3:9 says, 'Surely the Lord God will do nothing, but He revealeth His secret unto His servants the Prophets.' In this case, He only hinted at what was to come."

"Sounds cryptic."

He nodded and continued his tale. "They all turned out to see me off. The whole town, I mean. I don't know how word leaked out, and I suspect more than a few were there hoping I'd shower them with gold before I left. But it at least afforded me a chance to say goodbye. There was also someone there I did not expect, nor did I know how to answer."

She burst through the door without knocking, startling Nicky as he stuffed the last of his clothes into a sack. "Is it true?" she asked.

"Johanna," he acknowledged. "What are you doing here?"

She came into the room and stood before him. Her hands fidgeted. "Are you leaving?"

He tied off his sack. "I'm going on a pilgrimage. To the Holy Land."

"Then I'm coming, too."

"What?" He stared at her. "Don't be ridiculous. Why would you do that?"

Her fingers curled into fists. "Why shouldn't I? Do you think I love the Lord any less than you?"

He stared at her. "Of course not. No. I never said that. But you shouldn't come on this voyage just because I'm going."

"Well who said I am?"

"No one," he conceded. "But... are you packed?"

"Well, no."

"Have you told your father? Your sisters? Did you even purchase passage on the ship?"

She looked at the floor. Gently, he touched her cheek and raised her face so he could see her eyes. She took his hand in her own and held it there. He felt a lump in his throat. There was more in this touch than he wanted to admit. "You are very beautiful, and I am very fond of you."

"Fond?"

"But I am a monk. I have dedicated my heart to God."

"And that means you cannot give it to another?"

He pulled his hand away. "I have to go." He started toward the door.

"And when will you return?"

He stopped, his hand on the door post. "I'm not coming back." With that, he pushed away from the door and hurried down the path.

"Nicholas, wait!" she called after him. He kept moving as if he had not heard. "Nicholas! I love you!"

He winced, and kept going.

After saying his goodbyes at the dock, Nicky hurried on board *The Hatmehit*. His heart felt wrenched apart. Fear, longing, and regret plagued his mind, filling him with doubts. He'd hastened below, scared witless that Johanna might come to the dock, and that seeing her standing there would make him forget his vow, that regret would pin his feet to the pier and prevent him from leaving. Even now, a hard ache squeezed his chest and drove hot tears down his cheeks. He buried his face in his elbow, and tried to pretend it was homesickness that made him cry.

And, of course, it was a lie.

When he closed his eyes, all he could see was Johanna's dark eyes pleading with him. He remembered the thrill that coursed through him when she took his hand in her own.

*This cannot be! I belong to God. What right have I to reclaim my heart and give it to another?*

"I made a vow," he whispered to God. "I promised You I'd

always be Yours. How can You now test me thus?"

No answer presented itself. After a while, he dried his tears and made his way to the deck of the ship.

Captain Qennios stood midship, barking orders to his men, who scurried about casting off lines and unfurling the sails. The ship rocked gently on the waves. Nicky glanced up as the wind filled the sheets, and felt the ship move forward. He turned to the gunwales and waved again at those few who remained on shore. But of course, most of them had left as soon as he went below deck. And what did he hope to see? Someone to make him stay?

And yet—his heart fled his chest, stretching wings across the water to the shore of his home—there she was, keeping pace with the ship, her hair loose and whipping in the wind that drove him further and further away. He dug his fingers into the wood, half tempted to jump into the sea and swim toward her.

"I will go where You send me, Father," he prayed, "but I must confess, I'm leaving my heart behind. How she managed to claim it, when I never offered it to her, I do not know. But neither can I deny it is in her hands." With that, the tears broke once more, running free down his face as if all his sorrows were in a rush to rejoin the sea.

Johanna reached the farthest point she could walk and stopped suddenly, as if startled she could go no further. She stood there, watching the ship depart, growing ever smaller with the distance, until at last she was lost to Nicky's view. At long last the town itself dwindled into obscurity, and Nicky turned away.

After a day at sea, Nicky had begun to trust in Captain Qennios, who proved himself a capable seaman, despite Nicky's father's forebodings. He ran the crew with a hard but even hand, and even invited Nicky to dine with him that supper, where they traded stories of his old man, as Qennios put it.

But that evening, as Nicky lay on his bunk, he was tormented by dreams. In his nightmare, a massive storm rolled in, swamping the ship and scattering the crew upon the waves. Nicky thrashed in his sleep, seeing the craft shatter into flotsam before the onslaught of the sea. He tried to cling to a piece of wood, but a sail caught him and held him fast, and the sailors who were drowning kept pulling him under.

One of them struck his face.

Nicky woke, and realized the hands and the slap were real. But the sail was his own blanket, and there was no storm, only the morning sun shining in its brilliance.

"So you are awake now, eh?"

Nicky glanced toward the seaman who'd struck him.

"You were crying out in your sleep. Dreaming, yes?"

He nodded. "Nightmare."

"Ah. Then I am not sorry to wake you. I am Marcus."

"Nicholas." He shook the man's hand.

"So, Nicholas of Patara. What did you dream that made you thrash about so?"

He swallowed and sat up. "It was nothing."

Marcus waggled a finger at him. "It was more than that. I think you are not being truthful with Marcus, hmm?"

"It was just a dream. I saw a storm. It rolled the ship. We broke apart in it and started to drown."

Marcus's eyes widened. "That is a dreadful dream. Perhaps the gods have spoken to you."

Nicholas gave him a wary eye. "There is only one God."

Marcus blinked. "You only have one god?"

"He's all I've ever needed."

The swarthy man frowned. "I have many gods, and none of them have ever done me any good."

"Perhaps you should try mine."

His mouth split into a wide grin. "Perhaps I should. Does he send dreams?"

Nicholas almost said no, but he caught himself. "Sometimes."

"So perhaps he has sent you this dream. Come! We must tell the captain."

"No, I don't think—!"

But Marcus caught him by the hand and hauled him onto the deck. "Captain! This man has had a dream!"

Qennios was at the helm. "A dream? Is that you, Nicholas?"

91

Nicholas came forward, his cheeks flushing. He noticed the rest of the men slowing their work and gathering around. "It is."

"And what is this dream you have had?"

"Go on," Marcus poked his side. "Tell him."

*Oh dear God!* he prayed. *I don't want to discredit You. If I tell them this dream, and nothing comes of it, will they not say I have testified falsely? But if I do not warn them, and the dream is of You, will they not blame me for their misfortune?*

He noticed the men pacing nervously. He swallowed the lump in his throat and said, "I had a dream. A storm came up from the northeast. A great gale of wind stirred up the waves into a tempest, and they crashed upon the ship. It overturned and was broken to pieces. Many perished."

The men around him muttered darkly. Some said, "It is an omen." While others chided, "He is a frightened child. He knows nothing."

To the men, Nicholas said, "I do not think God sent this dream to no purpose. It was given as a warning not to punish or frighten, but to save. Captain, if we drop our sails and turn the ship away from the wind, we will be driven before it, and not capsized."

Qennios came down from the helm and folded his arms. "You forget your place, Nicholas, son of Theophanes. I know what your father said of me. That I am reckless. Heedless. But I am captain here."

"You mean to prove him wrong then?"

Qennios opened and closed his mouth, as if suddenly aware that he'd backed himself into a corner. Finally, he said, "I have outrun many storms in my day. I keep my sails unfurled and let the wind drive me ahead of it, then I turn to the north and slip its fury 'ere it does me any harm. But if this storm of your dreams should rise, we will do as the son of Theophanes suggests. There may not be as much sport as in outwitting Neptune, but neither has your father ever lost a ship, eh?"

Nicholas opened his mouth to thank the man, but was caught off by an ominous rumble from aft of the ship. All heads turned, and beheld with sudden shock the dark, billowing clouds that rushed down on their tiny ship like a Roman siege.

"Captain!" Marcus cried. "It comes, just as he said!"

Qennios stared at the storm, then at Nicholas, his mouth gaping.

"Heed the warning," Nicholas said. "God will yet save us." He turned to the men as they scrambled for the lines. "Have no fear! You will see the salvation of the Lord this day. God shall protect us!"

Qennios pointed to the sails. "Secure those lines. Helmsman! Steer a course directly away the path of the storm. Let it drive us before it till it passes o'er us!" He turned to Nicholas and put a hand on his shoulder. "I'll ne'er doubt your God again. Pray to Him for us."

Nicholas nodded, and then dropped to the deck, folding his hands in prayer.

In mere moments, the storm was upon them. *The Hatmehit* groaned as the waves lifted and dropped it. Gales of water sprayed upon the deck, soaking them to the bone and glazing the wood. A crack of lightning struck the main mast, which caught flame for a moment before the heavy rains doused the fire. Nicholas closed his eyes tightly and prayed more fervently. Just then, a sudden pitch in the ship sent him sprawling sideways. He collided with the rails and felt his skull smack against the wood. He opened his mouth, and caught a face full of seawater as a massive wave surged over the gunwales and thrust him back against the wood.

Marcus stumbled beside him and grabbed his shirt collar. "What are you doing? Pray! Your God battles Neptune for our fates!"

"Secure the rigging!" Qennios's voice sounded small over the thrashing of the ocean. Nicholas reached a hand up and wrapped it around the ropes, hanging on for dear life. He stared through the water beading his eyelashes as Marcus grabbed the rope and scurried up the ratlines toward the mainsail. The man reached the spar and started drawing the sail tighter about the beam. Just as he finished lashing it, the ship pitched yet again. He lost his footing, and slipped off, dangling from the mainspar by his arms.

"Marcus!" Nicholas cried.

The man clung desperately to the beam, but his body shifted down, buffeted by the winds.

"Oh God, no!" Nicholas pushed to his feet, releasing his hold on the ropes.

Marcus lost his grip. His body fell, plunging to the deck which pitched, rising upward as if to catch him. He struck with a heavy smack and lay listless, shifting about as the boat rocked beneath the storm.

Nicholas rushed to his side even as other sailors hurried to their fallen comrade.

"Marcus?" Nicholas touched his face, but the man's head lolled to one side, unresponsive.

The other sailors stared wide-eyed and silent. Qennios reached them. He pushed the others out of the way and bent down, putting his ear to Marcus's chest. After a moment, he raised his head and shook it.

"He's dead."

*God, no.* Nicholas stared at the man. *Please no. Hasn't there been enough death already? He does not know You! His soul is lost without You. Please, God. Bring him back.*

Qennios put his hand on Nicholas's shoulder. "Enough! Your prayers are no more use here!"

Nicholas stared at him, his lip quivering. He hadn't realized he'd been speaking out loud. He felt something warm, bordering on anger, welling in his chest. "Marcus, hear me! Jesus Christ commands you: wake up and live!"

Nicholas stood, glaring once more at the captain, and then raised his hands at the sky. "Peace! In the name of God, be still!"

*The Hatmehit* shuddered once more in the waves, but then the storm clouds relented, and, impossibly, the rain stopped. All the men stared at the sky as the wind abated, and then at Nicholas. A sudden cough drew their eyes down to the deck, and a cry of wonder rose.

Marcus coughed again and opened his eyes, sucking in a huge breath.

"Impossible!" Qennios declared.

Nicholas lowered his hands, turned, and caught Qennios's gaze. "Nothing is impossible to them that believe."

 **Eight**

"Wait a second," I said. "Let me get this straight. You brought the guy back from the dead?"

The Abbot shook his head. "I have no power to do such a thing. Marcus was healed by God. That is the only explanation."

"Yeah, but you told him to wake up, and he did. After the captain checked his heart. And then you told the storm to quiet down, and it did."

"Jesus once said to His disciples, 'You will do greater things than these because I go to the Father.' Is it so hard to believe that He meant what He said?"

"Yeah, but miracles?"

He cocked his head at me. "Why does this strain your credulity?"

I gaped, searching for the words. "Miracles don't just happen. I'm not talking about seeing a sunset or having a baby kinda miracles. I mean the truly supernatural, 'Hey, look! I just raised the dead,' or 'Hey, look! I can walk on water!' kind of thing. They don't happen."

"In your experience."

"In anyone's experience!"

"They've happened in mine."

My ability to find the words to voice my instinctive objection to what he said was fading rapidly. "I-I just find this really hard to believe."

"For those that do not believe, no proof is sufficient. For those that do, no proof is necessary."

"No, wait. I'm not saying I don't want to believe you. I mean, your story is incredible. But, come on! Raising the dead?"

The Abbot heaved a breath. "Let me repeat myself. I never said I raised the dead. Only God has power to do such a thing. If you believe in God, nothing will be impossible for you. If you do not believe in God, nothing will be possible. That's just how it is, Brett. As it stands, I did not say I raised the dead. What I can tell you is that Marcus fell from a tremendous height. Hit the deck. And when Qennios put his ear to his chest, he heard nothing. To me, that was unacceptable. How could God allow this pagan, so close to learning the gospel for the first time, fall and pass away like that? That was why I said what I did. And when I said those words, Marcus opened his eyes. That is what I know. What I believe, is that God raised him up in answer to my prayer."

"So it's possible he wasn't dead at all?"

"I am not a mortician! And it isn't the point of the story at all. I'm not sitting here trying to convince you I have magical powers. I don't! What I am telling you is that God has all the power over life and death, and He alone decides who lives, who dies, and who lives again."

It wasn't an entirely satisfactory answer. Nicholas seemed to be telling me that he'd either brought about—or at the very least witnessed—a bona fide miracle. I couldn't accept that. Not if there wasn't an alternative, rational explanation. Certainly to Qennios and to Nicholas, it must've looked like Marcus had died. And maybe the impact had caused a temporary arrhythmia that corrected itself moments later. And that freaky business about calming the storm could've just been a convenient coincidence. A freak synchronicity. Nothing more.

Evidently, Nicholas wasn't satisfied by my answer, either. "Faith is a choice, Brett. You choose to believe, and you will find the evidence to back up your belief. You choose not to believe, and you will also find the evidence to back up your unbelief. But don't fool yourself into thinking that belief or unbelief are not your choices to make. God will not force Himself upon you. Not yet, at least. A day is coming when every knee will bow, and every tongue confess that Jesus Christ is Lord. But for this day, this moment, it is up to us to choose Him, or to reject Him. And we either want there to be a God because we want the world to have meaning, or we don't want there to be a God because we do not want the world to have meaning."

"Just wanting there to be a God doesn't make Him real," I insisted.

A sly grin tugged at the corner of his mouth. "And just

wanting there not to be a God won't make Him go away."

I heaved a breath. "So what happened then?"

"Well, as you can imagine, a great many of the sailors came to faith that day. Qennios himself did not, and neither did he invite me to sup with him after that. But Marcus believed, as did a number of his shipmates. And they asked me to teach them the ways of God the rest of the journey. Which I did. I organized the men into groups according to their watch, and taught them the Word of God three times each day. Thus, I occupied myself with the ministry of the Word for the duration of the voyage. By the time we put into port at Tyre, I had baptized seven of the crew. By Caesarea, another three. Just before leaving the ship, Qennios asked me to come see him.

"Nicholas," Qennios said. He glanced around as if wary that any of his men might see him talking to the young man. "If you have a moment?"

"Certainly." The young monk followed the Captain into his cabin.

Once inside, the Captain closed the door. He took a heavy breath. "I never properly thanked you for what you did that day of the storm. To be truthful, I've thought of little else since then. I struggled to find words for it. And I cannot."

He motioned Nicholas to a seat. "You strike me as a common man, Nicholas son of Theophanes. You are a devout and holy man. Anyone can see that. But you take your share of work. You laugh readily and heartily with the men. And you treat every man as equal, regardless of father, faith, or fealty. And that is why I don't quite know what to do with you. To my every sense, you are as normal as I. But there are two things I know with certainty. I know that when I put my ear to Marcus's chest, I heard no heartbeat, and yet you bid him awaken, and he stands among us today. And I saw you raise your hands and rebuke the storm. I know this. I also know, though you are as normal as I, that I could not have done either of these things.

"So what are you? Are you a god?"

Nicholas almost laughed and shook his head. "No. Of course not! And you are right. I am as normal as you. What you must know is simply this: I, Nicholas of Patara, did nothing. I calmed no storm. I raised no one to life. But there is a God in heaven Who listens to prayer. He watches over each and every one of us because He made us and knows us, and believe it or not, He loves us despite ourselves. He is the One Who raised Marcus to life again. And the storm stopped at His command, not any word of mine."

Qennios shook his head. "How is this possible?"

"Why is it not? Is anything impossible with God?"

"But that He should choose to consort with mere mortals—"

"Captain," Nicholas started, but they were interrupted by a knock at the door.

One of the men poked his head through. "Captain? You are needed on shore."

Qennios nodded and rose. He apologized and shook Nicholas's hand. "Someday you must tell me more of this God you serve."

"Gladly," Nicholas replied. "And if it is all right, I should pray that you meet Him even as I have."

But as Nicholas left the ship behind, he bore a sinking feeling that he'd missed a moment, and that he might never see Qennios again.

"So did you?" I asked. We were sipping tea, now, Brother Don having cleared away the dishes after we finished our meal.

Nicholas gave me a furtive smile. "I'm going to hold off on answering that just yet."

Just then, Brother Don appeared at our table. "Pardon the interruption, but Brother Stephan has asked if you could come down to see him in a few hours."

"Indeed? Does he imagine he'll have the order ready?"

Brother Don smiled widely. "He said not to tell you, that it would spoil the surprise. But he did want to be sure you came down tonight, after vespers."

The Abbot checked his watch. "That should be fine. Is Heinrich leading the service this evening?"

"He is," Don's eyes widened, "and I hear he's got something special as well."

Nicholas managed a wry grin. "Everyone is putting on their best show for you, it seems."

"Oh?"

"You must forgive us. We so rarely have visitors this far north. Everyone is excited you are here."

"Why are you this far north?"

"Oh come now!" he leaned back. "You are really getting ahead of the story."

I put my hands out. "I withdraw the question, so long as you'll answer it in time."

"In time," he mused. "Speaking of which, we should return to Brother Oleg. If he wakens and we're not there, I'll never hear the end of it."

Together, we returned to the upstairs room where Brother Oleg had been sleeping. As soon as we opened the door, I knew we were in for it.

"I've not got so much time left in this world," Oleg reproved as we walked inside, "that I wish to spend it staring at these walls alone."

"It's my fault," I said quickly. "The Abbot noticed my stomach rumbling."

"And Brother Don would have been quite useful in bringing you some food, rather than you both traipsing on down to the kitchen, leaving me to suffer alone," the monk answered.

"But that would've involved Brother Don navigating the stairs," The Abbot replied, "and you know how quickly that tires him out."

Brother Oleg made a face. "Yah? It seems to me Brother Don could use a little tiring out. The exercise would do him good."

"And a little rest would've done you some good," The Abbot replied.

"Bah. I'll have plenty of rest soon enough."

I turned to the Abbot. "Is he always this grouchy?"

"It's one of the symptoms of senility."

"I am not senile!"

"Denial is the other one," The Abbot finished as he closed the door.

Oleg gave him a baleful glare. "You are incorrigible."

"After so many years? You are just now figuring that out?"

"Matches that temper of yours."

"But nothing is a match to yours. Come," he took his seat beside Oleg's bed. "We'll pick up where we left off."

"Where did you leave off?" Oleg groused. "I have missed half the story."

"You only missed the storm at sea, and I've told you that one already. I just finished telling Brett how I came to Caesarea. From there, I traveled on foot to Jerusalem, joining with a small band of pilgrims making the same journey. And that is how I came to the Holy City."

"And what did you do there?" I asked.

"Today we would call it sightseeing. Back then, there were no tours to guide us—at least, none that would rip you off."

"How's that changed?" I returned.

He snorted. "Point taken. At any rate, I visited the sites, walked the Via Dolorosa. Prayed at Golgotha. And spent time contemplating the empty tomb. You can imagine the impact that had on me."

"Considering what you just went through? Of course."

"And I also visited the cave in Bethlehem where Christ was born."

"Yah. Talk about impact," Brother Oleg murmured. The Abbot raised an eyebrow at him, and he winked in response.

"So was it all you'd hoped it'd be?" I asked.

The Abbot stroked his beard. "Difficult to say. It was overwhelming, on the one hand. And on the other? Bewildering."

"Why?"

He shifted in his seat. "I suppose because I thought I'd find answers there. A sense of direction. A sense of calling. Anything to tell me what it was God wanted me to do. And yet, after visiting all the sites and spending much time in prayer, I was no closer to finding an answer to the question than I had been aboard *The Hatmehit.*

"I spent most of that first week sleeping out under the stars as I wandered about, benefiting from the hospitality of the locals and blessing them as I had opportunity. Giving them news of the goings on in Patara and other parts of the world turned out to be a greater service than anything else I performed, though. The world was in turmoil, not unlike today, and people wanted to know the thoughts and opinions of one who'd come so far just to visit them.

"But after storm clouds rolled in the next day, I sought refuge with the brothers at Beit Jala."

"What's that?"

"It is a small village southwest of Jerusalem, about a mile or so from Bethlehem. There were a series of caves and some small houses there where the brothers had built up a small monastery. I spent the next three years living and serving among them, waiting for an answer to my prayers."

"Long time."

"It was. But I had to learn patience. I had to learn that to merely walk where Jesus walked was not to walk His path. Such would require greater sacrifice and commitment on my part than I had yet attained. I began to question myself, my faith, my whole reason for being there. I even began to question God, Who'd allowed my parents to die. I suppose this is a test many in the faith must undergo, to decide whether we believe because it is convenient, or if we believe because it is true even when inconvenient. I remember vividly, one night, coming to pray at the only Church left in Jerusalem at the time. The Church of the Room of the Last Supper, on Mount Zion. It seems strange now, to speak of there only being one church left. For so long Jerusalem had been the center of Christian life—and yet the world had moved on. Rome had taken preeminence, and the place where it all began remained an historical curiosity, but nothing more."

As he talked, I put my finger on the heart of what bothered me about The Abbot's tale. He talked of all these places as if he'd been there. And yet clearly, these were things that had happened long, long ago—far longer than a man of his age could have experienced directly. I started to suspect that I was the recipient of some grand oral tradition, perhaps passed down from generation to generation over the years so that its truth would remain intact. Maybe they wanted me to finally write this down, so that it could be preserved in its best form. Though why they should have waited so long to do so made little sense to me.

"I suppose," The Abbot continued, "this is how we lost Jerusalem to the Muslims. They took nothing more than what we had already abandoned. Strange that so many died in those futile wars to win back what we clearly had no real interest in maintaining. At any rate, I came to the church late at night, feeling compelled in my spirit to pray there, and found the heavy doors locked securely. I wondered how I would find entrance to do as bidden in my spirit. But as I came near, the doors swung open of their own accord and admitted me. That's when I knew I was where I was supposed to be. That I was doing as the Lord willed. I fell to my knees, my heart overflowing with thanksgiving to God. And I committed, then and there in a way I never had before, that I would go anywhere, do anything, say any word, that my heart, my life, my soul was His to do with as He saw fit. All other questions and doubts fled from my mind, and in the cool shadows of that sanctuary, I finally received my calling."

"Which was?"

He smiled. "To go home."

## Nine

"Home?" I repeated. "That was it?"

He nodded. "Yes. That was it."

I couldn't suppress my grin. "So you travelled all those thousands of miles just to learn that you never had to leave in the first place."

Oleg snorted, and the Abbot frowned. "No. Not remotely. I travelled all those thousands of miles in order to see my life in perspective, to discover who and what I was. You must understand, as a youngster, I could think of nothing more desirable nor fantastic than escaping my home by way of the sea and travelling to far distant lands. Now I had, after a fashion, done so. I had lived for three years among a people who knew me as no one else, who'd never seen me grow up, who had no sense of who my parents were, no preconceived notions of what I ought to do or how I ought to live. I encountered a freedom in Jerusalem I had never really known in my home country—the freedom of being just a man in Christ. But now, basking in the freedom of Christ, I also knew that I could best serve Him amongst my own people. And so that is what I did.

"I took my leave of the brothers in Bait Jala and the friends

I'd made there, returned to Caesarea, and booked passage on the first ship home."

"Qennios?"

"No. This was *The Mollusk*, captained by a man named Matthias. An altogether unpleasant fellow who made me very glad the voyage was short and uneventful."

"Why so disagreeable?"

Nicholas shrugged. "Perhaps his shoes were too tight. I don't know."

I glanced at Oleg. Was this an example of the famous temper he kept mentioning? He winked at me, as if reading my thoughts and confirming my suspicions.

"What I do know," The Abbot continued, "was that he took it upon himself to relentlessly attack the faith. He disparaged Christ and His Apostles with no end of accusations and slander, severely testing me, I might add. I think, in retrospect, it was a test from God, to see whether or not I would control my tongue and restrain myself, or would I simply tear him a new one. I must confess, I was sorely tempted. Believe me, if I really kept that list people say I have, his name would still be at the top."

"List?"

He smiled at me. "Love keeps no record of wrongs. Anyway, by the time we reached port, I'd had enough. As soon as I walked off the ship, I turned and loudly blessed him in the name of Christ Almighty, The Holy Spirit, the Blessed Virgin and every saint he'd maligned during the entire voyage. I must've gone on for five minutes. And then I told him he'd done so well as captain that I would give him my heartiest recommendation to all my Christian brothers, and prayed he never lacked for two or three Christians on his ship, just to plead to God for his health and safety." He laughed and slapped his knee. "I'll never forget the look on his face!"

At that moment, there was a knock on the door. A monk I'd not yet met poked his head in when Nicholas announced it was open and begged our pardon. "It's Brother Stephan," the man said. "He would like a word."

"I'm given to understand we'll be visiting him later."

"Yes, but he's asking for you—just you—at the moment."

"Did he say why?"

"How to put this delicately? He's run into a bit of a snag."

"I see. Please tell him I'll be right there." To me he said, "I apologize, Brett. It seems there is something I must attend to before vespers."

"Okay. No problem. I guess I can wait here till you return."

He nodded and started for the door, then turned abruptly. "Oleg? Why don't you pick up where I left off? You know the story well enough."

"It's supposed to be your story," Oleg groused.

"And it is, but if we delay much, we'll run out of time before we run out of story."

"*Svært vel.* But you owe me one."

Nicholas rolled his eyes and shut the door behind himself. After he'd gone, I faced Oleg.

"*Vel,*" Oleg said. "He didn't go back home exactly. He stopped in to see his uncle, but God had other plans."

"Okay."

"It started when the bishop in Myra died."

"Myra?"

"Yah. Today it is known as Demre. It is near to Patara, only about fifty miles east as the crow flies. As I said, the bishop had died."

Bishop Lucian looked up as the last of his fellow elders entered the room for the conclave, and lifted his eyes to heaven in silent thanksgiving. None of them had been captured or killed. Things within the Empire were once more getting out of hand. The emperor, Augustus Diocletian, had begun to make noise again about tradition, by which he meant pagan idolatry. His fellow Caesar and son-in-law, Galerius, blamed his military losses on the disapproval of the gods, and was pushing the entire tetrarchy toward an edict against the Christian faith. Lucian had prayed that Augustus Maximian and Caesar Constantius, the remaining members of the ruling tetrarchy, would restrain the impulses of the other two, but it was unlikely.

Troubling times indeed. Days like these made the gatherings of Christians difficult. The assembling of so many bishops in a single place, however, was downright dangerous.

Nevertheless, what choice did they have? Myra's See was without a Bishop, and a new one needed to be appointed.

He shook his head. For more than thirty years, there had been peaceful co-existence between the Christians and the pagans. Why should that change now? And yet, ever since his ascension, Diocletian had showed contempt for those who thought differently than he did. He'd driven believers out of the army, and had condemned to death the followers of Manichee. While the persecution of the Manicheans did not involve the Christians directly, neither did it bode well. Diocletian surrounded himself with public opponents of any faith but his own. Lucian shivered. The future would be dark indeed.

And yet, the Lord had determined in His wisdom to perfect His Church through suffering. Tertullian had said the blood of the martyrs was the seed of the Church. Certainly this was true. And yet, hadn't the faith been growing and spreading during the peace spawned by the previous emperor, Gallienus? They'd even built a church in Nicomedia overlooking the imperial palace.

But now, all that might come to an end. In his spirit, Lucian felt this to be true. In a real way, whoever they appointed to this position—by the grace of God—they would be sentencing to a life of suffering or worse. This, more than anything made the selection of a bishop a challenge for all. Not only must they be sure the man they select is designated by God to lead His Church in this city and its environs, but they must ensure the man is prepared to endure the trials that inevitably come from those who despise the faith, and do so, as Saint Peter said, with gentleness and respect.

"Brother Lucian, are we all assembled?"

The voice broke him from his reverie. He glanced up. The speaker was Dionysius, a gentle, learned man. Lucian looked over the assembled bishops and, after a moment, nodded. "Let us pray," he said.

And they prayed. For hours they prayed, begging God to give them a sense of who among the See of Myra might be the one the Lord had chosen to lead His flock. The prayer taxed them, pushing their mental and spiritual reserves. Sometimes, one of them would mutter a name, and the others would lift him up, begging God for confirmation, for some sign that the name posed an answer to their requests.

But nothing came.

The candles dwindled to waxy stubs, until the wicks themselves flickered and fell, drowning their flames in the residue of their own burning. Outside, the sun vanished beneath the horizon, and a blue darkness deepened as night overcame day. Slowly, one by one, the bishops rose, crossed themselves, and slipped out of the church to find their own beds. Lucian lifted his eyes and watched them go, fully conscious the prayer was not finished—would not be finished until the new bishop was named—but even Christ recognized the limitations of human endurance.

The spirit is willing, but the flesh is indeed weak.

He shook his head, crossed himself, and rose from his knees. First to arrive, last to leave. In a way, he felt it was as it should be. He followed the men from the room, pausing only at the door to listen. Perhaps the Lord would see fit to speak now.

Nothing.

He sighed, a heavy breath drawn from deep in his lungs and expelled as if disgorging the weight in his soul. He shuffled outside, shut the door, and retired to his room.

As he lay down that night, staring at the shadows quivering in the dark, he voiced his own prayer to the Lord. Lacking formality, he spoke from his heart, begging for clarity.

*I fear the future, God. I fear what You might ask of this new bishop. I know that he will suffer. I can read that much into the times. And how can I accept the responsibility of subjecting one of Your children to such a fate? Oh, forgive me, please! I know it is not my choice to make, nor even that of the conclave. It is merely our responsibility to name. The choice belongs to You and You alone. But how can I not feel this burden? Is this what weighs on Your Own heart? You, Who knows the future and fate of us all? Even knowing You would raise Lazarus from the dead, still You wept. Even knowing Your own victory over the grave, still You sweat drops of blood in Gethsemane. I feel that burden, too. And I fear placing it on the shoulders of another.*

*Perhaps that is why my ears are so dull. Perhaps that is why none of us knows the name You have chosen. Dear God, please relieve us this burden! Speak the name to Your servant and be done with it!*

He waited a moment in the dark, hearing nothing. At last, he closed his eyes.

*Nicholas.*

He opened them almost immediately. The name came from the darkness, spoken without sound to his conscious mind.

*Watch the doors at matins. The first person to cross the threshold of the church in the morning named Nicholas shall be the bishop in Myra.*

He opened his mouth, awed by the clarity with which God had spoken. Then he nodded slowly. "So be it, Lord," he answered, and closed his eyes.

116

The next morning, when the conclave had gathered and the doors were shut before dawn had broken, Lucian lifted his hands and addressed them. "My brothers, has the Lord spoken to any of you this past night?"

Exchanged glances all around. Then Cassius nodded his aged head. "He has spoken to you, Brother Lucian. Hasn't He?"

Lucian nodded. "He has. As I lay on my bunk asleep last night, seeking the Lord's will in this matter before us, I heard Him speak a name. It is not any one of us here, nor, to my knowledge a brother within this fellowship whom He has selected. As I prayed and listened, the Lord said to me, 'The first person to enter this church at Matins named Nicholas is our new bishop.'"

A low murmur ran through the conclave. Then Dionysius said, "Let us pray for confirmation of this word."

"And perhaps our learned brother should keep an eye on the door," Cassius added. "For I see the sun is about to rise, and Matins begins."

Lucian nodded somberly, and moved to the door. On the other side, the sun poked over the horizon and sent a slender, golden ray gleaming over the fields and gentle hills. He lifted the latch and pushed the heavy door open, hearing it creak against the ponderous hinges. The morning air washed over his face like a mother's caress, and a gentle breeze brushed at the few locks of silver hair that still crowned his head. He squinted against the brightness as the sun climbed higher, and in its brilliant glare saw the first forms of the faithful as they paraded toward the church for morning worship. He felt his pulse quicken as they arrived, and tried not to look disappointed when the first one there was an elderly woman, supported by her grandson. Next came a family with two small children, the daughter with her arms wrapped around her father's neck as he carried her in his arms. Lucian smiled and welcomed them in, and yet couldn't avoid feeling a twinge of disappointment, knowing they were not the Lord's chosen.

And so it went. Farmers, craftsmen, fishermen and their families. Young, old, and all those in between sauntered into the church, taking their places in the pews for the morning service. And none of them was the man the Lord had chosen. At last, the church was full, and the stream of humanity had dwindled to a trickle, and then ended.

Perplexed, he turned around and met the eyes of the other bishops gathered by the side. He shrugged.

Cassius stepped forward and spoke to the assembled believers. "Beloved friends, is there one among you named Nicholas?"

After a moment, a young man gingerly raised his hand. Slowly, he stood. "I am Nicholas," he said. Lucian recognized him as the young man who'd come in with elderly woman—the very first person to walk through the doors that morning, in fact. He'd been sitting among them the entire time.

Lucian broke into a broad grin, and strode forward, raising his hands in greeting. "Brother Nicholas, friend and servant of God. We have been expecting you. For your holiness, you shall be bishop of this place."

"So, bishop, just like that?" I asked.

Brother Oleg shrugged. "More or less. There was a great celebration once the bishops explained matters. Nicholas, I think for a moment, tried to refuse. Wanted to, actually. He didn't feel himself worthy—being so young and inexperienced. But what could he say? He himself had been praying mightily for the Lord's direction. It was mere happenstance that he was in Myra at all. His uncle had learned the conclave was gathered there, and sent Nicholas to them with the intention of asking some of the bishops to visit New Zion monastery before they returned to their respective homes. He hadn't seen some of them in many years. And, I suspect, he wanted to introduce them to his nephew. His uncle had no notion that Nicholas himself would be appointed Bishop in Myra. It was as much a surprise to him as it was to anyone.

"But they believed the Lord had spoken. The vision or dream Lucian had from the previous night had come true. And so, Nicholas was placed in the bishop's seat, and in short order went through the confirmation process. They ordained him a deacon and then a priest to preserve the tradition, and then immediately confirmed him as their new bishop."

"Isn't that a little unusual?"

"Yah, certainly! In fact, it has only happened two other times, to Saints Ambrose and Severus."

"Hmm. And who were they?"

He gave me an irritated look. "Ambrose became Bishop of Milan around 374. He was originally the Governor of Aemilia-Liguria in northern Italy, and was known to be very conciliatory in his approach. Milan, at the time, was overrun with Arians, and they—"

"I'm sorry. What are Arians?"

"I am beginning to see why the Abbot asked you not to interrupt."

I raised my hand in surrender. "Apologies. I'm just a little lost here."

"Arius was a heretic. He did not think Jesus was God in the flesh, and insisted on teaching many others this very troubling, very false doctrine."

"I see."

"As I said, Milan was overrun with his followers, and St. Ambrose, as Governor, was attempting to bring peace to the discord in the church after the previous bishop had passed. The people were so impressed by his oratory, they demanded he become their bishop. Thinking they would get a sympathetic ear, the Arians agreed. He turned out to be quite harsh with them. The other saint I mentioned—"

"Severus."

"Yes, Severus, was Bishop of Barcelona. By trade a weaver, the people of Barcelona witnessed a dove landing on his head, and took this to mean the Holy Spirit had descended upon the man, so they elected him bishop."

"Wait a second—a bird lands on the guy's head, and he gets a bishopric out of it? Good thing those guys had never been to Central Park. They'd be ordaining statues left and right."

Oleg snorted. "Times were different then. People were less educated, and more apt to believe things the educated man would miss. As it is, the people of Barcelona did not choose badly. A number of miracles are associated with Severus. He died in the persecutions of Diocletian. The soldiers scourged him with a flagrum—a multi-thong whip—and then drove nails into his head."

"Dear God!"

He nodded. "Yah. The persecutions of Diocletian were among the most brutal the Church has ever endured. It's amazing any survived."

The door opened, and Nicholas came back in. Oleg raised his eyes. "Most didn't," he finished.

**Ten**

"All set then?" Nicholas asked.

Oleg nodded, and shifted back into his bed, pulling the covers up to his chin. "Yah. I just finished telling him about your unusual ordination. We compared it to that of Ambrose and Severus."

"Hmm," he grunted. "Honorable men, both."

"Everything go all right with... whatever the big mystery is?" I asked.

"I'll never tell," he grinned. "Oleg has finished telling you how I became bishop of Myra?"

"I said I did," Oleg groused.

I ignored his outburst. "It must've been quite unnerving," I told the Abbot.

"And it was. I had no real notion what I was getting into. What would be expected of me. After they ordained me, I pulled Lucian and Cassius to one side and begged them to tell me what to do. My experience with bishops was limited to mass and the few times I'd seen them serving in various functions. I had no real concept of what a bishop did day in and day out."

"Did they clear things up for you?"

"Not really," he laughed. "But in time, with the prayer and

support of my flock, I learned the ropes well enough. After a few months, my uncle came to see me."

"How'd that go?"

He sighed. "Not as well as I'd hoped."

I frowned. "Was there a problem between you two?"

"No. It was who he brought with him."

Nicholas stared out the window of his study at the morning sun, pondering the letter he'd received earlier that week. His uncle was coming to see him. In his letter he spoke of Nicholas's ordination to the bishopric in glowing terms, and yet somehow, Nicholas couldn't shake a feeling of dread over it.

He'd spent an hour in prayer already, searching his soul, trying to discern the source of his unease. He'd initially suspected that he had some unconfessed anger toward his uncle for sending him here in the first place, as if the errand his uncle had entrusted to him was merely a ruse to get him out here. And after a fashion it was—Uncle Nicholas wanted to introduce him to the larger sphere of bishops in hopes that one of the men would take him on as a disciple, perhaps ordain him as a priest or help him discern his calling. And he'd known that when he agreed to come. Neither of them could have predicted it would lead to this!

But no, there was no anger there that he was conscious of. He did not hold his uncle responsible—and even if he did, it was hardly something for which the man should apologize! Truth be told, Nicholas enjoyed his new role. He found great satisfaction in both preaching and counseling. Tending to the needs of his flock gave him great joy.

Then he'd begun to imagine he might be experiencing some measure of guilt—though for what, he could not say. He searched his heart and his memory to discern whether or not there remained any promise not kept, any commitment he'd made to his uncle as yet unfulfilled. Once more, he came up empty.

What weighed on his heart most of all, he'd begun to realize, was the incredible burden he felt for the city. Myra was in the midst of a famine. Plague had swept through the country not long before he'd arrived—it was this that took the previous bishop's life, in fact—with the result that many of the fields had been left unsown. Consequently, there was too little food to feed the surviving population. Nor had the subsequent drought helped matters any. The grain was dying in the fields, burned from the heat of the summer sun, and as harvest neared, what they did bring would be insufficient to feed the hungry or do much for the poor.

This, he realized, was what bothered him. Not merely the burden of caring for his flock, but the feeling of impotence in the face of such desperation, and with it, the fear that he had or was failing in his new role, and would prove a disappointment to himself and to his uncle, and perhaps even an embarrassment to God.

It wasn't true, of course. He knew that as a matter of faith. But it was difficult to convince his mind of this.

Uncle Nicholas would be arriving any hour now, and he, as Bishop, had the responsibility to greet the Abbot and welcome him with a meal. But what could they possibly serve that would not take food out of the mouths of his parishioners? Should he explain the matter to the man, or should he just offer the best meal possible and take the loss?

On the other hand, his uncle would be horrified if Nick insisted on feeding him at the expense of others. He knew the man well enough for that. But that meant being fairly clear about the desperate state of the town, and he did not wish to burden his uncle unduly.

He crumpled the letter in his fist and tossed it into the brazier, watching as the flame curled the parchment until it caught fire in a burst of smoke. In moments, all that remained were what looked like charred leaves with tiny glow worms inching about on the edges.

Nicholas watched the fire a moment, reflecting on how quickly the paper vanished in the flame, and he reflected on the words of James, the brother of Jesus. *What is your life? You are but a vapor that appears for a little while, and then vanishes.*

He shuddered, and turned back to the window. When he did so, he saw two figures appear over the crest of the hilltop, moving slowly along the road. One he recognized instantly as bearing the portly gait of his uncle. The other... he stared. The other was a woman with dark hair like a raven's and a determined gait.

Johanna? His heart thudded at the prospect of seeing her face again. Last time he'd talked with her she had confessed her love for him, and he'd run away, fleeing below deck even as she gave chase along the shore. What would he say to her now?

"Uncle, it is so good to see you!" He heartily embraced the older man.

"And you. You're looking well as a bishop. I see the ministry suits you."

"It does, it does indeed." He helped the old man into a seat. When he straightened, he turned to the woman. "Johanna."

"Nicky. I-I mean, Bishop—" She blushed.

"It's all right. I'm still getting used to it myself. Can I offer you anything?"

"A little wine if you have it," the Abbot replied, giving them both a careful glance.

"Of course." Nick rose and found the decanter and cups.

Johanna moved to intercept it from him.

"Allow me," she said.

"Nonsense." He poured a cup and handed it to her. "You are my guests. And I am honored to serve." He poured a second cup and handed it to his uncle, then a final one for himself, which he promptly downed. *That was unseemly,* he told himself, and carefully put the decanter away.

"I'm told," the Abbot began, "that Myra is in the midst of some difficulty."

"We are," he sighed, recognizing there was no point in disguising the truth. "Plague and famine."

"One tends to follow the other."

"Yes. And Death follows after, with Hades in its wake."

"Is there anything we can do?"

"Pray. I'd request further assistance, but the farmers here would be too proud to take it. Even the poorest among them is more apt to suffer in silence than to seek aid."

"Yes," his uncle tipped back his cup. "It is a perverse form of pride to suffer in silence rather than permit another the opportunity to show charity. Or love."

Nick glanced at him, and his uncle held his gaze until Nick turned away. The Abbot handed the goblet back to Nicholas. "I should like to see these fields."

"I can arrange for you to see them after supper if you like."

"I think now would be better. My legs have not yet stiffened from the journey."

"As you will," he replied. He rose and received Johanna's cup, and when he did so her hand touched his own. The feeling was so electric he nearly dropped the goblet. "Yes," he stuttered. "It would be good to... I'll show you now."

He led them outside to one of the large fields growing on the hillside behind the church. His uncle walked on one side, and Johanna walked on the other, and Nick found himself struggling not to look at her as they climbed the hillside. Nevertheless he still had to take her hand when they reached a particularly steep place, and she refused to relinquish it when they crested the rise.

"Ah," his uncle bent down and ran his hand through the dusty soil. "I see now the devastation. The ground is parched. And not a cloud in the sky."

"The summer has been long and hot."

"Are all the fields like this?"

"Most, though not all."

His uncle grunted, then rose to his feet. "I find myself suddenly overcome from the journey. I think I should like to lie down and rest a bit."

"I'll see you back."

"No, no. You two stay. Johanna was most anxious to see you. I'm sure you have much to catch up on. I'll see myself down."

Helpless, Nick watched as his uncle left him there on the hillside with the one person he both wanted to see and wished to avoid the most.

After an awkward silence he cleared his throat. "So. H-how are you?"

"You never came back. You knew that I was waiting for you. Three and a half years without a word."

"I did come back. I was in Patara up until a few months ago."

"And yet you never gave a thought to me."

"That's not... true," he confessed. "I did think of you. Often, in fact."

She faced him, her eyes piercing in their accusation. "And yet you never said a word? Knowing how I've felt. What I said at our last parting, and yet you never said a word."

He swallowed and turned his eyes at the lifeless fields. "What was I supposed to say?"

"How are you? It's nice to see you again. I've missed you."

"All true."

"I love you. You could've said that."

After a moment he nodded. "I could have."

"But you won't."

"I can't."

"You're lying!" Her voice broke, and it sounded like a mirthless laugh. "You love me, Nicholas. I know that you do. I know that's why you ran away from me on that ship. And I know that's why you never came to see me once you returned. And I name you a coward for it."

"Coward?"

"You are afraid to love. You loved your parents dearly. I know you did. And they left you. And so now you are afraid that if you love again, that once more you will be bereft. That is why you protect your heart, hiding it behind the walls of a monastery, and now those of a church. You think you will be safe here. Safe from loss. But you are not. Nicholas, look at me!"

With effort, he turned his eyes upon her, and when he did so, he found he could not look away. She reached forward and took his hand, and then placed something within his palm. Reluctant and confused, he glanced down. It was a tiny sack of gold.

"Recognize it?" she asked.

"T-this is my gift to you. How can you return it to me?" He stared at her, dumbfounded.

"It is my dowry. I am giving it to you, because I will never give it to another. I have loved you from the first day we met, and I will love you till I close my eyes in death."

"No. Don't vow this!" He tried to give the gold back, but she thrust it in his hands and held it there with her own.

"You have my heart, Nicholas." Tears streamed down her cheeks. "Where else should my treasure be?"

He opened and closed his mouth, but no words came out. Turning, she fled away from him, hurrying down the hill, leaving a cloud of dust in her wake. Nicholas stared after her, unable to see for the tears that stained his eyes.

When Nicholas returned to the church, Johanna was not in sight. The Abbot had taken Nicholas' seat by the window, studying the landscape outside.

The young bishop came in and shut the door.

Without turning, his uncle asked, "Did I err, bringing her here?"

He sighed. "I wish you hadn't."

"So you don't love her?" When he didn't answer, his uncle turned around and regarded him coolly. "I remind you that you are a bishop and a Christian, and you are obligated to speak the truth."

"I know."

"Do. You. Love. Her?"

"How can I?"

"How can you? How can you not? Look at the woman! She is beautiful and young and has eyes only for you. Devoted to the Lord, she would make any man a fine wife."

"And she would."

"So why not yours?"

Nick stared. "Uncle, do you hear yourself? I am a bishop! I have given my life over to God. How can I possibly now take a wife? What message would that send?"

"Is not marriage ordained of God?"

"Of course it is."

"And is there anything within sacred scripture that says a bishop should not marry?"

"Well, no, but—"

"But what? May I remind you of St. Paul's words to his disciple Timothy? In his first epistle, does he not say, 'a Bishop therefore must be unreproveable, the husband of one wife.'"

Nick shook his head, incredulous. "But I belong to the bride of Christ."

"As do we all."

"And St. Paul also said, in his letter to the church in Corinth, 'The unmarried cares for things of the Lord, how he may please the Lord. But he that is married, cares for the things of the world, how he may please his wife.' In that same place, he also says, 'It were good for a man not to touch a woman.'"

The Abbot raised a finger. "And do you know what it is he says right after that?"

Nick hesitated, then quoted, "'Nevertheless, to avoid fornication, let every man have his wife, and let every woman have her own husband.' But that is what I seek: to avoid immorality." He'd read the passage recently.

His uncle smiled. "Then marry the girl."

"But I am bishop!"

"And bishops marry. Not all do, but many. Even St. Peter, the first bishop of Rome, took along with himself a believing wife. Nicky, I beg you—for your sake and for hers—see what is right in front of you. Open yourself up to this blessing of God. Not every good thing that happens is a temptation, my son."

Nick took a seat across from his uncle and propped his chin on his elbow. "I am torn. I do not know which to choose. On the one hand, I would very much like to take Johanna for my wife. To know the joy of marriage, of children, and have a family of my own. But on the other, there is the simple reality that I have committed myself to this church—and while that may not be a contradiction, neither will it be an easy task. The rumors I am hearing warn me against doing anything that might bring Johanna to harm. Caesar Galerius is against the Christians, and he has the ear of the emperor Diocletian. If I marry Johanna, and even if the church embraces her as I might, that does not mean all is well. What am I to do if they come for us?"

"Do you really think it will come to that?"

"I do not know. But in my heart, I fear that it might."

The Abbot pursed his lips. "Emperor Diocletian is old. This may pass."

"And he will be succeeded by Galerius. Do you think we'd fare better then? Or worse? How could I subject Johanna, or anyone, to such risk?"

His uncle sighed. "It is not your decision alone to make, Nicky. Johanna has a mind of her own."

"I've noticed," he said dryly.

"So do you not think that perhaps she deserves a chance to weigh in on this?"

Nick pushed away from the table. He crossed to the window and clasped his hands behind his back. "She has already made her intentions clear."

The Abbot managed a chuckle that sounded a bit like a cough. "Do you mean to suggest that she proposed to you?"

"No. Of course not. But she did give me this." He turned and tossed the bag of gold to his uncle. The Abbot frowned when he caught the purse, weighing it in his palm. "It's the gold I gave her father," Nick explained. "Her dowry. She told me I have her heart, and asked where else should her treasure be?"

The Abbot put the coins on the table and touched them gingerly with his fingers, almost caressing the bag. "All I can tell you is this: if our roles were reversed, I would marry her."

"And leave your position?"

"If I felt God calling me to, then yes. I did not enter the ministry because I had no interest in marriage, Nicky. I entered it because I had no opportunity. Mind you, I was in love. And she was beautiful. And I think, she even loved me as well. Her father, however, was not interested. He had other ambitions, and thought a strategic marriage would advance his position in society. To this day, I regret not running away with her when I had the chance.

"Nicky, I would not have you live your life with regrets. It will poison your ministry, and you may come to find yourself resenting the Church you claim to love. Promise me you'll at least consider it."

Nick sighed. Without looking back he said, "All right then. I will consider it."

Eleven

"You're not Catholic, are you?" I said.

"Hmm?" The Abbot looked up, as if startled that I was there. He'd grown a faraway look in his eye, the same kind of expression I'd seen in soldiers who'd lost a brother-in-arms. The question immediately felt strangely out of place, as if I was intruding on something sacred, and asking for something grossly inappropriate.

"I'm sorry," I instantly apologized.

"No, no. It's fine. You want to know if I am Catholic."

"I mean, I just assumed..."

"Yes. Assumptions are dangerous. I don't think I can answer the question as you have phrased it. You mean to ask if I am Roman Catholic, as opposed to Protestant or Orthodox or Coptic or Nestorian or any of a hundred other divisions in the body of Christ. Would it shock you to learn that I recognize no such divisions? At the first, there were none. There was only one Church. The term Catholic means this, of course."

"It means universal, or something, right?"

"It means there is only one Church. That is all our Lord recognizes. *Roman* Catholic is an oxymoron. The divisions in His

136

body are like the scourge marks He suffered at the hands of sinners. They divide His flesh and bring about pain, and yet somehow, even through this, His grace shines through." He sighed. "Why do you ask?"

I felt relief, because it went to the heart of my question. "Well, it's just that you were talking about getting married as a bishop, and naturally, that is contrary to the Church's teaching on celibacy."

"This isn't quite true, you realize. Even the Roman Catholic church has married priests. What they require, however, is that within the confines of a marriage, that their married priests remain celibate. It is unfortunate to require it, however, for it speaks against Paul's words in First Corinthians chapter seven verse five. 'Defraud not one another, except it be with consent for a time, that ye may give yourselves to fasting and prayer, and again come together, that Satan tempt you not.'"

"So you disagree with the Church's teaching?"

"Rather, I agree with Saint Paul's teaching. Husbands and wives ought not defraud one another of their conjugal rights. But to the matter of whether or not priests ought to marry at all, remember that at the time, I was quite conflicted on the matter. Paul gave his opinion that it would be better that men not marry at all, and in view of what he termed, 'the present distress,' he further advised against it. It did not take much to extrapolate a principle from those words—the very same principle that led, in fact, to the Church's stance on celibacy. Marriage must be taken seriously, but so also must the commitment to serve the Church. And sometimes, those conflict. When they do, it is the marital commitment that takes precedence. This is why marriage was not encouraged for the priests or bishops, so that they could give their full attention and devotion to the cause of Christ.

"All this weighed on my mind with my uncle's suggestion. I knew he would not lead me astray, and certainly there was a sense in which he was attempting to prevent me from incurring the same regrets he himself experienced. But I can hardly fault him for that."

"So did you marry her?"

A half grin tugged at his mouth. "Let me tell you the story."

That night, Nicholas led the congregation through evening worship, saying the words by rote and hoping he did not err too much or too noticeably. Both Johanna and his uncle were in the congregation, sitting on the left in the back, their eyes affixed on him throughout the liturgy in such a way that it became impossible for him to look in their direction for fear that he would break into a blush or a cold sweat, stumble on his words and forget himself before them all.

When it came time to serve the Eucharist, they both took

their place in line as he distributed the bread and wine. Person by person they approached, until at last Johanna herself stood before him, carefully watching him with the deep wells of her brown eyes. He felt lost in them, and as he lifted the wafer to her lips, he could sense what it would be to feel her lips on his fingertips, the heat that would flood through him. For a brief moment, he felt as though he would drop everything then and there and take her in his arms, pressing his lips to her own and declaring quite publicly his love for her.

A sudden intake of breath, and he realized he was still there, still holding the wafer, while she waited before him with her mouth slightly open. His uncle cleared his throat.

Quickly, he recovered himself and placed the wafer on her tongue. She closed her lips and moved on, and his uncle took her spot. Uncle Nicholas measured him with his eyes. He swiftly passed the wafer and moved on.

After wrapping up the service and returning everything to its place, he went out to stand by the door, ready to receive his parishioners. His uncle and Johanna came out together, near the front of the line. "I need to talk with you," he said to her. "Will you wait for me?"

"It is late."

"On the morrow, then?"

"We are starting back tomorrow. Best to get an early start."

His heart fell. Was this the Lord's will? To bring him to the edge of giving in, and then withdraw the temptation? It did not seem right. "Please," he persisted. "It won't take long."

His uncle broke in. "I think we can spare a few moments."

"All right," Johanna answered, and tipped her head to one side. "I will see you tomorrow, then."

"Yes. Yes, I look forward to it."

His uncle rolled his eyes, took Johanna's elbow, and steered her away. Nick watched them go, and then turned back to the rest of his congregation. As he greeted the rest, he noticed a young man hurrying toward them up the path.

"Bishop!" the man cried. "A ship!"

Nick turned to the young man, caught him and held him by his shoulders as he struggled to catch his breath. "Darius, did you run the entire way from the docks?'

"Aye," he nodded, his hand on his chest. "I did."

"A ship, you say? What of it?"

"A grain ship. Has put into port here. The captain is asking for you."

Nick dropped his hands. "A grain ship?" Without a second glance at Darius or the rest of his congregants, he hurried past the man, running full stride down the path toward the docks, his vestments flying about him. When he reached the harbor, he caught his breath and his heart soared. The ship was *The Hatmehit.* He hurried toward the dock.

"Hoy there!" he called. "Is Qennios still Captain aboard this vessel?"

A moment later, a grizzled face appeared over the gunwales. "Who's asking?"

Nicholas stared up at the care-worn face of his former companion. "Is that you? You old sea-dog!"

"Young Nicholas of Patara? As I live and breathe! Come, come aboard!"

Nicholas hurried toward the gangplank and ascended to the ship. When he stepped onto the deck he was thrust into a quick and hearty hug by the Captain. "I never thought I'd see the day when our paths should cross," Qennios said. "But here you are, as plain as day and looking fatter and healthier than ever. And what's this? You wear the robes of a bishop now?"

"Yes, it is true," Nicholas replied.

"Has it been so long?"

"Nay," he laughed. "They ordained me just weeks ago. An answered prayer, if you can believe it."

"Aye. I could believe that."

"Personally, I think they ought to have prayed harder. I'm sure God could have found someone far better for the job."

"And that I could not believe."

"Are any of your old crew here? I'd love to see them again."

"Ah, sadly no. A few are, to be sure, but none of those who took to your faith. I left them in Alexandria."

"Oh? And why is that?"

Qennios grimaced. "It, ah, it became too dangerous to sail with them."

"Dangerous? They are not violent men."

"Nay. That is true. Your God did a number on them on that account. How can I put this delicately?"

Nick put a hand on the Captain's shoulder. "Bluntly would be preferred."

"Hmm. The world has grown a dangerous place for Christians. And for those who harbor them."

"Why? The edict still stands. We are still tolerated throughout the Empire."

"There are rumors that is changing. Surely you have heard such."

"I have, but I think them only rumors."

"Were it that easy. Many of those who crew with me would not take kindly to berths given to those that bear the name of Christ. They would say I was taking work away from more qualified men. Some of them make a sport of trying to coax their fellow seamen who call on your God into a fight, tormenting them with beatings and other insults. They call it cheek-turning."

Nick felt his face grow hot. "I should think these men, rather than those of faith, would be less qualified to serve aboard your ship."

"Aye. 'Tis true, 'tis true. But you must understand, a vessel captained and crewed by naught but Christians would make a tempting target for pirates and could easily be seized by governors or other provincial rulers eager to make a positive impression on Rome. It came down to a matter of keeping my ship, and keeping peace aboard it."

Nick frowned. "Qennios, those who make a friend of the world make themselves an enemy of God."

"Oh Nicky. I was hoping you'd understand."

"I do understand. You chose money over principle."

Qennios glared at him. "I chose life over death. I thought you'd understand that. Even your God should understand that."

Nick shook his head. "Forgive me. I-I'm upset by the whole thing. My fight is between me and the Emperor. You got caught in the middle."

Qennios snorted. "You want to take on the Emperor?"

"No. I simply want him to leave us alone."

"Pity. I'm beginning to think you're the only one who's man enough to do it."

"Pray that we never find out."

They shared a laugh, and for a moment Nick simply enjoyed the feeling of the sturdy wooden deck beneath his feet, the way the ship rocked gently on the surface of the waters. Then he glanced up the hillside at his town. "I mean to ask you something. Your cargo. Where is it bound?"

"Alexandria. We've just come from Italy, and are putting in here at Andriaki harbor before heading south."

"I see. How many ships are with you?"

"Five."

"Qennios, the people of Myra—my people—there's just no easy way to put this. Our situation is desperate. Plague and famine have ravaged our town. Many are near starving. I want you to sell me some of your grain. I have gold. I can give you a fair price."

Qennoios grimaced. "Nicholas, as much as I would like to help, I cannot. The wheat we carry is meted and measured. It is meant for the Emperor's garrison at Alexandria. I must deliver all of it, or I shall have to answer for the shortage."

Nicholas reached into his pocket and brought out the gold that Johanna had given him back. Her dowry. It seemed he would need it after all. He held it out to the Captain. "Please. You know me well. I will not treat you unfairly, nor falsely. We need this grain."

Qennios stared at the sack of gold. "The grain is measured. What am I to do?"

"Sell it to us. Trust me." He took hold of Qennios' hand and placed it over the sack of gold. "Trust my God. When you arrive in Alexandria, you will have no problems."

Qennios shook his head. "That is not possible."

"Neither is bringing a man back from the dead. One hundred bushels from each ship. No more. No less. You will have the gold, and you will make your delivery with a full cargo. I assure you this is true."

"So your God is the God of bread, too?"

Nick grinned. "He once fed five thousand people on five loaves and two fish, with enough left over afterward to take up twelve basketfuls."

"Did He indeed?"

"Aye. And He Himself raised the dead many times."

After a moment, Qennios nodded. "All right. I cannot believe I'm doing this, but for the sake of Marcus, and for the changed lives of my former crew, I will do as you ask."

"The Lord bless you and keep you, and make His face shine upon you, and give you peace."

"Aye. I hope that He does." With that, he turned and gave the command.

"So what happened?" I asked.

"They unloaded the grain as they said. Five hundred bushels of wheat. The town of Myra fed on that grain for two whole years, with enough left over to plant seed and harvest when the drought finally stopped."

"And what about the ship? *The Hatmehit*?"

"Oh, I never saw her again. They left the next morning, caught a favorable wind, and headed straight for Egypt. I did learn later that the grain was supplied within their holds exactly as I said it would be. And for that miracle, Qennios gave his life to God."

"Incredible."

"But true. And so, you see, that answers the real question. Without the gold, I could not have bought the grain to feed the town. Without Johanna giving it to me as her dowry, I would not have been able to do anything at all. And so, her coming to me was of the Lord. Her love for me saved our town. Saved Qennios's soul. And that is why I had to marry her. Besides, I couldn't pay back the money!"

 # Twelve

"This is quite irregular," Lucian grumbled. He'd arrived from Antioch the previous night, less than a month after Nicholas sent him an urgent request, begging him to come. Nick stood shoulder to shoulder with the older bishop now, staring at the fields as the villagers worked to harvest what little they could from the parched soil.

Nick cleared his throat. "So is appointing a young man a bishop, and him not a priest or deacon beforehand."

Lucian glanced sideways at him. "Do you say we should not have done so?"

"No." He tucked his hands beneath his armpits. The light from the rising sun sent tangerine rays spilling across the field. "You ordained me because you believed, as I believe, that the Lord had called upon you to do so, even as He called upon me to serve. But in like manner, I also believe He sent Johanna to me, to unite us together for the express purpose of saving this city. What other purpose He might have remains a mystery to me, but I'm learning to trust His will in the matter."

Lucian snorted, as if he didn't quite believe the young man. He clasped his hands behind his back and turned, heading with

Nicholas back toward the church. "And where is the girl now?"

"She's gone back with my uncle to Patara."

"And have you proposed to her?"

After a moment, he confessed, "Not yet."

"But you intend to."

"I do."

He nodded. "I thought as much. I did not believe you were asking my permission."

They stopped long enough to let some sheep wander across their path, following a shepherd who tipped his cap to the holy men as he hurried along his way. The sheep followed, bleating plaintively.

"I'm asking for your support," Nicholas replied. "When word gets out that I have taken a wife, the rest of the bishops may not understand."

"That may be an understatement."

"I know that many of them accept the common wisdom that we should not marry. Better to remain single and celibate, and dedicate ourselves to the task at hand. And for the most part, I agree."

"We serve as members of the Bride of Christ. Our marriage is to Him."

"Just so."

"But you feel a divine call, nonetheless."

"I do. I cannot tell you why. Just that I am certain I am

supposed to marry."

"Do you love this girl?" Lucian studied his face, as if searching for an explanation for what he was hearing.

Nicholas smiled a little and nodded. "I do. Sometimes just seeing her hurts, as if being separate from her is an unnatural state. I don't know how else to describe it."

"Well, that sounds like love sure enough. And this girl? Ja—?"

"Johanna."

"Johanna. Yes. She feels the same?"

"She says so, and I've no reason to doubt her word."

"Hmm." He pressed his lips into a thin line and stared downward, as if studying the dirt. "Rumor has it that you called a dead man back to life again."

Nicholas shook his head. "You know how rumors go."

"So did you?"

"Aboard ship, on my pilgrimage to the Holy Land, a man fell injured. I prayed to the Lord. The Lord healed him."

"So it is true."

"He did the miracle, not I."

"It may take a miracle to convince the other bishops you've not lost your senses. But I will tell them this: that you do what you do because you believe in your heart the Lord has called you to it. Who has known the mind of the Lord, that he should instruct Him? His ways are not our ways, and His thoughts are not our thoughts. As high as the heavens are above the earth, so are His thoughts above our thoughts, and His ways above our ways. It is a mystery. Marriage is a sacrament. It is not the unholy alliance that some make it out to be. I know many men in my Church who are married who wish they were not. And what many do not realize is that their wives are equally unhappy. Perhaps you are meant to show them all a better way—to show them what marriage was meant to be."

Nick shook his head and shrugged. "I don't know that. I only know what I am told. What the Lord has revealed to me. I should no more disobey Him in this than I should in anything else."

Lucian nodded. "As you say."

They'd reached the church door, which Nicholas opened for them both. But then he stood to one side as Lucian entered, and did not follow. "Thank you for your understanding, Brother."

Lucian frowned. "You're not coming in?"

"If I am to marry Johanna, then I must go to Patara and ask for her hand."

"You mean to leave now?"

"I've delayed long enough. The Lord has spoken, and I am eager to obey. I shan't be gone long. When I return, it will be with Johanna by my side."

"And what of your church?" Lucian gestured inside the empty chapel. "Have you told any of them?"

"All of them, actually, when I explained where the money came from to buy the grain. They could hardly object when they were filling their mouths with the Lord's provision."

"I see. Clever."

"Wise as a serpent, innocent as a dove. Isn't that right?"

"So it is."

"I've asked several of the older men to be praying for me specifically. They will know when I am gone how the Lord has answered."

"Have you considered bringing her back here, and then having the wedding in Myra?"

"I did. But then who would perform the service, since I am bishop? My uncle will do the honor in Patara. He's the only family I have, and all Johanna's sisters with their husbands and children are there. Not to mention the many friends we both have there."

"Well." Lucian raised his eyebrows. "You'd best be on your way. I think I can manage here till you return."

"Thank you, Lucian."

He clapped a hand on Nicholas's shoulder. "Give my regards to your bride." And with that, he let him go.

The wedding was the talk of the town, and not least because it was so unusual to have a bishop giving vows. A few openly grumbled that it went against tradition, and some said against the Church, though no one could exactly say why.

But before that, Nicholas had to ask Johanna's hand. This proved harder than he'd thought it would be.

He found her serving in the monastery, washing the dishes as he once had under the careful eye of Brother Francis so long ago. He cleared his throat when he entered, but she did not turn around. When he tried again she said, "Are you too proud to pick up a dish rag and help? Or have you forgotten how to wash a plate?"

"I-I'm sorry I didn't—I—uh—h-how did you know I was here?"

She nodded at the open window. "Saw you coming up the path."

"Oh."

She washed another dish, and then turned and held it out for him. "Oh," he said again, and then hurried forward to pick up a rag to dry it.

"So what are you doing here?" she asked after another plate.

"I came to… I came to…"

"I hope it wasn't to wash dishes, because you're dreadfully slow."

"I came to apologize," he blurted.

"Apologize?" She raised an eyebrow. "For what?"

He took a breath. "For getting on that boat, and sailing away from you. I ran from you like a coward. And I was wrong to do so."

After a moment, she nodded. "Hmm. This has been weighing on your mind, has it?"

"A little, yes."

"Very well then." She returned her attention to the dishes. "I forgive you."

He took the plate from her. "I also came to apologize for staying away as long as I did. And for not coming to see you when I returned. Again, I was a coward. And I am sorry."

She cleared her throat, as if something had gotten stuck in it. "I forgive you. You can go."

He reached into the water and drew out her hands. "And I came to apologize for not speaking truthfully when you came to see me in Myra. For hiding behind tradition. For being afraid to love because of what it might cost."

"Don't."

"Don't what?"

"Do whatever it is you think you're doing. I'm not here to salve your conscience. How can I forgive you when seeing you is torment?"

She pulled away from him to leave the room. He held fast her hand and swung her back to face him. Then he got down on one knee. "And I came to apologize for not asking this question sooner. And I hope you will forgive me, but I mean to ask it now. Johanna, will you marry me?"

Her eyes filled with fear and doubt as she stared at his face.

153

He licked his lips. "I prayed about this mightily. I've spoken to the church. I've consulted with some of the other bishops. What I propose is unusual, but not without precedent. I mean you to come back with me to Myra. As my wife. The wife of a bishop. If you'll have me."

She looked away, searching for her voice. "How can you do this?" she whispered. "How can you come to me now after all this? I've given up on you." She shook her head. "No."

"No?"

"No. I don't accept."

He frowned. "I don't accept you not accepting."

She cocked her head. "What?"

"I don't accept your refusal. You love me, Johanna. And you want this. I know you do."

"Nicholas, you broke my heart. How can I marry you?"

He rose to his feet, putting her hands against his chest. "I aim to mend it. Will you now break my heart? And out of what? Revenge? I promise you. I will love you till my dying day. Till my last breath. I will pour every energy into healing the wound that I have made on your soul. I was afraid before, but I am afraid no longer. My love for you has made me as bold as a lion. I could stand and face down the tetrarchy and all their legions with you by my side. You make me a better man than I have ever before dared to be. And I might as well be lost without you."

"Ask me again. Quickly."

"Johanna, will you marry me?"

A smile and a quickened breath. "Once more."

He took his hand and swept it through the lock of hair hanging down across her face, tucking it behind her ear. "Marry me." He leaned in close, their lips almost touching. He met her eyes, and saw his answer etched there. "Marry me!"

She nodded. "Yes."

With that, he pressed his lips to her own, and felt the world shift beneath them.

Six days later, in the church bedecked with flowers, Nicholas waited at the altar as his bride swept down the aisle in her mother's white dress. At his side, his uncle waited, beaming. When she came to be presented before him, her father took Nicholas's hand and whispered in his ear, "I could not have asked for a better man to be my son. My only regret is that you must live so far away!"

"You are welcome in our home any time, small that it may be."

Antonius stepped back and gripped his shoulders in both hands. "As you are in mine. And I expect you to take me up on that."

"We shall."

He nodded, and then stepped out of the way so his daughter could take her place at Nicholas's side. His uncle raised his hands and blessed them both, read scripture from the Old Testament and from Saint Paul's first letter to the Corinthians, and enjoined upon them both the responsibilities that marriage entailed.

Then he said, "Nicholas of Myra, it is unusual that you as a bishop would be taking marriage vows. I suppose we ought to ask the Lord His opinion on the matter." With that, he looked, as if listening for a few moments. Then he nodded his head. "We'll take the Lord's silence on the matter for His approval, for certainly there is nothing in holy scripture that enjoins you from marrying a bride."

Later, Nicholas asked him privately what he would have said had it thundered at that moment. His uncle chuckled and said, "Then I would have said the Lord has spoken aloud His approval!"

Thus establishing Nicholas's right to marry, he led them through the exchange of vows before draping the cord over their palms that tied them together. Then he said, "I now declare you to be husband and wife. What God hath joined together, let no man put asunder. You may kiss your bride."

As they kissed, the church erupted in spontaneous cheers.

Nicholas broke contact long enough to stare out at the assembled guests, thinking he could not have lived a happier day had he lived a thousand years and more.

"And it was the happiest day I've ever known," the Abbot said. His eyes misted over, and he put his thumb and forefinger at the corners, wiping away the tears that gathered there. "Sadly," he continued, "it was also a very short marriage. What I feared came to pass more quickly than I could have imagined."

I stared at him. "What happened?" I wondered if someone in the Church didn't put the kibosh on the whole affair. His answer stunned me.

"Galerius happened."

# Thirteen

"Who was Galerius?" I asked.

Nicholas managed a pained smile. "He was part of the tetrarchy, and was Diocletian's son-in-law. Diocles was paranoid of the future. I've long suspected it stemmed from his fear of judgment and the condemnation from his own stricken conscience. The more time bore down on him, the more anxious he grew to know the future. In Antioch, he consulted the soothsayers and mutterers, slaying a number of animals so he could study their livers and predict what was to come, or so he imagined. While thus engaged, some of our brothers were outside praying that God would frustrate this demonic scheme. These men were attendants of the Emperor, and longed to confront him with the Gospel. They felt his conscience and constant fear of the future would be relieved when he turned to Lord. I suppose, in this regard, they cannot be faulted. They meant to do what was right, and to convince the Emperor to do the same.

"And God answered their prayer. He frustrated the soothsayers. The priests could do nothing, no matter how many animals they killed or how many livers they examined. But

Diocles would have none of it. The soothsayer priest, a man called Tages, accused these brothers of obstructing the rites, and the Emperor, in a rage, ordered that all present be compelled to make a sacrifice to the gods or be scourged. He went further, sending letters to all his commanders ordering the same throughout the army and the court. Any who refused would be dismissed.

"Evidently, Galerius thought this a really good idea, and he began pressuring his father-in-law to do something about the Christians 'consuming the empire,' as he put it. For two years he kept at it. Finally, his persistence paid off. It was a cold and wet February morning when we received word."

Nicholas awoke with a start, hearing the rain pattering down on the shingles of the small house the believers had built for him and his wife nearby the church. He turned his eyes to the window, and through the slats in the shutters he perceived the cold dark of night. Morning wouldn't come for at least another hour or two, but even then the sun would be veiled by the storm. It sounded like ice pellets hitting the roof. He listened for a moment to the wind lashing the walls with droplets, wondering what had wakened him. A glance at Johanna revealed her still sleeping form in the bed beside him, dark hair splayed upon the pillow like a cast off veil. She stirred, but did not wake up. Her belly was swollen and distended from the pregnancy. In another few months they'd learn what child the Lord had blessed them with.

Gently, he bent forward and lifted a few strands of her hair away from her cheek. A familiar foreboding tugged at the edges of his mind, and he knew now he would not get any further sleep. Carefully, he rose from the bed and crossed into the next room, where he lit a lamp and set it near the window. The chair creaked when he pulled it away from the table, and he winced. He did not want her to hear his prayers, lest she think something was wrong.

But something was wrong. In his heart he knew it. *Have I sinned?* He turned his eyes heavenward, searching the ceiling for answers. *Did I misunderstand Your purpose in Johanna? Was this love never meant to be?*

He felt his pulse quicken. It was the only answer he'd received ever since the warning first came to him. An unnamable, persistent dread that weighed down his spirit, dulled his thinking, sharpened his temper. Ever since she'd come to him with the news that he was to have a child, he'd felt it, a dark voice whispering to his soul that this child would never be born alive.

Cautiously, so as not to reveal his concern, he'd spoken to the midwives of the town, old women with many children of their own, and even a passing physician whom he'd arranged to come to the house and examine her. All assured him that Johanna was fine, that the pregnancy was proceeding precisely as it was meant to go, and who gently chided him for worrying himself unnecessarily.

He told himself that they were right. Laughed off his earlier fears as the product of an overactive imagination, or even of a lack of faith, and for a time he felt better.

Until he didn't.

The further into her pregnancy she grew, the greater the certainty that neither she nor the child would survive.

And so he sought the Lord. Begged assurances from Him that all would be well. Searched and studied the scriptures to see whether or not he had erred in his choice to marry, and even corresponded with both Lucian and his uncle.

But he learned nothing.

Neither Lucian nor his uncle had any words of wisdom for him that he hadn't heard already. The scriptures revealed nothing more to him other than what he already knew from studying them, and not even the few writings from the early fathers that he'd found in the church's sparse library offered any consolation or wisdom to understand what he feared.

"Dear God," he prayed, "please comfort me. Give me that sweet repose only You can provide. I know not whence these fears come, but they consume me and steal away my joy like a thief pilfering coins. Lord, I need You. I need Your presence. Only

You can possibly understand what I'm going through, and whether or not any of it shall come to pass. Please, Father, I beg You: tell me what I must do."

He folded his hands and waited while the fire burned low in the lamp. Around him the shadows lengthened even as the fire grew smaller. Soon it dwindled to a guttering, blue flame.

How foolish of him! He'd forgotten to put more oil in the lamp. He reached for it, but as soon as he lifted it, he knew that wasn't the case. He could feel the oil sloshing within the cavity of the lamp. Then was it the wick? He turned the lamp toward himself to see when abruptly, the flame winked out.

A loud banging rattled the door. Johanna murmured, "Nicky? Is that you?"

He rose from his chair, the lamp forgotten, and went to the door. He lifted the latch just as the banging resumed. He swung the door open. On the front step, a man in a hood bearing a shielded lantern pressed a finger to his lips and pushed his way inside.

"Timotheus? What is it?"

The man shut the door and faced Nicholas. "I am very sorry to disturb you at this ungodly hour, my bishop, but we must hurry."

"Hurry? To what?"

Timotheus moved past him into the house. "It is bad. Do you have a bag you can pack? We haven't got much time."

"What is going on?"

"Travel will be difficult for Johanna with the baby, but I've secured a donkey for you."

"Travel?"

"Nicholas, they've done it. The edict has been passed."

"What edict?"

"Nicky?" Johanna's voice came louder. She'd risen from the bed and come to the door of their room, her shoulders draped in the blanket. "What is going on?"

Timotheus turned to her and barely blushed. "My lady, get dressed. Be quick about it."

"Timotheus," Nicky persisted, "what edict?"

The man put his hands on Nicky's shoulders. "The Roman Empire had declared war on Christ. They're arresting disciples, demanding they make a sacrifice to the gods and recant their faith. Any who refuse are thrown into prison. Any who resist are executed on the spot."

Nicholas shook his head. "We know about this edict. It has been applied chiefly in the west."

Timotheus shook his head. "You know about one edict, yes. But Diocletian has issued a second. And now all bishops and priests are subject to arrest regardless of where they are."

"Why?" Johanna asked.

"Please, my lady," Timotheus begged.

"It's because of what happened in Melitine and Syria," Nicky surmised. "The riots and protests."

"It matters not why," Timotheus said. "Only that it has been done. Now if you don't mind, we must hurry. Cresca says she knows of some caves she used to explore when she was a child. We'll hide you there."

Nicholas nodded, and Johanna shut the door to dress herself. Timotheus said, "I'll be just outside. I don't know if the guards have come from the governor yet, but they are on their way. They'll go to the church first, unless you are betrayed."

"Surely others besides our brothers know we've built a house nearby."

He shrugged. "I only hope they are delayed."

Nicky turned wordlessly and went into the other room where Johanna had pulled on a dress and was wrapping shawl about her shoulders. He pulled his old travel bag down from the rafters—the same one he'd used to carry his clothes when he boarded *The Hatmehit*, and started stuffing garments into it. In moments it was full. Johanna swept the blanket off their bed and followed him out. They tugged open the door. Timotheus waited on the step, shifting his feet nervously and watching the church. His face was slick with rainwater, but he paid it no mind. He ushered them forward with a quick wave of his hand.

"Wait." Nicky turned back, heading for the shelf above the table which held his favorite treasure.

"There is no time!" Timotheus hissed. "Hsst! The guards are

already at the church!"

Nicky retrieved the codex from the shelf—a wedding gift from his uncle, the codex held all the writings of Saint Paul, the Four Gospels, and Saint Luke's Acts of the Apostles. He'd even considered adding the Apocalypse of John to the back, if he could get his hands on a copy and find sufficient paper.

Quickly, he wrapped the book in oil cloth and tucked it under his arm, then hurried back to rejoin his bride and Timotheus.

"They would have burned it," he explained.

"They'll burn you if you don't hurry."

Together, the trio went out into the night.

Timotheus led them to the outskirts of town, making their way inland past the fields that had been sown with the last of the grain Qennios had sold to them that fateful day. This Spring there'd be a bountiful harvest, enough to not only feed the city for another year, but sufficient also to sell at market and turn a profit.

It was small comfort.

Timotheus kept them at a rapid walk. Johanna had initially refused to mount the donkey, preferring to trudge alongside them as they slipped away from the city and so keep a faster pace, but by the time they'd reached the outskirts of town her steps had faltered, and Nicky insisted she ride the rest of the way.

Timotheus held the reins as Nicky helped her up and then draped their blanket around her shoulders. Once she was settled, he gave a nod to the man, and they continued.

As they crested a rise, Timotheus pointed toward a dim light flickering in the hills. "The caves are just over there. Cresca awaits with food and warmth."

"She should douse that fire," Nicky observed.

"I told her not to build it up. It might give us... away."

His steps and voice faltered as a ring of soldiers stepped out from behind a mound of rocks. Their eyes glinted in the dim firelight, and their swords rang discordantly as they drew them from their scabbards.

"Nicholas of Myra, Bishop of the outlaw Christian sect," announced their commanding officer, striding purposefully toward them, "you are under arrest."

Timotheus, his face slick with rain, slowly turned, stammering, "Nicholas, I am sorry."

Nick glanced at Johanna as two soldiers took hold of his arms and held them fast. Her eyes widened in fear. He opened his mouth to say something, but the strong dread that had waked him earlier rushed to the fore, throttling the words in his throat. He looked instead to Timotheus. "It's all right," he told him.

"I only wanted to keep her safe," Timotheus replied.

Nicholas furrowed his brow, unsure what the man meant. The rain continued to pelt them in vast sheets of water, veritable waves pulsing across them from the heavens, driven hard by the wind and guttering the flames even in the sealed sconces of their lanterns. To the commander, Nicholas said, "I'll come along quietly. Please let these others go."

The commander reached into the pouch on his belt and withdrew a small, drawstring sack that he tossed to Timotheus. When Timotheus caught it, Nicholas heard the distinct clinking of coins. His heart surged to his throat, erupting from his lips in a harsh yelp, "Timotheus?!"

"It was the only way."

"No!" Johanna screamed, swinging her leg off the donkey's back, her eyes fixed on Nicholas.

"Johanna, no!" he cried.

Timotheus moved in front, "Lady, please!"

"Timotheus," Nick called again.

Johanna whirled on the man. "You! How could you?" She beat him with her fists. Nick yelled to her, but she didn't seem to hear him. Two soldiers broke ranks, moving to intercept her. Nicholas screamed as one of them raised his sword. Without hesitating, the soldier smashed the pommel of the weapon down on the crown of her head. She collapsed to her hands and knees, and took a hesitant shuffle forward. He hit her again. She fell into the mud and lay still.

"No-o!"

Nick tore his arm free of the guard who held him and shoved the other off balance, his eyes fixed on his fallen bride. He rushed toward her. Three steps away, strong arms wrapped around his waist and drove him into the ground. He tried to push forward, but they pinned his arms behind his back and lashed them together with cords. Nick stared at Johanna, as if willing her to open her eyes, groaning at the blood that ran down her cheek from the back of her head, washed away by the incessant rain and soaking into the earth.

I stared at him, my pen faltering on my notepad. His eyes bore a haunted look, as if he'd stared long into an unimaginable horror and forgotten to look away. After a moment, I cleared my throat. Still, it took him a few seconds before he looked up. He seemed startled to find himself in the room with me by his side.

"You..." I cleared my throat again, "you didn't make that up."

He stared at me, the corners of his mouth turning down ever so slightly. I realized then that I'd let on to my disbelief in the whole tale—that the entirety of it was implausible, a clever put-on serving a purpose I had not yet guessed.

"I-I mean that, obviously, this affected you deeply."

He coughed and looked away. "It was a long time ago."

"What happened?" When he didn't answer, I said, "Abbot Nicholas?"

Wordlessly, he rose and walked out of the room. I watched him go, wondering whether or not to follow. Oleg's voice was low behind me. "Give him a moment."

"I didn't mean to—"

"It's all right. He isn't mad at you. Speaking of Johanna and his unborn son pains him still. Even after all these years."

"Unborn son?"

He nodded.

"What happened?"

A sad smile tugged at his mouth. "She died. Timotheus meant to care for her, knowing the danger she was in because of her marriage to Nicholas. But his betrayal came at the price of her life. She lingered for a month without regaining consciousness. There was some hope of saving the baby, but she died before he could be born. They cut open her womb and pulled him out. Sadly, the baby was already dead.

"Nicholas didn't receive word until almost a year later. It is what finally broke him."

I opened and closed my mouth, unsure how to respond. The story was incredible. Impossible, even. And yet, it was either true, or I was in the presence of some of the greatest method actors in the world. Finally, I shook my head. "I just don't know what to believe now."

Oleg blew a breath out. "Let's you and I cut to the chase, shall we? You want to know how this man has the experiences and memories of someone from more than seventeen centuries ago."

I nodded. It was exactly what I wanted to know.

# Fourteen

I gave it my best shot. "Is it some sort of past life regression?"

In reply I received a burst of laughter, and frankly I felt a little put off by it. I do admit: past life theory has not been fully validated yet, but I knew of numerous case studies—researched on my private time—that lent credence to the idea.

I did not expect to be laughed at.

I tried again, "Well, what else am I supposed to believe? That Nicholas has been wandering around alive for nearly two thousand years like some kind of vampire or... or zombie?"

His laughter intensified, and he shook his head, unable to speak. Oleg's face turned beet red and his eyes squeezed shut in tears. He started coughing, and I began to fear he might die on me. When he finally calmed I said, "Okay, so not a zombie or a vampire, and not past life. So was he like, frozen out here and you found him encased in ice or something?"

"Yah? Like a popsicle?" More laughter. "Oh my friend, you have brought such joy to an old man!"

I sat back in my chair and folded my hands in my lap. "I give up. You tell me how the impossible can be true."

He took a breath and dried his eyes. "When the impossible is true, then by definition, it is not impossible, yah?"

"I suppose it would have to be."

"You suppose. And do you suppose that someone who was once dead could be alive again? And I don't mean a zombie."

I thought a moment. "Resurrection."

"Yes. Let me think how the English translation puts it. 'Christ being raised from the dead dieth no more; death hath no more dominion over Him.' Saint Paul's Epistle to the Romans."

"But that's talking about Jesus."

"Yah. So it is."

I furrowed my brow. "Are you saying He's Jesus?"

He started laughing again.

I ran a frustrated hand over my mouth. "Oleg, please! Will you just spit it out already?"

He reached from the bed and took my hand, and after several breaths, he began to explain. "Nicholas died, yah? In prison, shortly after they told him his wife and son were gone. He succumbed to his injuries, to deprivation and want—and he died. And when that happened, he saw Christ. He saw his mother and father. He saw his beloved Johanna and his unborn son, cradled in her arms. And Christ came to him, and gave him a choice. To stay, or to return and finish the work God had for him. I do not know his reasons. I do not know why he should choose to remain here on this earth, especially after suffering so much pain. Such intolerable cruelty. Nor can I imagine why he should choose to

172

remain among us for so long as he has. What I do know is this: he does not age. He does not get sick. And he does not die."

"So he's immortal."

He nodded. "Yes. As we all will be one day, who believe in Christ. The Lord spoke to the sister of Lazarus, to Martha. He said, 'I am the resurrection, and the life: he that believeth in me, though he were dead, yet shall he live; and whosoever liveth and believeth in me shall never die. Believest thou this?' I tell you with assurance: Nicholas believes. That is why he lives. Rather, how he lives. Why? I do not know."

From the other side of the door came the Abbot's muffled voice. "To serve."

A moment later, Nicholas pushed the door open. He appeared to have been leaning against the wall the entire time, and he still did not raise his head to look at us. "I live to serve. It was my oath, my promise to God. Had I seen Him when they arrested me, I would not have chosen to come back. But then they took my family from me, and threw me into that dungeon. I, and my fellow believers. Several of them bishops like me. We were beaten. We were lashed with whips to within inches of our lives. The Romans spared themselves nothing when it came to cruelty. A number were burned alive, refusing to recant their Lord even to gain mercy from the flames.

"More than twenty thousand of us perished under the Great Persecution. People began to weaken and recant. When word reached me that Johanna... I gave up. A guard—I forget his name—mocked me when he told me what had happened. He asked me what I thought about my God now. I said to him, 'My God is all I have left. You have taken everything else of value from me.' He asked, 'What about your life?' I told him I did not value it. Not anymore. Sometime after that is when I died."

I swallowed. "Did it hurt?"

"No," he said quickly. "It was a relief. A release of all that pain. And suddenly I was free. I could see my body, and the walls of the prison around me, and then it all dropped away, like waking from a dream."

I swallowed again, and still could not get rid of the odd lump in my throat. "Why did you come back?"

"I knew that I had given up. It wasn't the sacrifice I was meant to make. I sensed it, standing there in His presence. Standing before all of them, I sensed there was more—much more—that I could do, especially for my brothers who were weakening in faith. I wanted them to know it was real, to encourage them. And I even felt angry that such evil would be done against my Lord and His Bride. But that was fleeting.

"And so I came back. And I have never regretted my choice. Even now, I know there is much to be done."

"All this time, though. You've been up here?"

He shook his head, a wistful grin pushing away the grief of moments ago. "No. Not for some time, actually. After coming back, I was still in prison, believe it or not. But I had hope, now. And power."

"Power?" I picked up my pen again. "What power?" I hadn't decided whether or not I believed him, but I was willing to suspend disbelief—at least for the time being. There seemed no other way to get the rest of the story, as incredible as it was.

"Well," he came back into the room and returned to his chair, "for one thing, I'd become impervious to wounds. It made me fearless before them. I can't say that I had courage. Courage is showing heart—even love—in the face of fear. I had no fear whatsoever. The guard noticed the change first. You can't imagine how unnerved they were."

"You! Get up!" The harsh tones rang through the stark cell like the warning growl of a lion.

Nicholas opened his eyes, breathless from the vision of glory receding, but still present in his mind. *Had it been real? Oh my God! It felt so utterly real!*

Next came a banging on the prison bars. The faint glow of torchlight cast the far wall in pale shades of orange and yellow.

"Come on, now! I know you're alive. I can see you breathing, see? Now get up!"

Nicky felt an incredible warmth flow through him, from the

top of his head all the way to the soles of his feet. It was intoxicating, but at the same time invigorating, with none of the mental dullness that came from wine or strong drink. He heard everything: the sound of a fly buzzing about the straw—even hear the distinct beats of its wings. The dripping of water from the ceiling down along the walls into the cracks of the floor. He listened, following the droplets further into the bowels of the earth till they joined an underground stream, wending their way through the secret places in the bedrock till they rushed out to sea. Far above, he could feel the warmth of the sun baking the streets of the city, feel the air rushing through the windows of the prison, reaching even as far as his solitary cell. He could smell the sweat glistening on the back of the guard standing outside his door, could feel the man impatiently shuffling his feet. Could even hear the moment the guard made his decision to enter the cell.

The keys jangled as the guard lifted them from his belt.

"Is it not a beautiful thing," Nicholas asked, "to be alive?" He opened his eyes.

The keys faltered, just outside the lock. "Eh?" The guard said after a moment. "What's that?"

Nicholas rolled over and sat up, pulling his legs beneath him and resting his hands on his knees. "Do you not feel it?"

"Feel what?"

"Life. Such a glorious gift our Lord has given us! Life flows through the air, the water, the earth, the fire of your torch. It fills all things—the very will of God spoken that holds all things together, that binds them one to another. If you but open your eyes, your ears, your nose! Even your soul to this—you will realize that life does not end. Death can have no more dominion than a cloud can hide the sun."

The guard licked his lips. "What in Tartarus are you talking about?"

"It is why He rose from the dead." Nicky shook his head. "Christ. He is life itself. And love. And all good things."

The guard set his jaw. "You done cracked your head."

"No. I've been opened to the truth. And you can be, too. Acanthus, isn't it? The grace of God is free and meant for you as well as me."

"Hey now," Acanthus warned, "we'll have none of that."

"Don't you see? The gods of your people are nothing more than ideas—and not very good ones at that. They're not real! And they can do nothing for you. Your prayers to them are vain, and your sacrifices a waste. But there is a God Who is real and Who does answer prayer—and Who has already provided a sacrifice for you far greater than any you could ever give. Turn from this life of sin and give yourself over to Jesus Christ."

Acanthus grunted, and then motioned with his hand. Nicky closed his mouth, sad for what was to happen next. The key turned in the lock and the man shoved the door open. Nicholas pushed to his feet and folded his hands in front of him, nodding in greeting at the two other guards who followed Acanthus in.

"We got ourselves a live one here," Acanthus said. "Thinks he be converting me to his pagan ways. Worshipping that dead guy, Christos."

"He's one of them bishops," one of the other guards replied. "A true believer. Likes to set an example to the flock, ain't that right?"

"Speak when you're spoken to!" the third man cried, and cuffed Nicholas across the face.

Nicholas sensed the force of the blow, but curiously, felt no pain. It was as if someone had merely caressed his cheek rather than struck him with the back of his hand.

"You are right," he answered. "Tatius. That is your name, isn't it?"

"Shut up!" Tatius bellowed, and hit him again. Then he turned to his fellow guards and laughed.

"He thinks he's an example, perhaps we oughtta make an example outta him, eh?" Acanthus loosened a flail he kept in his belt.

Nicholas smiled and thought of Johanna. "Do what you will. It matters not."

"Strip him down."

They turned Nicky around and tore the coarse garment off his back, shredding down the middle. In the shadows on the wall,

Nicky watched as the man raised the flail and brought it down hard across his back. He heard the crack of the whip, but felt nothing greater than the brush of a feather on his skin.

*Curious*, he thought.

Acanthus reared back and hit him again, and again and again. Nicholas watched the whip's shadow on the wall as it fell each time.

*Do they mean to tickle me into submission?*

"Hey now, hold a moment," the second guard said. The flail halted in mid air. "Why ain't he bleeding?"

The guards muttered briefly, and then the flail came down again with no more force than if the fly Nick had heard earlier had landed upon his back.

*I feel no pain*, Nicholas marveled. *None whatsoever!*

"He ain't bleeding, Gordianus. Narry a drop o' red!"

"Maybe he's cursed."

"Maybe I'm blessed," Nicholas replied. He turned around and faced the men. "Gordianus, Tatius, and Acanthus—listen to me. The Lord Jesus Christ has appointed you to hear this message. I am your prisoner, and the Lord has graciously chosen you to know His salvation. Do not despise this day of salvation. It is time you put away your whips and swords. They will not avail you here."

Gordianus snorted. "We'll see about that."

In one smooth motion he drew his dagger and thrust it

through Nicholas's heart, embedding the hilt in his chest. Nicholas glanced down, and then looked up again at the man. Gordianus's triumphant snarl faded into confusion, and then panic.

"Peace," Nicholas urged. "Be still."

Acanthus and Tatius fell to their knees, their jaws open. Abruptly, they put their faces to the floor, bowing before him. Nicky opened and closed his mouth, and then put his hand over Gordianus's, and gently withdrew the blade. Gordianus stumbled backward and fell to the floor, staring wide-eyed up at him.

The dagger withdrawn, Nicholas turned and offered it back to him, hilt first. "Put this away. And you two: up. Up with both of you. I am but a man. Worship God alone."

"'Tis impossible!" Gordianus cried.

"Nothing shall be impossible to him that believes," Nicholas replied.

"Wait," I objected. "He stabbed you. Through the heart."

"Yes." The Abbot nodded and tapped his solar plexus. "Right here."

"Naturally, it didn't leave a mark."

I mean, it couldn't have. Because it never happened. I willfully suspended disbelief for the sake of the story. My question wasn't meant to challenge him. I only wanted to confirm for myself how the story would unfold. This better be what Marshall was looking for. Either way, it was one hell of a story.

But the Abbot's words stunned me. "Of course it did. I bear the scars to this day."

"Scars."

"Yes. The wounds do not cause me pain. Nor do they harm me in any way, but I do not leave this world unmarked—whenever it is that time should arrive."

I frowned, not quite sure what to do with this.

"You don't believe," Oleg stated.

I shrugged. "In the absence of evidence."

"Evidence?" He started coughing uncontrollably, and the Abbot bent over him, and then turned him to his side while he hacked and struggled to breathe. I opened my mouth to say something, but Nicholas waved me off.

"You've upset him," he said brusquely.

"I didn't mean—"

Oleg's continued fit interrupted me. For a moment there, I feared he was dying before my very eyes. I stared as Nicholas closed his eyes, his lips moving in fervent prayer. At last, Oleg spat, a long line of drool hung suspended from his lower lip and fell to the floor. The Abbot wiped Oleg's mouth with a tissue, and the old man collapsed onto the bed, exhausted.

"I'm sorry," I muttered.

"How?" Oleg asked.

"Sorry?"

"How can you say... absence of ... evidence... when he is standing right in front of you?!" He straightened and almost shouted this last part at me. Then he fell back to the pillow, exhausted.

"Easy, friend," Nicholas murmured. "Be gentle with the man."

Oleg gripped the Abbot's hand. "You... you must show him."

The Abbot shook his head. "It is unseemly. You know I do not do this."

"He is not a brother!"

"Show me what?"

"What difference does it make?" Nicholas persisted. "Belief is a matter of the will, not proof. For those who do not believe, no proof is sufficient. For those who do, none is needed."

"Show him," Oleg insisted. "Even Christ showed Thomas."

"What is he talking about?" I asked again.

Nicholas sighed.

"Vær så snill!" Oleg insisted.

"Som du ønsker," Nicholas muttered. He stood and undid the belt holding his cassock together, and began unbuttoning it from the top. Before I could object, he pulled the whole ensemble off and stood there with his back to me, wearing nothing but long under-breeches.

His back was a mass of heavy scars. In the center, puckered a bit around the spine, was the remnant of an ugly, star-shaped wound.

"Dear God," I muttered.

He turned around, and there, in the middle of a hairy, somewhat burly chest, glowered the source of the wound in back.

I've seen puncture wounds before—both those that have healed and those that never would. Nothing looked quite like this.

"Satisfied?" Nicholas asked.

I raised my eyes to his face, but he'd already turned to glare at Oleg. Oleg wagged a finger at me. "Now? Do you believe?"

# Fifteen

"I must apologize for my friend." The Abbot took a seat beside me, fully clothed again—mercifully—and clasped his hands in front of his face, resting his forehead on his thumbs as if praying.

We'd left the room almost a half hour ago and gone outside. I, because I thought I was going to be sick, and Nicholas, because he insisted that Oleg get some rest.

I had no objection. I needed a break.

Above our heads, the stars glistened, piercing against the velvet black. A half-moon crawled the heavens along the roof of the monastery, providing just enough light reflected in the snow at my feet to see.

My mind spun, still trying to sort out the meaning of it all. I grasped for threads that would anchor me to reality—to how I knew the universe worked—and they broke like cobwebs falling to dust in my hands.

Nothing made sense any more. The world in which I lived, which had always been rather normal, predictable and, well, scientific, now seemed utterly at odds with reason.

A dead man walked the streets, and now sat beside me.

Those wounds had to have been faked! Clever make-up and special effects!

Except that I knew they hadn't been. Couldn't have been.

Had to have been.

I shifted uncomfortably away from him, and dearly wished I hadn't given up cigarettes.

Nicholas reached into his pocket and pulled out a packet of tobacco and a pipe. "Smoke?"

"You're kidding."

"If it bothers you..."

"No! No, that'd be great, actually."

He grinned and pulled out a second pipe. "Thought you could use something to help you relax."

Deftly, he filled each pipe, handed me one of them, and then struck a match and held the flame to his own before offering it to me. "The brothers don't like it when I smoke. Do you think they're afraid it will kill me?"

I laughed nervously.

"'The stump of a pipe he held clenched in his teeth. And the smoke, it encircled his head like a wreath,'" he quoted, and then blew out a fragrant cloud. "It's one of the few things dear Clement got right in his silly little ditty."

"A Visit from Saint..." I turned and gaped at him.

He grinned and sucked his pipe. "You're starting to put two and two together."

"Santa Claus." I shook my head.

He chuckled. "Not quite."

I breathed a sigh of relief and drew in a draught of smoke.

"Thomas Nast was mostly responsible for that myth," he explained. His Harper's Weekly illustration. Though he based it on Clement's description. Tell me truthfully: do I look jolly and plump? A droll little elf?"

"Droll?"

"Elf?" He grunted and sucked his pipe. "Santa Claus is a cartoon. An invention of American Main Street meets New York City Wall Street—a means of putting a stamp of approval on the crass commercialization of what is otherwise a sacred holiday. Don't confuse it with me."

"But you are saying that you are... Santa. The real thing."

"I am not *Santa*. I am Nicholas of Myra. I am as real as you are. True, my existence—my presence before you—is a miracle. But it is a miracle of God. Not marketing. Not Main Street." He drew in a draught and blew out a cloud. "And certainly not *A Miracle on 42nd Street*. Ridiculous movie. They should never have colorized it."

"This is impossible."

"With God, all things are possible." He met my eye and winked. "Even me."

"But how—?"

"Really, Brett," he chided, "is there even a point to that

question? I tell you it is a miracle of God. Might as well ask how the sun comes up, or how a child is woven in its mother's womb."

"But we know how," I objected. "The earth rotates on its axis. Babies grow from cellular division and differentiation. This," I pointed at his chest, "is entirely different."

"Is it?" He smiled. "Does knowing how the sun rises or an infant forms make them any less miraculous? Perhaps it does, but I wonder whether we're the better for it. You Americans are so inquisitive! You treat mystery as a thing to be solved, and not as something simply to be enjoyed and pondered. Perhaps I am exactly what your country needs: a mystery they cannot explain. A puzzle box they cannot unlock."

I took the pipe out of my mouth and stared at it. I could easily picture what would happen to a man like Nicholas if he came to the United States and openly declared his secret. First, he would be laughed at. Scorned. Even vilified. They'd lock him away in an asylum, like they tried to do to his carton self in *Miracle on 42nd Street*. But if he proved he was who he claimed, then it would be even worse.

They'd stuff him in a lab, somewhere. Study him. Run all manner of tests to unlock the secrets of his immortality, his healing. The justifications would all be in the name of the greater good, but they'd unleash hell in the process. And worse yet, if they succeeded, then they'd try to keep the secret only for the select few—the elites who could pay the largest price. If it ever did break out onto the open market—no death for anyone—global overpopulation would surge, along with a pandemic of crime.

The secret he'd shared is one that would undo the world.

"I have to think," I muttered, my hands shaking, "that your secret revealed... would be very bad... for the rest of the world."

He smiled kindly, but his eyes were sad. "Indeed it would, if it were merely a drug others could take without relying on God. Now you know why the Lord sent Adam and Eve out from the Garden of Eden before they could eat from the tree of life. For if He hadn't, they would have lived forever in sin. Hell on earth."

"And yet you sent for a reporter—a news reporter—to tell your story to. Why would you do that?"

"Because it doesn't work without God. There is no fountain of youth, no secret elixir of life you can take to cheat death. The only way to live forever is to die and be raised again by Christ." He tipped his pipe at me. "But let us briefly suppose your fears are justified. Do you think for a moment that your news story would ever be believed?"

"Of course not," I scoffed. "Santa Claus is real? Hell no. No one would buy it."

"I'm not—"

"I'm just telling you what the headline would be."

"I should hope you could come up with a better headline than that."

I put my head down and stared at the ground. "That's more Marshall's department, anyway. I'm sure he'll come up with something better. If it goes to print at all."

"Well," he patted my knee, "I'm sure you'll do fine telling the story. The miracle, however, is quite real. It is the truth, and, my friend, I suspect your reluctance to tell the story has more to do with your reluctance to believe in miracles than it does with whether or not your story would be believed."

I shivered from a sudden chill. The Abbot tapped out his pipe. "Come, you're getting cold. I'll have Don warm us up some hot chocolate."

I followed him back into the monastery, and stared agape at the activity going on inside. Monks hustled to and fro, giving Nicholas and myself broad smiles and polite nods, but hurrying on their way. Several of them appeared to be carrying tools of some kind or another. I tapped the Abbot's shoulder. "What's going on?"

He grinned slyly. "You'll see. Let them finish their preparations first. We'll have vespers soon, if you would care to join us. And then the brothers have something special they wish to show you."

"This surprise I keep hearing about?"

He pursed his lips and shrugged, and led me down the hall. As we moved toward the kitchen area where we'd dined earlier, we passed a glass display case built into the wall. I'd passed it before and paid it no mind, but this time I stopped.

Within the glass case, mounted on a wooden frame like those seen in a dressmaker's shop, hung a ratted set of crimson robes. I stared at them, now, perhaps seeing them in perspective for the first time.

Nicholas returned to my side. "One of the earliest members of my order made me promise to keep them. For years they simply hung in my closet, unused. About a hundred years ago, a follower brought them out and insisted on building this display case."

"Your followers wring many promises out of you."

"It is part of the grand bargain they make. Each of them promises themselves to God, and they sacrifice so much for the sake of His glory. In exchange, I make each of them one promise—whatever they ask, if it is within my power to do, I will do for them."

"That's a bold promise."

"It is. But since they only get one, they tend to choose carefully."

"So," I breathed, "this is where it comes from? The whole suit of red fur?"

"More or less. These are my bishop's robes—rather, what's

left of them. You will find a great many of the traditions associated with that legend have their origins in benign and rather plain facts—beyond the miracle itself, of course."

"So am I going to find eight tiny reindeer around here somewhere?"

He chuckled. "We have trucks for going into town. No sleighs. But there was a time..."

"You're kidding."

"We didn't always use motor vehicles, Brett."

"You've got to tell me how you wound up here. This is a long way from the Mediterranean."

"So it is." He turned from the display and led me into the kitchen. "And I will, but first I have to tell you what happened after Diocletian."

The light hurt his eyes, despite the fact that so little did bring him pain now. Nicholas blinked as he emerged from the prison, with brothers Tatius and Acanthus opening the gates before him, deferentially guiding him back toward the street.

In the year since his death and resurrection, Nicky had trained his senses to shut out the din of the world, the constant awareness of everyone and everything. Those first few months of his new life on earth had bordered on agony—except that he could not feel pain as he once had. That is not to say he no longer suffered. Far from it. But now, his suffering had less to do with his own physical sensations and much more to do with the afflictions of those around him.

He laced his prayers with the reality of human misery— bringing his fellow inmates, guards, believers, doubters alike before the throne of grace. He prayed for those outside the walls, walking the streets above where he could almost feel their steps, painful and slow shuffling through the dust and gravel. He prayed for those in power and those in slavery, for pagan priests and holy men, for merchants and thieves, for women in labor and men with one foot in the grave.

And for children—he could sense their delight, their confusion, their hunger and hope—and he lifted all before the Father.

In time, though, he realized that many of his prayers remained unanswered, if not downright ignored by heaven. Surely the arm of the Lord was not too short to save! Then at last he recognized that God did not intend to remove suffering from the life of man, much less to remove man from a life of suffering.

Pain was redemptive. Transformative. Necessary to the growth of the spirit. His own suffering had brought him to the point where he no longer wanted to live, until at last his spirit broke under the weight. Now reborn and returned to walk once more amidst the furnace of affliction, he realized what all his

192

suffering and losses had finally done—they had broken his grip on the earth, and freed him to take hold of heaven.

With both hands firmly grasping the firmament, he walked among mortals now as an ambassador of eternity, an agent of hope in a world of despair.

So yes, the light hurt his eyes. He tempered what he saw and what he heard and felt, pushing it in the background of his awareness so that he could focus on what lay in front of him.

It was easy to get distracted. Especially when the background noise threatened to overwhelm him, as it did so now. He almost couldn't hear Tatius over the din, and shame-facedly, he asked the guard to repeat himself.

Tatius gave him a curious stare. "D'you not hear them, man? They're crying for you!"

Crying? What are they crying?

He took a few more steps forward, reaching the top of the rise where the prison steps opened out onto the market. His eyes widened at what he saw: a mass of humanity, arms suddenly raised in triumph and giving glory to God.

"Nicholas!" they cried. "Nicholas the Confessor!"

I raised my hand. "Confessor? What did they mean by that?"

Nicholas took a sip of his hot chocolate before answering. "It came to be a title, but at first it was simply a statement of fact. A confessor is one who confesses Christ, who does not recant his faith even under the direst torment, who remains faithful unto death. I was hardly the only one. But if you want to know the reason why the Catholic faith considers me a saint, you'd start there."

"I'd have figured the miracles. Your resurrection."

"No one knew about that but Tatius and Acanthus, and I'd sworn them both to secrecy."

"And Gordianus. He knew."

He shook his head. "Gordianus, sadly, refused to recant his pagan faith. He would not believe."

"But he saw!" I objected. "He was the one who stabbed you, right?"

"Indeed. I've often wondered if that wasn't why he refused. Guilt will more often drive a man deeper into sin as draw him out of it, especially if he refuses to accept what his guilt reveals of his nature. Men do not willingly embrace the true darkness of their own hearts. We desperately want to believe we are good. And when we prove otherwise... it can be devastating. Some men would rather die than face the truth. Such was Gordianus's fate. He drank himself to death. Rather, he drank until he passed out on duty, and was executed for it."

"That must've been—"

"Agonizing. I was with him when it happened." He tapped his

head. "Up here. I'd been reaching out to him. Tuned in, if you will, in hopes of finding a way to get through to him. When they caught him, they killed him on the spot. I felt his soul leave his body. I felt him scream as he entered judgment. There is no sound so terrifyingly pitiful as that of a soul who realizes all hope is utterly lost."

I blinked. I was going to say 'that must've been relieving,' thinking how Gordianus got what he deserved, and that Nicholas was at least assured his secret was safe. My cheeks flamed.

"At any rate," he put his chocolate down, "I was now free, and with two loyal disciples, along with a host of admirers. It was a little overwhelming, to say the least."

"I imagine so. What did you do?"

He shrugged. "I went home. The village of Myra received me as a welcome hero. Even those in Patara came to greet me. I wanted for nothing except time. Were it not for Tatius and Acanthus, I might not have had a moment's rest—especially those first few weeks."

"Did you need rest?"

"Not physically. Tiredness, like hunger or thirst, is an affliction of the mortal body that I no longer experience. But I still eat. I still drink. I still sleep. I even still dream. I simply no longer suffer consequences if I don't. That being said, there is a weariness of the spirit I can and do experience. Even God can be wearied."

When I raised an eyebrow he explained. "It's in the words of Isaiah, the prophet. The Lord testifies the prayers of the impenitent and faithless weary Him.

"In my case, it wasn't the impenitent and faithless so much as it was the constant awareness I felt. Most of the people who came to see me, with their problems, their pain—they came looking for a miracle. They'd beg me to bless them. Bless their babies, bless their animals, bless their houses. But what they really wanted was for me to make their pain go away. And how could I do that, knowing that pain was what God wanted them to experience? Not because God was cruel or vindictive or malicious in any way—far from it. Simply because God knows that our suffering can be transformative. Even redemptive. It's not that God wants us to suffer. It's that suffering has a purpose: to bring about the transformation of our character so that we become like Christ. The masses wanted their blessings, but what they needed was something else entirely. And yes, that did weary me."

"In any case, I soon found a better way to restore my spirit."

"And what was that?"

He grinned. "Destroying temples."

# Sixteen

Nicholas stared at the abomination, and felt a deep, growing well of anger surging in his spirit. The hot sun beat down on his brow, unalleviated by the warm breeze blowing up from the sea. The breeze was mild, and did little to remove the stagnation the bishop felt in the area. *Like the odor of death,* he thought, and grimaced.

It was not the scent he'd expected when he returned to Myra, and for a moment he wondered whether the city actually smelled different—or if he was just now noticing what had been under his nose all along.

Before him, the abomination rose with a massive façade of stone. It had taken years to build. Hands belonging to some of his dearest friends and disciples had worked that same stone— repair work and maintenance, mostly—because the money was good. Indeed, what Nicholas had in mind would harm the economic interests of the city. *Short term harm for long term good,* he mused.

Four columns entwined with vines supported the peaked roof. Like the stone, the vines hadn't grown overnight. They wound their way around the columns from the good soil, finding purchase in the cracks and crevices in the stone surface and would, in time, accomplish the same purpose he now intended. As if the earth and all of nature justly rejected the abomination this structure contained. Peering between the columns, he could make out the massive carved figure—nothing more or less than a perversion of the feminine ideal. The many-breasted goddess looked down from her pedestal with what seemed to Nicholas a daunting leer.

She was far smaller than the famous one in Ephesus, some two hundred ninety miles away to the northeast. That same temple figured prominently in the book of Acts. Saint Paul had ignored it, concentrating his mission on reaching the heathen within the city and its environs rather than directly confronting the idolatry of the goddess. Still, a confrontation had erupted nonetheless. Demetrius the silversmith had gone to his fellow craftsman, complaining that Saint Paul's preaching of Christ was so effective that their trade in silver goddesses and amulets was falling into disrepute, and that if left unchecked, the singular attraction of the many-breasted goddess, Artemis of the Ephesians whose image supposedly fell from heaven, would fail.

*Oh, you fell from heaven all right, foul demon of the abyss!*

This version of Artemis was less impressive, but no less dangerous. Tolerating her presence in his diocese was tolerating sin, allowing the same evil that had killed his beloved wife and unborn son and had thrown countless brothers and sisters into prison or an early grave to fester and grow.

Idolatry was a pernicious weed despoiling the fine garden of God's grace. Left unchecked, it would soon choke out the plants and render the ground inhospitable and wasted. The only solution was to tear it out by the roots.

Starting here.

A shadow appeared behind him. He knew already it was Prefect Eustathios puffing up behind him, answering to the bishop's summons. Without waiting for the man to announce his presence, Nicholas said, "Thank you for coming."

"Your—ah—apologies, sir. I don't know what title—"

"Titles mean nothing to me now. But if you must have one, you may call me Bishop Nicholas." He turned and regarded the man, observing his round, flushed face and thinning white hairs poking from around his ears. The man's girth hung over his belt, giving him the shape of an enlarged pear. "I know you are not a man of God—" he continued.

Eustathios interrupted, "Well, that is, ah, we in the council have the utmost respect for you and, ah, the masses you represent—"

"The majority of the city, you mean."

"Ah... yes."

"And soon, the empire as well." Nicholas clapped a reassuring hand on his shoulder. "Our new emperor favors us."

"Yes," Eustathios wrung his hands, "and allow me to be the

first to say how dreadfully sorry we all are for you and the suffering you endured at the hands of the previous administration."

He was hardly the first, but Nicholas didn't tell him that. "You mean Galerius and Diocletian."

"Of course."

Nicholas turned from him and stepped toward the abomination. "Constantine learned from their errors. You cannot kill that which cannot die. Try to stamp us out, and we come back stronger a hundredfold. Bleed us, and it is the very seed by which more are saved every day." He reached back and tugged on the Prefect's shoulder, who flinched. Nicholas smiled and kept his grip firm, pulling the man along. "No apology is needed. It is an honor to suffer for Christ. My wife and my child await me with the Lord, and to them I shall go, when my task here is completed."

The Prefect quailed beside him, but couldn't seem to tear his eyes from Nicky's as they walked, leaving him to stumble a bit on the road. "And what is that task?" His lip trembled.

Nicholas grunted and gestured toward the temple with his crozier. "Diocles and Galerius tried to crush out Christianity. They tore down our homes and burned our churches with fire, and yet here we still stand. Tell me, magistrate, do you think those who love Artemis would stay faithful if our new emperor were to treat them as they treated us?"

"... uh, I don't... uh, surely you don't mean to..."

"Have no fear, Eustathios. I do not intend to beat, imprison, or kill anyone. That is not our way. A day will come when every knee will bow and every tongue confess that Jesus Christ is Lord, but until that day comes we invite you to worship with us. We do not force it."

The Prefect managed a relieved smile. "I'm grateful to hear that."

"That being said, this temple before us must be uprooted from its foundations and thrown down."

Eustathios stopped short, backpedaled slightly. "Beg pardon?"

"It is an abomination, an offense to God. And to the faith of our Emperor. Tear it down."

The Prefect wrung his hands, shaking his head. "Surely you jest! The temple of the goddess is, by far, the most exquisite structure in all Myra. People come from miles around just to worship at her feet and see her beauty!"

Nicholas stamped his crozier on the ground. "All the more reason it must be removed. It is a cancer upon the land and its inhabitants!"

The Prefect found his conviction. Nicky watched it surge over the man's face from somewhere within. "Those inhabitants depend upon the trade this temple inspires! Devotees flock to this place, a-and they buy and sell—and trade with us! Your own

201

offerings for the poor depend upon the commerce this temple—what you dare call an abomination—inspires!"

Nicky felt his stomach churn. Money! It always came down to money. "Doubtless you fear the loss of revenue—"

"Of course! As should you!"

"On the contrary. I know the Lord always provides. And He shall provide for you and for the city as well, if you would but put your trust in Him."

Eustathios curled his lip. "Trust him? A god I can't see?"

"Yes. Precisely that. It's called 'faith', my brother."

Eustathios wagged a finger at him. "Don't be calling me 'brother,' Bishop. I'll not fall for your old wives' tale of dead gods who live again. Crucified saviors indeed! I believe in solid things. This temple," he ran his hand along the column nearest him, "that's solid. That I can believe in. And facts, like what will happen when the people no longer flock to Myra because her glory has been torn down by the likes of a vengeful religious zealot!"

"Prefect—"

"The council shall hear about this!" Eustathios gathered his robes about him, backing away toward the street. Nicholas watched him go, frustrated. A crowd had gathered, gawking at the disruption between the two, some sneering openly. Nicholas whirled about, addressing the abomination directly.

"Know this, foul corruption! You shall be torn down till not one stone is left standing upon another. Your very foundations shall be ripped up and laid bare, and this abominable pile of carved rock you call a god shall be cast down from its pedestal, broken asunder and cast into the sea!"

With that, he struck the column with the butt end of his staff. For a brief moment, he half-expected the stone to shatter. Indeed, the crozier vibrated in his hand, but the stone held fast against his assault. *Of course,* he reasoned. *The Lord shall not abide this temple, but far better it will be when the people take it upon themselves to tear her apart with their own two hands. That will be the real miracle.*

A few more snickers erupted from the crowd—likely the same scoffers who'd sneered at him at first. He turned a baleful glare upon the crowd, daring the scoffers to show themselves. A pair of lads whispered to each other in the back of the crowd, glancing at him with a cruel delight in their eyes. They had dark, unruly curls framing their faces, and the ruddy tint of their skin told him they'd seen many days in the sun, but the lack of heavy muscle on their arms suggested their days were spent in idleness rather than in something more redemptive, like hard work.

*These boys mean trouble,* he realized. He leaned his crozier against the ground and steadied himself upon it, staring at the boys. Gradually, the crowd shuffled away, almost parting before him like Moses parting the sea. But the boys slipped away, disappearing into the throng. Nicky snorted. He straightened and smoothed out his robe, and then headed back toward the church.

He'd not gone thirty feet when the first missile flew out. It was a tomato, and it struck the wall beside him with a liquid smack, dribbling its guts down the brick to land with a plop in the earth by his feet. He regarded it only a moment before a second tomato flew. It hit his mitre, knocking it from his head. He drew in a breath, spun on his heel and faced his assailants, who remained hidden behind a cart, snickering and congratulating each other on their exceptional aim. Spreading his arms wide, he stared at them, catching glimpses of their impish grins as they poked their heads above the cart.

"Well, go on," he dared. "Surely I present a tempting target."

Another tomato flew out, striking his robe before rolling to the street. He ignored it. The boys poked their heads above the cart, their smiles fading. The taller one let loose another round. It hit Nicky smack across the forehead. He felt the pulp sag off his face, the juice burning his eyes. He blinked and kept his gaze steady, steeling himself against the pain. The boys came out from hiding now, hurling fruit after fruit till their hands and pockets were empty. Nicholas continued to stare at them, bearing the brunt of their assault, their attempt to shame him. Silently, he waited.

The faded smiles turned into angry snarls. He was supposed to be embarrassed, he knew, shamed by this insult. It angered them that he was not.

The younger picked up a rock, hefting it in his hand. Then he threw it. The stone struck Nicky's shoulder before clattering to the ground. "By all means," he spoke in a low voice. "But wait." Reaching a hand around, he undid the clasps on his robe and let it fall to the ground. Quickly, he tugged his shirt off as well, till he stood exposed, half-naked before them. The scars across his chest and back puckered his skin, screaming the abuse he'd suffered at the hands of Diocletian and Galerius. "Now, go ahead."

The two boys stared at him.

"Go on," he urged. "Do your worst. I can take your hate." When they did not move, he bent forward and grasped a few larger stones. "Here, try these!" He tossed the rocks toward them. The boys flinched, but the stones scattered harmlessly at their feet. "Use the larger ones. They will inflict more pain. That is what you want, isn't it? To hurt me? You think to cause me shame? Humiliation? Suffering? It does not compare the suffering I already feel in my heart for you! I pray the Lord forgive you your sins, and I do not hold this against you. It is an honor to bear in my flesh the brand marks of Jesus."

Abruptly, the boys dropped their stones and ran, disappearing down a side street. He watched them go, ignoring the gaping stares of the passersby, and then put his shirt back on. Bending forward, he collected his robe and his mitre, planting it firmly on his head before walking the rest of the way to his church.

It was days later when he saw the boys again. They were dressed cleaner, now, their unruly curls shaved off as if attempting to disguise their identities, and they stood in the back of the church as he gave the sermon. He'd chosen his text that morning from Luke's testimony of the Acts of the Apostles, describing in great detail how their neighbors in Ephesus had repented of their sorceries and magic arts, burning the scrolls. Then, as he moved on to the story of Demetrius the Silversmith rallying the crowds of Ephesians to protest Paul's preaching and provoking a riot, and how it all stemmed from the illicit trade and worship of the false god Artemis.

"It is demonic," he concluded, and then pointed his finger in the general direction of the temple, "and that same demon calls our beloved city home, doesn't it?"

There were a few scattered "Amens," and some nervous shuffling in the congregation. He stepped out from behind the lectern, folding his hands in front of him and speaking to them from his heart.

"How long? Hmm? How long will we tolerate its presence among us? How long must we endure our taxes being confiscated and used to support the vile passions of such idolatry? How long will we suffer before we tell our civic leaders that enough is enough? Or do you think the Lord on high will consent to grant His blessing while we turn a blind eye to that vile abomination, or worse—even celebrate it as a source and symbol of greatness? I tell you no. It is not the time for us to live in peace with the domain of darkness. For what fellowship hath righteousness with unrighteousness? And what communion hath light with darkness? And what concord hath Christ with Belial? Or what part hath the believer with the infidel? And what agreement hath the Temple of God with idols?" He raised his voice, thundering to the crowd, "For ye are the Temple of the living God! As God hath said, I will dwell among them, and walk there: and I will be their God, and they shall be my people.

"Wherefore," and now he lowered his voice and extended his hand, gesturing toward the two young men hiding amongst the congregants, "'Come out from among them, and separate yourselves,' saith the Lord, and touch none unclean thing, and I will receive you.' This is the word of God to you. Now is the acceptable time, my beloved. Now is the day of salvation. Oh turn not yourselves away but that you receive the grace offered to you! Repent of this idolatry, that the calamity of the Lord's judgment fall not upon you!"

With a cry that startled those nearest, the younger of the two boys ran toward Nicholas, falling to his knees in front of him, bawling. Acanthus made a move as if to restrain the lad, but Nicholas stopped him with a quick shake of his head. A low murmur rippled through the congregants. Nicholas paid them no mind. He bent forward, and lifted the boy up, pulling him into an embrace as the youth sobbed. Glancing up, he caught sight of the older brother lingering back, a look of pain on his face. Quickly, Nicky motioned him forward. The lad came, reluctantly at first, and then faster as if his feet had a will of their own, till he too fell down before the bishop. He clasped his hands in front of his chest, barely daring to raise his head. "I am unworthy," he managed to mutter.

Nicholas knelt quickly and put his fingers under the lad's chin, lifting his face till he could look in his eyes. "We are all unworthy, but the Lord loves us still. And if you open your heart to receiving Him now, you shall be forgiven everything."

As the boys sobbed before him, Nicholas raised his head and met the gaze of the congregation. "Rejoice with me," he cried, "and be glad, for this son of mine—and his brother," here he tussled the hair of the younger, "were lost, and have been found. There is rejoicing in the presence of the angels of God this day."

With that he knelt, bowed his head with the boys, and prayed.

"Those two boys became like sons to me," Nicholas said, "second among my most loyal disciples. We gave them new names: Justin and Stephanos."

"What were their original names?" I asked.

He shook his head. "It does not matter. Their old selves died that day as surely as I died in that prison. They were born anew. It turned out, however, that they were the sons of one of the temple priests. You can imagine the consternation that caused! The priest of Artemis complained to the magistrate that I had stolen his sons. We had quite the row. But what could he do? Hundreds witnessed his sons conversion. That man, nonetheless, persisted to oppose me—and I, he—for the remainder of his days. It was ten years before that temple came down. But as I'd declared it was fulfilled, within half a generation. His own sons swung the picks and manned the ropes that pulled the idol down, and together we scraped every stone from its place and overturned the foundation. Some say the demons shrieked in agony as the light of God poured in on that place. In time it was nothing more than an utter ruin, never to be rebuilt."

He swung his empty cup of chocolate across the tabletop, listening for a moment to the sound of the ceramic as it scraped across the wood. "Some wanted to incorporate the stones of the temple into a new church, but I wanted nothing of it. Instead, we dragged the remains of the shrine all the way down to Andriake and dumped them in the harbor. We made a great progression of it, something I was certain would send a clear message to all devotees of that demonic cult. Nevertheless, the demise of goddess worship had less to do with any zeal of mine and far more to do with the shifting political winds. This was something I learned firsthand when I received a particular letter."

"What letter?"

"One from Emperor Constantine himself. A summons to a great council at Nicea."

#  Seventeen

The letter came sealed in wax, with the stamp of the emperor glistening in wax upon it. Nicholas took it from the hand of the courier, frowning deeply.

"What is it?" Tatius asked. He waddled over to see.

Nicholas glanced at the man and made a solemn promise never to let himself get quite so big. "It is from the Emperor," he said.

"The emperor?" Justin piped up. "You get letters from the emperor?" Awe filled his voice. Though he'd recently come into his own adulthood, in many ways he remained a child.

Nicholas patted his head. "Not usually, though he is known to respect the bishops. Far more than his predecessor did, at any rate."

"Doubtless it's about the Ancyra synod," Tatius said.

"Open it," Stephanos urged. The elder brother had come into the room following the courier, and now stood tall behind his sibling, his arms folded across his chest. Another figure shuffled in after him. Acanthus, with his arms folded inside his sleeves. Somehow, he managed to fill the doorway despite his thin frame.

Acanthus spoke in a steadying bass, "Give his grace a little space."

Nicholas's eyes crinkled. *Such a diverse and marvelous family You have given me, Lord,* he thought.

He took a seat, holding the letter before his chest, hesitant to open it. *A letter from the emperor?* He cleared his throat and cracked the seal, stretching the scroll wide to scan its contents. After a moment's reading silently, he peered over the top of the scroll. Four pairs of eyes stared back at him, expectant and eager, and even a little fearful.

"His excellency the emperor Constantine writes:

*I believe it is obvious to everyone that there is nothing more honorable in my sight than the fear of God. Though it was formerly agreed that the synod of bishops should meet at Ancyra in Galatia, it seemed to us for many reasons that it would be well for the synod to assemble at Nicaea, a city of Bithynia, both because the Bishops from Italy and the rest of the countries of Europe are coming, and because of the excellent temperature of the air, and in order that I may be present as a spectator and participator in those things which will be done. Therefore I announce to you, my beloved brothers, that all of you promptly assemble at the said city, that is at Nicaea. Let every one of you therefore, as I said before, keep the greater good in mind and be diligent, without delay in anything, to come speedily, that each may be physically present as a spectator of those things which will be done.*

*God keep you my beloved brothers."*

He rolled up the scroll and set it to one side.

"He's changing the city," Tatius observed.

Nicholas grunted. "Another eighty leagues at least. We should expect up to a week's extra travel."

"At least," Tatius replied.

"But just think of it," Justin gushed, "a great ecumenical council! Such a thing has never been done before!"

"Nor has it been necessary," Nicholas returned, "but this teaching of Arius requires remonstrance, if it be as rumors tell it."

"What is his teaching?" Stephanos asked.

Nicholas grimaced. "That is yet to be determined. Rumors, however, suggest that he denies the divinity of Christ. He treats Him as a lesser god, if such a thing could even be believed. That being said, it is not wise to presume that Arius has, in fact, erred in this way. The Lord's brother James was oft misquoted by his followers to whit: that he taught salvation by works, and thus that all believers should not only be baptized but also circumcised as well, and enjoined to follow the Mosaic law. But this was not at all his teaching. It was a misunderstanding of a careful nuance, that faith which is alive produces works which can be seen. That is all he meant to say, and it is both correct and significant. And yet he was clearly misunderstood by the Judaizers of Saint Paul's day. It may yet be that something similar has happened with Arius's doctrine as well. Regardless," he grunted and stood, "we shall find out. The man has been summoned by the emperor like the rest, and he shall have to give an account for his faith. It is, perhaps, well that he does it now if incorrect, that he may be reproved and instructed more correctly in the way before he is called to give an account before God. His very salvation hangs in the balance. Not to mention that of his followers."

"When is the synod to take place?" Acanthus queried. "Still at the solstice? Or has that changed as well?"

Nicholas shrugged. "It does not say. I would imagine the time has not changed. Some having already begun their journey, it would be unwise to alter the date now. Regardless, we must make preparations. Tatius, I will leave you in charge until we return."

"As you wish, your grace." The man bowed his head, but could not hide the smile that spread across his lips.

Nicholas cuffed his shoulder. "Oh, come off it! I know you feared the journey."

"It is true. I prefer to stay in one place. My legs aren't quite what they used to be."

The bishop grunted. "Just don't let them keep you from your duties."

"They don't keep him from the kitchen," Acanthus chided.

"You have put on a little weight," Nicholas replied. "Perhaps a fast is in order?"

"Bishop, you wouldn't!"

"I think it meet that you should be in prayer for us on our journey."

"And I shall!" Tatius returned. "With every morsel, I shall thank the Lord I am not on the road with you, and shall pray for your safe return."

"I wonder if the Lord will be able to hear him with his mouth full," Acanthus said.

"Pshaw," Tatius scoffed. "A sour stomach is not the same as piety."

"You eat too much."

"I enjoy the blessings of life the Lord has given us."

"You both argue too much," Nicholas chided. "There will be plenty of that in a few days. I pray I shall not be worn out from it before I even arrive." With that, he pushed up from his seat and put his arms around the lads' shoulders. "Come, boys. You can help me pack. We'll leave these two to squabble on their own."

The journey took two weeks on foot, and during that time they paid visits to many innkeepers and farmers on the way, granting blessings to those that sheltered them as they travelled north. During the trip, Nicholas couldn't shake a strange feeling that he'd be travelling north again soon, though why that should be escaped him at the time. He prayed to God about it, but no clear answer came from the Lord. It was simply a feeling that tugged at him, as if he was trying to remember something that had not yet happened.

By the time they reached Nicaea, they were, to a man, worn out from the long journey. But they were not alone. Entourages from all over the empire had converged upon the tiny lake city. Bishops with their various attendants arriving from places both far and familiar, they soon fell into talking with one another as they journeyed along and shared campfires till they reached the city itself.

Nicaea stood at the eastern edge of a long lake, bordered by miles of stone walls standing some thirty feet high, with more than a hundred towers overlooking the lands outside the city gates. As they drew near, Nicholas felt a foreboding in his heart, a pressure sufficient to make him stop and take a step back.

"What is it, your grace?" Stephanos asked.

"I—I don't know," he replied. The others looked at him anxiously. "Something about this place troubles me." He glanced up, and saw the towers lit by torchlight against the night sky, while all around them arrows sang even as a troop of soldiers drove a battering ram against the gates. He open his mouth to cry an alarm, and just as quickly, the vision was gone, replaced by blue, day-lit skies and the caravans of peaceful churchmen filing in through the open gates.

"Nicholas?" Acanthus's voice was filled with concern.

After a moment, he said, "The city will be overthrown."

"When?"

"Retaken, and then lost again. And just like this, all over the empire." He looked around. "What we do here today, and henceforth, will have an untold impact upon both the Church and the world. The faith will be defended, but it will come at great cost. I fear we will lose our way."

Stephanos looked worried. "What do you mean?"

He shook his head. "I do not know. A warning in my spirit. That is all."

Beside them, others continued filing in. He studied their eyes, searching for any indication. None of them showed any sign that they, too, had seen the vision. Surely God would've revealed it to more than he!

He waved his hand. "I'm sure it's nothing."

"Didn't sound like nothing." Acanthus said.

He grunted and started forward again. "If the Lord wishes to reveal something, I'm sure He'll find others to share it with besides me."

At that moment, the door opened and Brother Don poked his

head in, "Apologies. We are ready, now."

The Abbot set his empty mug down and pushed to his feet. "Excellent. You ready?"

I glanced at my cold cup of cocoa. "Uh, wait, what happened at Nicaea?"

Nicholas exchanged a glance with Brother Don. "It was a momentous ecumenical council. We wrote the Nicene Creed."

I blinked. "That's it? The most momentous ecumenical council, and all you can say is, 'We wrote a creed?'"

"Yah," Don put in, "and he boxed Arius's ears but good."

"Wait. What?"

Nicholas shook his head. "It's nothing."

"Oh," Don objected. "That's not what the emperor thought!"

I sat back. "Listen, I know you've got something planned, but you can't just leave me hanging like this."

Nicholas smiled thinly, and Brother Don nodded. "I tell them to wait a little longer."

The Abbot took his seat. "For the most part, the synod was boring."

"Doesn't sound boring."

"It was. In fact, it got so boring that at one point I fell asleep. Right there in the middle of the proceedings."

"Do tell."

"It happened at the dinner hour. There were a great many speeches, and some of my fellow bishops had a tendency to go on."

"Long winded preachers, eh?"

He managed a wry grin. "Suppose so. At any rate, I fell asleep, and when I did, I had a dream. In it, I heard a great many voices calling my name. I didn't know why, at least at first. Then I saw that it was *The Hatmehit,* Captain Qennios's ship. The storm battered it something fierce. Sails were shredded. The masts split asunder like toothpicks. Wave after wave crashed over the bow, and it looked as though the ship would be swamped. The sailors cried out, begging me to pray to my God for help."

"What happened?"

"I raised my hands—in the dream, of course—and told the seas to calm. Like Jesus with His disciples on the Sea of Galilee, yah? I don't imagine I am the Savior, nor did I then. It just—it seemed like the thing He would've done. At any rate, God heard my prayer and the seas calmed. The storm abated. The sun came out, and the ship was saved."

"Was it real?"

He shrugged. "It was a dream. The sailors all thanked God, and I blessed them with the sign of the cross. When I woke, the other bishops told me that much had happened whilst I slept. 'Yes,' I told them. 'A great ship has been saved.' They thought I was talking about the ship of the Church. In retrospect, perhaps I was. Perhaps that's all the dream meant. At any rate, we adjourned shortly thereafter. The next day we heard Arius give his testimony."

Arius stood with his hands folded in the center of the room. Around him, more than three hundred bishops stood or leaned back against the wall, waiting.

"My conscience is clear," he said. "No matter what the decision of this council. I know what I believe is truth. It is eminently logical. God is Spirit. He is eternal. But His Son is begotten, as the Scriptures say. The Proverbs declare, 'I was the first of the ways of God.' Christ is the firstborn of God. He is first. But first implies sequence, does it not? And there can be no sequence without beginning. Thus, there was a time when Christ was not."

"Heresy!" the cries rang out. "Brothers, this is blasphemy most foul!"

"Blasphemy?" Arius returned. "Is it blasphemy to speak the truth. Behold, O Israel, the Lord is God. The Lord is one. Except now we say that He is three."

"He is one," Alexander of Alexandria replied. "As Christ Himself said, 'I and the Father are one.' The three are one."

"How can three be one? One in purpose. One in mind and intent, even as His followers are of one heart and mind. But not one and the same. God the Father is not the Son."

"No one has said they are the same," another spoke up. "they are, perhaps, of similar substance, if substance can be used of Divinity."

"If they are of substance," Alexander returned, "then they are of the same substance, even as water and ice and steam are of the same substance, and yet each distinct from the other."

"We are not discussing water," Arius replied, "but the nature of our holy God. And all I am saying is what has been said from the beginning. That God is one. That the Son proceeds from the Father, but is not the Father. Hence, He is a creature and not the Creator."

Once more, the room burst into loud denunciations, with some crying, "Then how can He be worshipped?!"

Arius raised his voice, "He cannot be. That is the point. Honored, to be sure, but worship belongs to God alone. It must embarrass Christ that you adore Him thus."

"And that's what tore it for me," Nicholas said. "I'd had enough. More than I could take from this pompous, arrogant fool. I ran across the floor and boxed his ears."

I gaped. "You didn't!"

"I did. And he deserved it. After I hit him I yelled, 'Unblock your ears and listen to what you're saying! Does not your conscience burden you?'"

"So what happened?"

"Well, I'd done this in the presence of the Emperor. And though he was none too savvy in the particularities of theology, he did at least recognize that arguments should not be settled with violence. My actions brought the proceedings to a standstill. Arius was temporarily dismissed, and I was seized. What I'd done was, technically, illegal. I'd struck a man in the Emperor's presence without leave. Constantine, however, chose to let my fellow bishops determine my fate. They decided I should not be a part of the proceedings any longer. I'd embarrassed them, being hotheaded as I was. They stripped me of my vestments and put me in chains, then led me away to the jail. I was so ashamed. My fate would be decided after the council ended."

I put my elbows on the table and rested my chin on the point of my fingers. This particular part of the Abbot's story was coming slowly, as if he was genuinely reluctant to tell it. He'd been similarly reticent with the revelation of his resurrection—a point of the tale I'd yet to make up my mind about—but at least he'd come out with it. With that part, it seemed his hesitancy had more to do with whether or not I'd believe him, but this—this felt like he was ashamed it had ever happened, and didn't want to discuss it at all.

He met my eyes and smiled thinly. "It didn't go down quite as they'd expected."

The cell door shut with a resounding boom, and Nicholas felt his heart sink. Though not quite as dank nor as cramped as his confinement in Rome had been, the jail at Nicea remained a cell, nonetheless. And he was chained once more, naked from the waist up.

"I have sinned against You, Lord!" he whispered. Then louder, "I have sinned against You!" He sank to his knees, still feeling the anger toward Arius that had had flushed his cheeks, and feeling even more the shame at being called to account for it. The heavy links of his manacles clinked against the stone floor.

"I know this was wrong. I know I ought to have let the court decide. Zeal for Your house consumed me! But vengeance is Mine, saith the Lord." He bowed his head, and continued to pray in whispered mutters, expressing his regret at his outburst through the remainder of the night, trying not to shiver despite the chill.

Darkness swept over his cell, filling it like ink soaking through parchment as the light from the single window in the outer wall dwindled to pale blue, then nothing. He suddenly felt a tingling at the nape of his neck, like he was being watched. His chains abruptly fell to the floor. He raised his eyes, and found the room filled with a dazzling illumination. It didn't seem to have a source. It was as if the entire room was made of light. His breath slipped from his mouth as he lifted his head.

"Why are you here, Nicholas?"

He gasped, and felt the words tear from his throat as if they had a mind of their own. "My Lord! My love for You brought me to this place."

"Take, and read."

He opened his hand, and a copy of the Gospels appeared in it. He clasped his hands around it and clutched it to his chest. Then he saw his arms. Lifting them, he saw that he wore the omophorion. The Lord had clothed him as a bishop again.

He felt warm.

The light was gone, but the moon shone bright and silver, filling the room with a pallid glow more than sufficient to read by. He'd have called it a vision, but the robe he wore and the book in his hand—not to mention the manacles lying uselessly on the floor—told him otherwise.

The emperor and the council of bishops had looked with disapproval upon his outburst, but the Lord honored his zeal.

When the moonlight passed out of the window, he lay the book across his chest and closed his eyes, passing into a dreamless sleep. He woke at first light, as the golden sun filled the room with warmth once more, and then turned back to the same passage he'd meditated on the night before.

He hadn't read far, or so it seemed, when there came a

rattling from the lock in the door. The jailor, he realized. He hadn't heard him approach.

The heavy door swung open, and the man took a step into the room. "Holy God," the man exclaimed.

"So it would seem," Nicholas glanced up from the Gospels. "Take care that you do not blaspheme. This place is holy ground, for the Lord has stood upon it."

The jailor stared, unmoving, his mouth not quite working right.

"Kindly inform his excellency and our gathered bishops of what you have seen," he instructed. "I shall await their judgment."

"I don't imagine they had a heck of a lot to say after that," I told him.

The Abbot shook his head. "No, not really. Constantine ordered me released, and I was fully reinstated as bishop. If the Son sets you free, you shall be free indeed. It raised a bit of a stir, of course, and while I don't believe the council would have agreed with Arius at any rate, it did little to help the heretic's cause. Still, the entire council went on for two months. My little outburst was a passing thing, after all. In the end, Arius was excommunicated for his views, along with his followers, and exiled to Illyricum.

"It is said that toward the end of his days, the emperor showed mercy and allowed Arius to return to his church. He even required Athanasius to accept him, which the bishop would not do. For that, Athanasius himself was sent into exile at the Synod of Tyre."

"Athanasius?"

"Oh! Sorry. Athanasius had been but a deacon during the Council of Nicaea, even though he formulated the primary defense of the faith. It was given to his mentor, Bishop Alexander of Alexandria to deliver the defense. Upon the bishop's death, Athanasius succeeded him."

I made a note. "Thank you. It's a lot of names."

"Ancient history."

"Right."

"At any rate, Arius never made it back. He suffered a grievous hemorrhage of the bowels and died the day before he was to return. Some think he was poisoned."

My eyes widened. "I had no idea church could be so blood thirsty."

He snorted. "It's what happens when faith is married to power. 'Twas a hard lesson for us to learn. I'm grateful that we have. As for Arius, I don't know that he was poisoned, only that some have suggested it. Others, of course, have claimed it was a judgment upon him for his pride."

"Would God do that?"

"Absolutely. He struck down Herod in much the same way. Herod knowingly accepted the worship of the Caesareans and did not give the glory to God, and for this reason he was struck down by intestinal worms and died on the spot. And, of course, Ananias and Sapphira attempted to lie to the Holy Spirit and make a claim that they had given all when, in fact, they'd kept plenty enough for themselves. Both were struck down and died on the spot. The Lord God is not to be trifled with. He is a fearsome judge. A loving and forgiving Savior, to be sure, but we are all living on borrowed time and dependent upon His mercy to continue."

I shivered, feeling suddenly cold, despite the crackling fire in the hearth. All this talk of God and judgment! "What about you? Are you living on borrowed time?"

He smiled. "I've borrowed far more time than any I've ever known. Speaking of time, we'd best get downstairs. I think we've kept them waiting long enough."

# Eighteen

He led me down to a lower part of the monastery, past the display case where his red robe still hung on the wooden dummy, and I wondered if this was the same omophorion put on his shoulders by the figure in the white light he'd said had come to him—or if I was just supposed to believe that. I was still having a hard time taking all this in.

Down another flight of wooden steps, and I caught the scent of cinnamon and pine needles wafting through the air. Nicholas reached a set of double wooden doors and lifted the latch. He winked at me and said, "Welcome to the workshop," before thrusting the doors wide.

As soon as he did so, a cheer rose up from those inside. A warm, bright light flooded the hallway, and inside I saw well over a hundred monks toasting me with frothing mugs of hot chocolate, while displayed on several tables inside the room were boxes and boxes of wrapped presents.

I raised an eyebrow. "What is this?"

"This is our ministry. One of them, anyway."

"Presents?"

"For orphans. We run one of the largest toy distribution

networks in Europe, with hopes to expand in future years to North America and Asia. Someday, I hope to be global."

"Toys. Santa's workshop."

He chuckled. "I told you: I am not Santa."

"Next you're going to tell me you don't have a sleigh."

"Of course not. We use FedEx."

*Naturally.* Someone pressed a cup of cocoa into my hand. I wanted to object that I'd already had one, but I was being toasted yet again and decided to just go ahead and play along. I bumped my lip against a candy cane I hadn't noticed soaking in the cup.

"How big is the operation?"

"Here," Nicholas said, "allow me to introduce you to Martin, our chief of distribution." He waved a man over clothed in a green apron, with wire frame glasses perched across his nose. We shook hands, and Martin showed me around the room. Nicholas followed a few steps behind.

"This is really something," I observed.

"Oh, and it is. A very old tradition, here at the north pole."

"North pole?"

He looked back at Nicholas. "You didn't tell him?"

"Not yet," the Abbot replied. "We're still at Nicaea."

"Oh my. You'll never get done tonight at this rate."

"There's a lot to tell," Nick replied.

"There is indeed."

I shook my head. "You distribute toys. At the north pole, or near enough to it, anyway."

"Depends on what you mean by north," Martin replied.

"Okay."

Nicholas clapped his hand on my shoulder, "You will find that the myth or legend you know of as Santa Claus is actually based on something quite real. Just a little blown out of proportion."

"We don't send toys to everybody," Martin put in.

"Right."

"But you know, give us another hundred years?" He glanced at the Abbot, who rolled his eyes. "Well, as I said," Martin continued, "this is a very old tradition. We've been at it for some time. Well, *he* has, at any rate."

"The monastery has," Nicholas corrected. "As I said, it is part of our ministry."

We'd reached the center of the room, now, and from what I could see, there had to be enough tables here to provide packages to thousands of children. It wasn't nearly as big an operation as the one Billy Graham's son ran, but it was still something.

"Is distributing toys all you do?"

"Of course not!" Martin replied. "Nor is this everything. We have operations like this in over fifty countries."

"Then how come I've never heard of it?"

"You have," Nicholas pointed out.

"I mean, besides the Santa thing."

"That's because we don't draw attention to ourselves,"
Martin said. "Everything is anonymous."

"Really? You don't solicit donations or anything? Give people
a chance to get involved?"

Nicholas folded his hands behind his back. "Sometimes, it is
better not to let the left hand know what the right hand is doing.
Our giving is in secret."

"So why are you telling me about it?"

He smirked. "Promises to keep."

"Of course."

"But as Martin said, our ministry is greater than just this, and
it is far more than distributing toys. We're also involved in
feeding the hungry, assisting with low-income housing, hospice
care, elder care, and, of course, caring for young mothers."

"That's a lot. And all of it behind the scenes?"

"All of it. Our goal is not to draw attention to ourselves, but to
Christ alone."

Martin spread his arms wide. "You are looking at the single
largest charitable organization the world has never known.
Without this man," he moved and put his arm around Nicholas,
"this planet would be a far darker place than it is now."

I thought of my recent time in Afghanistan. "No disrespect,
but it's still plenty dark."

"One man can only do so much," Nick replied. "Even if he
doesn't die."

"Oh, and it isn't nearly as dark as it used to be," Martin objected. "You reporters and your newspapers always write about the bad stuff that happens. You lose perspective on just how good it all is, how much everything has changed for the better in this world."

I shrugged. "You may be right, 'cause I don't see it."

"Like I said. Perspective. Think of the advances we've made in medicine, or in alleviating poverty around the world. Even wars have gotten less messy. The casualty rate for armed conflict is far lower now than at any time in history. And if you take those numbers as a percentage of world population, well, you can begin to see just how very much better it all really is."

I took a sip of the cocoa. "You're a very positive person."

"It's the elf in me. And working for this guy."

"Elf?"

Nicholas said, "Another story. I'll fill you in soon."

Martin opened his mouth, but Nicholas said, "In order. All things make sense when revealed in their proper time."

"Meaning you weren't ready to show me this yet," I surmised.

He sighed and steered me back toward the hallway. "I fear Martin is right, that we'll never get through everything there is to tell. I've lived better than twenty lifetimes now, and you have no idea how fast it has all gone. I blink, and decades are gone. Friends I've come to love are old, and soon must pass. All that's left to me is the work. The ministry serving the most needy in this world, which I shall do faithfully till Christ returns. Come, Brother Oleg may not live out the night, and I've no wish to be separated from him when his time comes."

"Are you sure?" I objected. "He looks so strong."

"It is his spirit that is strong. His body, however, is giving out."

He led us back up to the bedroom where Oleg lay, almost with a sense of urgency. The man had been sleeping peacefully when we left, and had otherwise seemed strong enough to last the night, at least. I wondered why the Abbot seemed in such a hurry?

When we reached the room, Nicholas paused, then slowly opened the door. He stayed there a moment, his body blocking most of the light from the room, then motioned me forward.

"He is asleep again," he whispered. "Do you hear his breathing?"

I listened a moment to the raspy intake and exhalation of air, then frowned. "Congestive heart failure?"

"It won't be long."

"Shouldn't he be in a hospital?"

"The closest hospital is in Hammerfest. And by the time we reached there, it would be too late. Besides, there's nothing they can do for him now."

"But—"

He silenced me with an upraised finger. "It is his dying wish not only that I tell a reporter my life story, but that he remain here among his friends—indeed, his family—until he passes to the other side. I'll not take that from him."

I smiled grimly and nodded my understanding.

Nicholas brought me back into the room and he stoked up the fire a bit, then we retook our places at the table.

"So what happened after Nicaea?" I asked.

"I returned home. By ship, this time. We went first to the Capital, Nicomedia, within the emperor's entourage."

"Wait, I thought Constantine's capital was Constantinople."

"It was, but not until about five years after the council. Byzantium was under construction at the time, and the emperor worked from the interim capital, where Diocletian himself had reigned, until it was completed and renamed Nova Roma. It did not take the name 'Constantinople' until after the emperor's death."

"Oh."

"At any rate, I took ship from there. On the way back, my companions and I travelled with three generals and their troops who'd been sent by the Emperor to address a revolt in Phrygia. They were Christians now, at least in name, and I gave much time to teaching and instruction in the way of righteousness while we sailed. Call it a 'captive audience,' I suppose. At any rate, we put into Andriaki before they were to continue, because the wind had died down. Some of the soldiers came ashore and went as far as Myra with us, hoping to buy bread and other supplies before returning to the ship. And that's when things got interesting."

"Bishop, what is happening?" Stephanos asked. They were nearing the church, and Nicholas was looking forward to a rest after the long journey. But at the youth's words, he glanced up, seeing a crowd of people hurrying past them toward the port.

"Perhaps they're hurrying to see the ship that has returned their bishop," Justin offered.

"And ignore the bishop himself?" Acanthus queried, "I think not."

"I'm afraid Acanthus is right," Nicholas replied. "Something is amiss at port."

As more people fled past them, the sound of shouting grew louder. He turned from his companions and hurried after them. Down the slope, he rushed, seeing a sizable crowd gathered near the ship that had just carried them home. The soldiers were out in front, and had formed a line with their shields and swords drawn. Before them, the townsfolk were shouting and waving their arms.

*Is this a riot?* Nicholas wondered. He hurried into the crowd, motioning for quiet with his hands. "Peace, brothers!" he called. "Peace!"

"Bishop Nicholas," one of the generals called to him. "Your blessing on our mission!"

Nicholas shielded his eyes in the glare off the sea and recognized the speaker's face. "General Ursus. What is the meaning of this?"

At once the townsfolk began raging again. Nicholas climbed onto the dock and held his hands up for calm.

"There is a complaint," Ursus said.

"I see that."

"Evidently, some of the townspeople believe soldiers in our ranks have caused a disturbance in the city."

"Aye!" one of the townsfolk cried out. "They were looting my stall! Made off with three chickens!"

"And I lost a basket of bread!"

"Three of my melons were squashed in their escape!"

Nicholas once more put his hands out for calm. "General Ursus, are these all your men?"

"Aye," Ursus replied. "Those that came ashore anyway." He raised his voice, "And I say to you now, that if any of my men are guilty of this trespass, he shall be dealt with in the most severe manner!" To Nicholas he added, "All have vouched for one another already. We did not do this."

"And what about our losses?" cried the baker. The others chimed in along with him.

"If you please," Nicholas said. He waved his hand, "before you stand the company of soldiers who came ashore. So which of these men is guilty? Whom did you see? Take care that you do not bear false witness."

The baker, melon-seller, and farmer with his chickens grunted and began going from man to man, conferring with each other as they reviewed the soldiers. At last, they faced the bishop. "We don't know," the baker confessed. "Can't say that we got a clear look."

"How many of them were there?" Nicholas pressed.

They shrugged. "Like he said, we didn't get a clear look," the farmer explained.

"I see. And yet here you are, demanding recompense and causing a riot, when you cannot even say for certain it was these men involved. My fellow countrymen, I have spent the last week aboard this vessel with these same soldiers. And they are a rough lot as soldiers are wont to be, but each one of them is a Christian, and each has listened attentively as the Lord has given them instruction through me during our time together. I do not believe you would find them causing trouble in this way. More likely, you will find the troublemakers amongst your own number, men who'd take advantage of the presence of strangers to deflect the suspicious eye from themselves and thus hide their crime from justice."

The merchants looked at one another, and then to Nicholas. "Then what should we do?"

Before he could answer, Tatius came hurrying up, red-faced and out of breath. "Bishop, you must come quick!"

"What is it, Tatius?"

"An execution," he hoarsed. "A grievous miscarriage of justice!"

Nicholas glanced at General Ursus, who nodded once. "I'll come. I'm sure Generals Nepotianus and Eupoleonis will want to come as well."

"At once, then," Nicholas replied, and hurried down to Tatius. "Now, tell me everything."

"It's the Prefect," Tatius said as they hurried. "He's taken a bribe—I'm sure of it. The three men were with me in the church when they are accused of murder. It is a plot to seize their father's olive grove. The deceased is their father's own servant. Without him and his sons, the man won't be able to tend his groves. He'll be forced to sell land that's been in his family for generations, leaving the guilty party to scoop it up for a pittance!"

"And the guilty party?"

"You'll love this. It's Kabeus."

"Are you sure?"

"Yes. The Prefect's cousin. Testimony from the lads told me how he threatened their father when he would not sell. Said he had friends in high places, and that he would force his hand."

Nicholas snorted. "I wouldn't half wonder if Eustathios

didn't put him up to it."

"From your lips to God's ears, my bishop."

As they hurried forward, a throng forming behind them, more townspeople recognized the bishop and ran toward him. "Bishop Nicholas! If only you had been here, three men would not have died needlessly!"

Nicholas's heart plunged. "Are we too late?"

"They bare their necks to the sword as we speak!"

"Where?"

"The executioner has them just outside the acropolis. But you'll never make it in time!"

Nicholas dropped his crozier and let his mitre fall from his head as he broke into a run. The crowd hurried behind him. A block ahead, he saw the crowd gathered below the acropolis. His feet pounded the paving stones as he fled toward them. When he reached the edge of the crowd, the executioner lifted his blade.

"Wait!" he cried. "Let me through!" Shoving his way forward, he caught the flash of sunlight on metal as the executioner swung his blade. Nicholas gave a cry and hurtled himself between the startled swordsman and his victim. The downward swing faltered. Nicholas grabbed the blade, snatching it from the man's hand and flinging it to the ground. It spun across the pavement and landed at Kabeus' feet. Kabeus stepped back, as if the blade were a snake crawling over his shoe.

Nicholas glanced down, where three young men still waited

on their knees, their hands bound and their heads covered by hoods. He tore the hood off the first man. "Rise and be free!"

The man stared at his bishop, relief washing over his face.

"You have no authority!" Kabeus sputtered.

Nicholas spun on him. "Here is my authority!" He thrust his bloodied palm at the cousin of the Prefect. Crimson flowed down his arm, staining his robe. "I would rather my own blood be shed than allow this injustice to go further."

Kabeus spat. "My cousin shall hear about this!"

"Indeed he shall! All of it!"

As Kabeus spun away, forcing his way through the crowd. Nicholas bent down and undid the bindings on the young man. Ursus and Nepotianus helped free his brothers.

"You have saved our lives!" the first man cried.

"And at cost," Nepotianus said. "That wound is deep."

"Here."

Nicholas glanced down at the hand offering him a clean, linen cloth, and then at the man who offered it. It was the executioner. Nicholas nodded, and the man bound his hand.

"I-I was only doing as commanded," the executioner mumbled. "I meant it to be quick."

Nicholas touched the man's hands with his unwounded palm. "The fault lies not with you, but with those who gave you command."

"Thank you."

"Go in peace, brother."

The executioner bowed out, and Nicholas turned to the three men and the generals who were still with him. "I should like to pay a visit to the Prefect, if I may impose upon your company a little longer."

Eupoleonis grinned. "You've more courage than half my men together. I wouldn't miss this for the world."

Together, the company of men followed the bishop back into the city, with a throng in tow, more than half the city, Nicholas estimated.

When they reached the Praetorium, Prefect Eustathios had just come out, responding to his cousin Kabeus's urgent petition.

"Is this how you conduct the affairs of our city in my absence?" Nicholas demanded. "Accepting bribes from your cousin and nearly causing the deaths of three innocent men?"

"Y-your grace? W-whatever do you mean?" Eustathios's eyes kept flitting to the three generals and the soldiers who'd accompanied them.

"You know well what I mean, Prefect. Your cousin paid you well, did he not? Theodosius's olive groves on the north of town have been in his family for generations. These here are his sons, recently condemned by your command."

"It is true, I gave the command," Eustathios replied. "It is because they are guilty."

"And what evidence do you have of their guilt?"

"I-I examined them. They confessed. Turned on one another they did."

"It is a lie!" one of the sons put in. Nicholas bade him hold his peace with his bandaged hand.

"And during your exam, did it not come up that these three men were someplace else during the night in question? That they were seen there by more than one witness?"

"If that is the case it is news to me."

"Another lie!" the brother cried. "We told him so. We all told him!"

"You expect us to believe under pain of death that these three innocent men would not give testimony to exonerate them?"

Eustathios sputtered again, and turned to his cousin, but Kabeus had already turned and fled, disappearing into the crowd.

"Pray tell me you will not still stand here and lie before these envoys of the emperor?"

Abruptly, the Prefect fell to his knees. "Mercy!" he cried. "Pardon, bishop! Pardon, I pray thee! What you've said is true. All of it! My cousin Kabeus begged me for my aid. He pressured me so, night and day. He was relentless! His lust for Theodosius's olive groves is widely known. He sought a pretext to claim them."

Nicholas studied the man in his debasement. Most of the townsfolk had heard it as well. Eustathios would never again command the respect of the city. It was a harsh lesson in God's justice for the townsfolk. But for all that, Myra needed also a lesson in God's mercy.

He made the sign of the cross over the Prefect and said, "Prefect Eustathios, inasmuch as you have confessed your crime and shown true sorrow for your sin, in Christ's name I absolve you of your guilt and restore you to your position." He bent down and tugged the Prefect's shoulder, drawing him to his feet. "Go now, and sin no more."

Eustathios stared at the Bishop, as if unsure whether or not the man was joking. "How can you do this? Forgive so easily?" he muttered.

"Come by the church on the morrow, and I shall explain."

The Prefect nodded once, then bowed briefly before turning and shuffling back inside the Praetorium. Nicholas heard angry mutters from the crowd. He gestured toward the Praetorium and spoke aloud, "And what did you see here today? A broken man, brought down by the lowly temptations of his own flesh? Who among you could say you would not likewise stumble when faced with the same? Be not secure in your own self-righteousness, but rather acknowledge that you share alike the same fallen nature, and but for God's grace, the same fall. We are all alike guilty before God, justified only by the blood of His Son."

With that, he dismissed the crowd. Soon, all that remained with him were the three generals, their forces, and his own companions.

"Very impressive, Bishop Nicholas," Ursus said. "In a single day you have rescued our soldiers and spared the lives of three innocents."

Nepotianus said, "And restored a fallen man to his post. I doubt very highly this Prefect will dare pervert justice in this city again."

"Your grace," Eupoleonis put in, "all has been done well, here. But our ship must soon sail. Perhaps we could retire for some refreshment before we take our leave of you?"

Nicholas dipped his head, "I would be honored to dine in the company of such fine men."

"Nay, Bishop," Ursus returned. "The honor is ours."

"Then please," Nicholas waved his hand, "join me at our church. We can have refreshments laid out there for you and your men."

As they ate in the early afternoon sun, Nepotianus spoke up first. "I have a confession to make, Bishop."

Nicholas raised an eyebrow. "We make speak privately, if you prefer."

"No, no," he waved his hand. "Nothing like that. More of an observation, really."

The Bishop nodded. "Please. Continue."

"I have been a soldier all my life. Starting long before the empire embraced Christianity. At first, I thought Christianity made you weak. All that business about confessing sin and turning the other cheek and so forth. Then I witnessed firsthand the courage of confessors such as yourself, and I learned that confessing does not make you weak. Far from it. But still, I wondered if a man could truly be a soldier—a warrior, if you will—and follow Christ. After all, what does a Christian basilica have in common with a battlefield? Even after his eminence Constantine bade us paint crosses on our shields at the battle of the Tiber, I still questioned it. Were we simply trading one god for another? It seemed political to me, a way to rally the great masses of believers who'd survived Diocletian's reign and posed a very real threat to the stability of the empire, were they willing to take up arms against us. In fact, I was convinced this was so, until today. Today you showed me a man of great faith willing to put his own life at risk, to put yourself beneath the swing of an executioner's blade without thought or hesitation of what harm may have befallen you—all to save the life of an innocent man whom you barely knew, let alone bore any allegiance to. And then from there to confront the Prefect! To accuse him of such venality without proof and nothing more than the testimony of the accused to back you up—I am convinced now that true Christianity requires tremendous strength and courage—and is more apt to make a man a worthy soldier than any other discipline we might require. And for that, sir, I salute you."

With that, he rose and extended his hand toward Nicholas. Abruptly, the other two generals stood and did the same.

Nicholas waved them down. "Please, gentlemen. Give glory to God, not to me. I have no fear for my life for it is in His hands to do with as He sees fit."

"If this is what the Lord does with His servants, then I would be honored to be counted among them," Nepotianus replied.

"And so you shall. Seek Christ, and you'll never falter."

 Nineteen

"And," the Abbot said, "that was the last time I ever saw them."

"That's it?" I replied. "What happened to them?"

He glanced furtively at Oleg. "Well, if rumors are to be believed, it was the last time I saw them, but not the last time they saw me."

"Oka-ay."

"The story goes that they completed their mission and returned as heroes to Constantinople, growing both in their faith and in their acclaim. This provoked jealousy from the Master of the Forces, who then bribed the Prefect of the city, a man named Ablabius, with gold to betray the three generals. Ablabius went straightaway to the emperor and convinced him that the generals he had just honored with a great feast were, in fact, guilty of treason. What reasoning or arguments he made, I do not know, but supposedly Constantine threw them into prison without so much as a trial.

"Still, this did not satisfy the Master of the Forces. With the generals in prison, it might still come out that they were innocent—the victims of a horrendous slander. Thus, Ablabius once more convinced Constantine concerning the men, telling the emperor they still plotted against him even from prison. Constantine ordered them beheaded that very night.

"The jailor warned the generals of their fate, and together they prayed, begging God for mercy and aid. Nepotianus, it is said, recalled what he had seen in Myra, how I had delivered the innocent men from the Prefect's hand. And he cried, 'Lord God have mercy upon us. Save us now, as you saved the three men who were unjustly condemned to death in Lycia. Saint Nicholas, servant of Christ, though you are far from us, pray to your God that we may be saved.'

"Now, for what happened next, I personally have no memory. Supposedly, however, I came to the Emperor Constantine in a dream and ordered him to free the prisoners, or else I would lead the world in revolt against him. He asked who I was and I told him, and then I went and did the same thing to the Prefect. Or maybe they had the same dream at once. At any rate, Constantine conferred with the Prefect who verified the dream, and the generals were released. They turned their lives into giving charity to the poor."

"It's a nice story," I replied.

He nodded.

"Except it never happened."

"That I did not say. I simply pointed out that I have no memory of it. I suppose it's possible that I forgot my dream.

Who's to say what they really remember from a dream anyway."

"So why tell me?"

"If you look into my life—the background stories that have been written about me—you will find a great many fascinating and quite fanciful tales, none of which would get you closer to the truth than you are right now."

"Like?"

"Well, for instance, there is the story of the three beheaded children whom I supposedly raised to life again. Or a different set of children who were butchered and eaten, whom I also raised to life. And then there's the time I supposedly convinced the emperor to lower our taxes. He wrote an edict and I immediately put it in a bottle and tossed it into the sea. He then changed his mind and sent for it, but I told him it was already in force, and upon investigating he learned that, indeed, it was in force, and that the currents of the ocean had magically carried the bottle with the edict all the way to Andriaki, where they drew it out and put it into effect without delay. Would you be very offended if I said it was pure poppycock?"

"Pity, actually. I was sorta hoping you could come to New York and do the same thing."

"Death and taxes: the two undeniable realities of life."

"Except you've managed to avoid them both."

He ran his hand over his mouth. "Yes, I rather suppose I have."

"So," I said after a moment, "are you going to tell me the rest? How you managed to wind up here? In Norway, of all places? It's quite a distance from the southern coast of Turkey."

"So it is. The peace of Constantine changed everything. The Empire, of course, would not survive much longer. Within a hundred years there were the attacks of the Huns, the rending of the empire itself in twain, the rise of the Caliphate, and eventually, the fall of Rome itself. Byzantium eventually succumbed to the Seljuk Turks. Christianity, meanwhile, pushed further north into Europe."

"Wait. Back up a bit. Where are you, in all of this?"

"Alone, mostly."

"How did it come to that?"

"My disciples—my friends—died. Nothing sinister. Simply old age catching up to them as it does with, well, nearly everyone. And I realized that I would either have to declare myself to the world, or go into hiding. I am not the only one rumored to still be around, of course."

"What?!"

He hushed me with a sudden glance at Oleg. "There are others *rumored* to be around."

"Who?"

"Some older than I. For instance, there is Loginus, the centurion whose spear pierced Christ's side. There is Cartaphilus, the so-called Wandering Jew who took the name

Joseph when he turned to Christ. He is said to still be around somewhere."

"But you don't believe that."

He almost laughed. "Who am I to say? These legends were around in one form or another in my day, and I knew the reason they were legends was that nobody could just go up and talk to them—at least knowingly. They were wanderers. Sojourners on the earth doing good and spreading the message of Christ with their good works and acts of charity. They were not bound in one place nor did they have a retinue of disciples all clandestinely trying to learn their secret. In short, they went into hiding. That, I determined, was what I needed to do as well. It wasn't easy."

"You want to what?" Justin asked. Nicholas bent forward and stroked the old man's hand.

"I want to die, Justin."

The man flinched, his hands shaking. "The Lord has blessed you with an immortal life. Here I stand on the edge of eternity, looking long and hard into the darkened abyss into which I must shortly plunge, and I would give anything not to be facing it. My hope and trust are in Christ and His resurrection, but I tell you the truth, with Him in the Garden would I also pray, 'Father, if it is possible, let this cup pass from me!'"

"I understand."

"No! How could you?" Justin remonstrated. "You still walk and move like a younger man. Your joints do not creak with the years. Your hands do not shake, nor do you find it impossible to stay warm. Do not speak to me of what you understand!"

Nicholas frowned. "Is this any way to speak to your bishop?" Then he winked.

Justin tried to stifle a laugh and wound up coughing instead. Nicholas bent forward and dabbed at his lips with a cloth till the dying man pushed his hand away.

"You cannot give your life up."

Nicholas put his hands down. "This is no life, Justin. Already I have the burden of watching every single one of my friends die. Soon there will be no one left who really knows me at all."

"That is by your doing."

"Do you jest? The danger of letting others in on my secret is too great! Already there are whispers and mutters amongst the people. Some wonder if I'm using some kind of magic, if you can believe it. Others call it a miracle, but do you know what they say about it? They call it the miracle of Nicholas, not the miracle of God! How can I live with myself if I become a distraction from my Lord? Far be it from me!"

Justin closed his eyes, waiting patiently. "Have you asked God about this?"

Nicholas shook his head. "He doesn't answer."

"Perhaps He already has, and you simply want it to be something else."

He shrugged. "I don't know. I don't know how to hear anymore."

"You once told me—after your vision—that your whole being was at one with the world, that you could sense every blade of grass, feel the shift of water in the earth, almost hear the thoughts of men. What happened to that?"

The Bishop looked heavenward. "I don't know. I've lost the sense of it. Perhaps it is too much time down here already. Too much time in the city. I've gotten so used to everything that it all fades into the background, like a shore man who can no longer hear the waves."

"Then perhaps, rather than dying, you should simply take a sabbatical. Go join the hermits in the desert. Learn to hear God again."

Nicholas shook his head. "There would still be rumors. People would come looking for me."

"Then disappear. Entirely."

"How?"

Justin sighed. "You said it yourself. Die. At least, make them believe you have died."

"You want me to lie? Pretend I am a corpse? And how should I pull that off? What shall I do when they send the physician to listen and see if my heart still beats within my chest?"

"All you need is a body, my friend. Dressed in a bishop's robe with a shroud in place. Out of reverence, the physician will not lift the veil to behold the face of the deceased. He will only listen to the chest."

"And where will I get such a body?"

Justin studied him with a calm expression.

Nicholas shook his head. "No."

"I've always wanted to be a bishop."

"Justin, you can't. You deserve, of all things at least this, to be buried in your own grave."

"Why? Who will know me? In less than a generation I shall be forgotten, with none to celebrate my life nor mourn my passing."

"But—"

"At least this way, my death itself can serve a purpose. I can offer you this last service, and so honor the gift you have given me."

"Justin—"

"Please!" He fell into coughing again. After a moment, he spoke hoarsely. "Give me this final jest. Let me set you free. Consider it my last request."

"I—"

"Promise me!" He fell into a haggard, wheezing cough, and then an exhalation escaped his lips. His eyes went vacant, his hands limp.

Nicholas stared as Justin's face blurred through the tears in his eyes. The ache made his chest feel like it would explode. "I promise." He nodded, patting his dead friend's hand. "I promise."

"That's how it began, didn't it?" I asked.

Nicholas brushed away fresh tears. "It is. The first promise. First of many."

"I can see that it had a profound effect on you."

"It did. In so many ways. I've had much time to reflect on that subtle deception, and I've often wondered how history might have judged me, or might've changed, had we not done it." He sighed and leaned back against the wall, crossing his arms over his chest. "Justin was buried in my place, and there was a great mourning at 'my' passing. I shaved my head and beard and took the raiment of a lowly monk. Actually attended my own funeral. December sixth, the year of our Lord 343. It was discomforting, to say the least. And a tad embarrassing. Humbling, actually. His remains were placed in my tomb in Myra." He half-chuckled. "After Byzantium fell to the Turks, mariners from Italy showed up at the tomb and spirited away 'my' relics to Bari, ostensibly to protect them from the infidels. There was also the whole matter of the myrrh."

"Myrrh?"

"It is said to be a sweet, fragrant oil produced from my bones."

"How is this possible?"

He shook his head. "I know not. Some strange quirk of anatomy? Or perhaps a miracle of God, honoring Justin's sweet sacrifice on my behalf. Because, you see, it worked. I was free."

"Okay. Free to do what?"

"Oh, that was the question, wasn't it? I'd spent so much time as a bishop, now that I was dead—what was I to do with myself? I travelled for a while. Did good as I was able. For a time, I took work on a sailing ship, but not for long."

"Couldn't hack it?"

"Quite the contrary. I had a knack for it. But it was on the first night's voyage that I fell asleep, and that's when I had the dream."

"*The* dream?"

"Yes. *The* dream. I saw the Lord Christ standing by the helm of the ship, and He asked me, 'What are you doing here, Nicholas?' Immediately, I fell to my knees and confessed what Justin and I had done. I begged His forgiveness for deceiving His flock. But He commanded me to stand on my feet and declared that I would be a bishop no longer. 'The time for that service is at an end,' He announced, 'and I now have another task for you. Take My gospel to the farthest north, where the descendants of Japheth are. Amongst those who know you not you shall find refuge and work worthy of your calling.'"

"Is that how you wound up here? As far north as you could go?"

"Eventually, but it took a long time to get here. When I woke,

I knew that I had received fresh orders from my commanding officer. I departed the ship at our next mainland port, which took me to Constantinople. From there, I journeyed northward through Thrace and Scythia, and then into the territory of the barbarians."

"Barbarians."

"Yes. The first people I encountered were the Alans. Nomadic tribes. But shortly after reaching them, the Alans were displaced by the arrival of the Huns."

"Huns? As in Attila the Hun?"

"Just before his time. Like the Alans, the Huns were nomadic, tribal. Largely uncivilized. I was unable to win many converts among them. But I did make a few. Those that chose to follow Christ were forced to follow me as well, for the rest of the tribes cast us out. Had they stayed, they would have been killed. I saw no benefit to leaving them to die a martyr's death so soon into their walk with Christ. There was so much to teach them, and I needed time to prepare them in the way.

"Like Stephanos and Justin, they took Christian names for themselves, to signify their new nature, and together we began a small colony of faith, even as we continued farther north. By the time Attila took over from his dead brother—whom many say he murdered—we were too far removed from the action for it to have any impact on us. But if you thought Attila the Hun was barbaric, you have no concept of what lay further north."

## Twenty

"Brother Nicholas, have you ever shot a bow?"

Nicholas glanced up from the fire, where he warmed his hands. Christopher sat across from him on a fallen log. Dressed in furs, his face glinted in the firelight, his dark eyes searching.

"I've never had reason," he replied.

Christopher cleared his throat. "Now you do."

"And that is?"

"Food. In this country, if you want to eat, you must kill." He gestured at the snow falling around them, blanketing the ground.

This, Nicholas knew, more than anything had been the biggest surprise of his journey to the north. He'd never seen snow before. Initially, it filled him with wonder. Now, it just made him damp, cold, and irritable. He pasted a smile on and tried to hide his feelings. "I've never hunted a day in my life."

"Then it is past time you learn."

When Nicholas did not rise, Christopher shifted on the log. "Does not the Scriptures say, if a man shall not work, neither shall he eat? This is now your work. Do this, and you will eat."

"My work," he stirred the fire, hoping to eke more heat from the coals, "is to do the will of Him Who sent me."

"And does God feed you as well?"

"He does."

"And does He feed you with the meat we provide?"

At this, Nicholas laughed. Christopher was nothing if not persistent. It was how he'd learned Greek so quickly while his fellow comrades still struggled with the alphabet. He ran a hand over his face. His beard, once shaved off to disguise his appearance in Myra, had regrown and was now a full, flowing mane of white framing his face. "He does," he agreed, "but if you think it wise to try to teach this old man how to hunt, then I will do my best to learn. I cannot, however, say that I will be successful."

"I only ask that try," Christopher rejoined. "Success will come if you attend faithfully to what I teach you."

"Why does that sound familiar?"

"It is the same thing you said to me, when you taught me to read the Scriptures."

"Very well. What do I need to know?"

Christopher clapped his hand on Nicholas's shoulder and helped him to his feet. Despite whatever gift the Lord had given him which delayed or permanently enjoined mortality from him, this cold still made his joints ache. "We will start with a bow. You must learn to shoot."

"I don't have a bow."

"In time, you will make one." Christopher led him from the

fire. "For now, we will borrow from Groar."

Nicholas winced. Groar had little use for him, he knew. If it weren't for his loyalty to Christopher, his brother, he wouldn't even be with them. Groar stood a head taller than Nicholas did, and had shoulders almost twice as broad. With the wolf-skin furs he wore, he resembled a bear, with a temperament to match.

On the far side of their encampment, the round tent of their *tirmä* stood out amidst the trees. Drifts of snow pressed against the sides, and the smoke that curled from the hole in the roof was blown horizontal and carried away by the wind, as if being dragged out of the home.

Christopher strode toward it and lifted the flap, holding it for Nicholas to climb beneath before following after him.

Inside, a wash of warm air smelling strongly of pine needles shoved back the cold as if rejecting an unwelcome guest. Groar sat cross-legged on the other side of the fire, still adorned in the same furs that made him look so much like a bear. He held a long bladed weapon in front of himself, diligently scraping a stone over the edge with intense deliberateness. A tiny spark flew off the end of the blade when he reached it. He flipped the blade over and did the same on the other side.

"What do you want, holy man?" he growled.

"Brother," said Christopher, "we wish to borrow your bow."

Groar levelled them with his eyes. "Was I speaking to you? I was addressing him."

Nicholas cleared his throat. "Christopher wishes to—"

"Who?"

"Mo-an wishes to teach me how to hunt."

Groar grunted.

"And I would like to borrow your bow, that I may learn."

After a moment, he snorted and picked his nose. "You with a bow. This should be rich."

"My thoughts exactly."

"And yet," he uncrossed his legs, leaning his elbow on one massive thigh, "you eat our food. Warm yourself by our fire, and believe your—contribution—shall include nothing more than old wives' tales, myths of your god, and telling us that lines drawn on skins speak words."

Nicholas folded his hands in front. "Do you doubt Mo-an can teach?"

"Oh, he knows the way. Whether you can learn it remains to be seen."

"If he can teach how to hunt, then I will learn it. And you will learn this: that lines drawn on skins do speak words, that God is no myth, and the things I tell you of His Son and His resurrection are not tales. They are truth."

Groar's eyes were steel. Abruptly, he shook his head, picked up his sharpening stone, and returned to his blade. "Go," he said. "See what you can learn, and do not trouble me with what I learn. The bow is over there."

Nicholas glanced to the left, where a recurved bow and a quiver of arrows hung from a supporting peg in the lattice-work inside the *tirmä.* He retrieved them both and returned to the front flap. "My thanks to you."

Groar said nothing as Christopher held open the tent flap, and Nicholas ducked beneath it.

Once on the outside, he immediately welcomed the cold. Somehow, it felt warmer than inside Groar's tent. Christopher came behind him and led him away into the woods. "Pay him no mind," Christopher said. "He's always like that."

"He doesn't accept your Christian name."

"Why would he? He doesn't accept Christianity. All he knows is we have been driven away from our tribe. Exiled here, because of the faith you taught me. He keeps hoping I will change my mind about it all, so we might return."

"I know he is your brother, and you hold out hope for his salvation, but have you considered sending him back?"

Christopher stifled a laugh. "No."

"Yes you have."

"It is not our way. Blood before everything. It's why he resents you—even fears you."

"Fear?"

"Yes. You have offered me new blood. Loyalty to Christ, which is greater than my loyalty to kin. He does not understand this."

Nicholas shifted the bow on his shoulder. "I never meant for us to leave the tribe."

"It was necessary. They would have killed you otherwise."

He grinned. "They would have tried. I cannot be killed, as I've told you. Nor will I die, as they would have learned. Death has no dominion over me."

"So you've said."

"So I still say. And we could return."

Christopher grunted. "If we go back, yours will not be the only life they'll take. They'll put my head on a spike, and Groar's as well. Along with everyone else's in this camp. And if they can do it, your own, too."

Nicholas nodded. "I know."

"So does Groar. He just doesn't like it."

"Think not that I am come to send peace into the earth, but the sword. For I am come to set a man at variance against his father, and the daughter against her mother, and the daughter-in-law against her mother-in-law. And a man's enemies shall be they of his own household."

Christopher frowned. "Where is that from?"

"Matthew's Gospel."

They fell to silence, and the only sound now came from their footsteps crunching in the snow, and the brush of the flakes as they cascaded through the trees, whipped into a frenzy by the gusting wind. Their breath came out their mouths in a misty vapor that drafted upward to disappear in the gray cast of the storm clouds above. Presently, Christopher drew them to a halt and pointed ahead to a large fir tree with a knob protruding from the trunk about four feet up.

"There," he breathed. "See that?"

Nicholas shrugged. "What of it?"

The Hun clapped his back. "That shall be our target. Watch." Deftly, he drew an arrow from his quiver and nocked it on the string. Drawing back, he let it fly with no hesitation. It struck the bole center on, a new limb for the tree. "Shoot with your eye. Release with your breath."

Nicholas raised an eyebrow.

Christopher grinned. "Trust me."

Awkwardly, Nicholas fitted an arrow to the string. Just as he was about to draw back, Christopher stopped him and corrected his grip and stance. Now repositioned, he tried again. The arrow flew past the tree, disappearing into the snowy underbrush.

"Should we look for it?"

"I'll show you how to make new ones. You'll need to learn anyway. Try again."

Nicholas tried again. It took him seven tries and nearly all the arrows in Groar's quiver before one finally struck the tree. It was a third of the way down from their target and slightly to the left, but still a hit.

"Very good. Again. Prove it's not accident."

"You are relentless."

"Must be relentless in the north. Only way to survive."

Nicholas grunted and drew another arrow. He focused on his breathing, clearing his mind of all else, and then drew and released the arrow. This time, it struck just below the knot on the tree.

"Again."

He reached back and grabbed the last arrow, then let it fly. It struck near to the center of the knot.

"Good." Christopher nodded curtly. "Now we go find arrows."

They spent the next hour finding as many of the arrows Nicholas had lost as they could. In the end, only three remained lost. By this time, Nicholas's fingers were stiff and unyielding from the cold.

"We should return."

"I agree. I could use some warming up."

"No," he shook his head. For the first time, Nicholas noticed he wore a look of fear. "Keep low, and follow me."

Wordlessly, Nicholas followed. The Hun moved cautiously toward their camp, an arrow nocked to his bow at all times. The barren underbrush provided little cover, and if anyone had been looking, Nicholas felt sure their tracks would have given them away. Except, he realized now, that the falling snow had already filled in their footprints and obscured their path. Were it not for the surety with which Christopher moved in these woods,

Nicholas doubted he'd have been able to find his own way home.

When they reached the outskirts of the glen in which they'd made camp, Christopher held up a hand, signaling halt. Together, they crouched low beside a copse of thorny shrubs, peering through the interwoven brambles to the four tents which they called home. At first, Nicholas could not discern anything amiss, though he saw no one. Then Christopher pointed. A dozen horses stood just outside the glen, with blankets draped over their flanks.

Now he understood. When the Huns had sent them away, they only let them keep two horses—enough to carry provisions for the small group. Nothing more.

So what were these horses doing here now?

Presently, an armored man stepped out of Groar's *tirmä* and moved off to the bushes to relieve himself. He wasn't more than ten feet from them. Christopher slowly lifted his bow. Nicholas put a hand against his and shook his head. Christopher frowned and jerked his head at the man, clearly frustrated.

"Stay hidden," Nicholas whispered. "I will go see what they want."

Glowering from his position, Christopher watched as Nicholas rose to his height and stepped into view.

The newcomer just happened to look up as he was finishing. His eyes widened.

"Peace," Nicholas said.

Hurriedly, the man struggled to bring his bow around, and finally fitted an arrow to the string just as Nicholas stepped in front of it. The arrowhead quivered a scant six inches from Nicholas's throat.

"You are my prisoner!" the newcomer barked.

Nicholas gently brushed the arrow to one side. "You are my guest. Welcome."

Again, the man tried to point the arrow at Nicholas's throat. Nicholas plucked it from the string and slipped it into his own quiver. "Arrows are for hunting food. For meat. Not for men. Come," He drew the man's arm down, "take me to your friends."

At a loss, the man turned with Nicholas and followed him into the camp.

"Brothers, welcome," Nicholas called as they reached the center of the encampment. "What little we have is yours. We share our bread and hospitality with any as has need."

At this, Groar's *tirmä* emptied, with two dozen armed men piling out, dragging Groar with them in chains. The man looked angry and belligerent, in utter contrast to the expressions the others wore. Their leader, an older man with a scar running down his face where his left eye should have been, bore a grim expression. The others looked on, curious.

"This is your holy man?" the leader asked Groar.

"I am," Nicholas answered.

"He is not," Groar huffed.

"Groar does not follow my God," Nicholas replied. "Not yet, anyway."

"You bear the look of Huns. Except you. Yours is a southern face."

"I am from Lycia in Anatolia. South of the Black Sea."

"I am familiar with the geography. These lands belong to us. Not Huns. And not you. But seeing as your kind did not attack our village, you will be spared. Kill the rest."

There was a sudden outcry as swords were drawn and Groar struggled to free himself. The leader turned away when Nicholas cried out, "Wait! Do not dare to lay a hand on these men! They are under the protection of the Holy Church!"

The leader turned, eyeing Nicholas warily. "What protection is that?"

"My protection. If you are going to kill these men, you will have to kill me first."

He snorted. "You are a holy man. A Christian. Are you even trained in combat?"

"I will not lay a hand nor blade upon you. But know this: no weapon formed against me shall prosper. My God shall defend me."

The man regarded Nicholas coolly for a moment, then sniffed. "Fine. Have it your way."

Quickly he drew his blade and swung it at Nicholas's head. Nicholas didn't even duck. The blade stopped a hair's breadth from his neck, and would not move. The man grunted, his face contorting as he struggled. Finally, he withdrew it. Then he tried an overhand strike, whipping the blade downward toward him. It carved a whistling arc in the air, and missed by inches. It struck the earth, burying deep into the ground where it stuck fast. He struggled with the hilt a moment, but the sword would not budge. Nicholas took a step forward, and the man fell back. Nicholas raised his hand and made the sign of the cross over him.

A sudden whistle from the side, and an arrow struck him on the side. Frowning, Nicholas reached down and plucked it from his rib. He held it aloft, showing the men the clean tip.

"No blood," one of the men murmured.

One at a time, and then in a wave, the men lowered their weapons and dropped to their knees, pressing their faces into the dust.

"No!" Nicholas cried. "Get up. All of you!" He went from man to man, gripping their arms and hauling them—unwillingly—to their feet.

"You are a god!" the leader exclaimed.

"Don't be ridiculous. I am a man just like you."

"A man would be dead."

"And I was."

This comment drew them to a silent standstill. He noticed that Christopher had come out from hiding, staring at the others. He frowned. "Did you also think it just an old wives' tale?

I died. Sixty years ago. The Roman emperors Diocletian and Galerius cast me into prison during the last Great Persecution of the Church. During that time, I died. I ascended into heaven, where I saw Christ. My wife and son were there as well. He offered me a choice: to stay, or to return here and continue the ministry to which He'd entrusted me long ago. I chose to come back," he pointed a finger at all of them, "to give warning to you and to all men. Eternal fire and damnation await all who do not repent and believe the Gospel. You are under judgment for your violence, your thefts, falsehoods and faithlessness. The time of this ignorance God once winked at; but now He commands all men everywhere to repent, because He has appointed a day in which He will judge the world in righteousness by that man whom He has ordained; whereof he has given assurance to all men, in that He has raised Him from the dead."

Groar whispered, "You are that man."

"I am not, brother. This same man that raised me is Christ the Lord. I was raised up by Him—the same that He shall one day to for all who call upon His name. But He needed no one to raise Him. By His own Divine power, He raised Himself, for He is God. The Son and the Father and the Spirit are one."

He bent down and withdrew the sword from the ground, holding it, hilt first, outstretched toward the man who'd tried to slay him. "So I say to you, believe on the Lord Jesus, and you shall be saved. And take this sword to be used only for His glory henceforth. One day you shall beat it into a plowshare, and never again learn to make war upon your brothers."

Reluctantly, the man took the sword. "What must I do to repent and believe in this one of whom you speak?"

Nicholas gestured toward the *tirmä*. "Come inside with your men, and I will explain it to you all."

# Twenty-One

"So you wound up with another church," I surmised. "Only this time, they knew your secret."

He nodded. "After a fashion, I suppose that's true. The men were a displaced tribe of Alans who intended to wreak a little revenge on the Huns they found."

"Meaning you, Christopher and Groar." I took time sounding out this last name as I wrote it on my pad. It was such an unusual name.

"And the others. After I shared the Gospel with them, they led us back to a river near their encampment. The whole tribe was baptized that day. More than two hundred souls were saved. And as an added bonus, I never had to hunt."

I cocked my head. "How's that a bonus? Some people like to hunt."

"There's a difference between hunting for sport, and hunting for survival. I do not object to meat, as some do..." he paused a moment. "Remember how I said I could hear and sense everything?"

"Yeah, but you lost that."

"And I left Myra to regain it. To some measure, I did. A

particular kind of sensitivity. Not as intense as my first experience in prison, mind you, but far more than the ordinary senses of man. I am particularly attuned to suffering, of both man and beast. I share the experience with those who hurt."

I nodded. "That's why you don't want to hunt."

"When the animal dies, I feel it. They drift into darkness and are gone. And there is confusion and fear. The suffering is not as intense as when a soul is lost in judgment—"

"Like when the guard Gordianus died."

"Precisely. But it remains unpleasant, nonetheless."

"Makes sense."

"At any rate, I lived and served among the Alans for many generations. As a tribe, we travelled far and wide, staying fairly near to the Black Sea, however. Occasionally, I would hear of events going back home. Or in Rome. I became known simply as 'The Old Man' to many of them. Others called me 'The Wanderer.' At the time, I thought it was because I often took long walks in the woods, seeking the counsel of the Lord. But then I discovered—to my horror—that a kind of cult was forming about me. I'd been conflated with another old wanderer known to the Germanic tribes. Seems the myth that I was a god never quite disappeared from their minds, no matter how often I tried to uproot it."

"Wait—they thought you were like, Odin or something?"

"Something."

I stifled a laugh, and he glared at me. "It isn't amusing."

"It is a little."

"No. It is not. Paganism is a pernicious weed. It must be pulled up from the roots, or it will flower again and again, choking out the fruitful garden God plants. That they conflated me with Odin or Wotan as he is called is no less a danger than your culture's confusing me with Santa Claus. And while you may not sacrifice children, virgins or livestock, you still sacrifice your futures and your souls upon the altar of consumption."

I protested, "That's a little heavy, isn't it?"

"Not at all. Christmas is meant to be a season of giving and receiving the gift of life from God. You have turned it into a season of shopping, of frantically rushing around in a mad dash to acquire things, to entertain yourselves needlessly, and to spend more than you earn, thus incurring heavy debts on the one hand as well as teaching yourselves and your children that acquiring things is the secret to happiness—which it isn't."

"Hmm," I muttered.

"What?"

I raised an eyebrow. "Oh? Nothing. Just thinking of an angle to the story."

"Angle?"

"Yes. Every story has to be written from a particular angle. It determines how I as a writer approach the subject."

"I see. And how are you thinking of approaching this

subject?"

"I was thinking something along the lines of 'Saint Nicholas' versus 'Santa Claus.'"

He folded his hands and leaned back. "I'd rather you didn't."

"Why?"

"Because I don't want to give any more ink to the myth."

"Oh, that's rather unavoidable, isn't it? People already put Saint Nicholas—you—and Santa Claus together. The whole Christmas motif. To not address it would, I think, leave a rather large and gaping hole in the story."

"Brett, if you tell people that I am the real Santa Claus, then what do you think is going to happen to this place? Hmm?"

I opened my mouth a moment, glancing about the room. "Well, I don't have to mention the monastery."

"Oh but you should! Don't you see? This is, after all, where I work. And it is at the north pole."

"Wait. The north pole is several miles further up. It's covered by ice most of the year, but it's pretty much an ocean."

"And how do you measure north?"

"On a map..." I shifted in my seat. "But geographic north and magnetic north are not the same."

"No. They are not."

"But this isn't magnetic north, either."

"Not any more. Not in a long time."

"Holy crow," I gaped. "You really did build the workshop at

the north pole."

"The command I received from my Lord told me to go the farthest north. And I did. Until I could go no further, because we'd already arrived."

"We?"

"Yes. The elves and I."

"Elves?!"

He smiled broadly. "That's what they were called."

The party trudged through the snow, pushing their way further into the woods. Darkness had fallen not so long ago, but shelter remained just out of reach. To warm themselves, they'd lit makeshift torches, which now glistened off the blanket of white and cast inky shadows stretching away into the woods that shifted away from them as they moved.

The sky above, where visible through the naked canopy of trees, showed a blizzard of stars in the azure vault. *No moon tonight,* Nicholas thought. It was just as well. Despite the centuries he'd now walked these lands, despite the ever-advancing spread of Christendom through the intervening years, the inhabitants still remained dangerously lawless.

He paused for breath, leaning his hand against one of the dormant oaks by their path, feeling the frozen bark beneath his palm. *I've been alive for a thousand years now. Longer than this tree. Longer than any still standing in this forest.*

Somehow, it still filled him with awe.

His disciples passed by wordlessly, their faces hidden beneath their monks' robes, gloved hands clutching the torches. So much had changed. So little had changed.

None of the men with him questioned his hesitation. They knew his secret. They knew despite exhaustion, lack of sleep, hunger and exposure, he'd still outlive them all.

The Roman Empire was gone, though not precisely forgotten. The Alans and Huns also had risen and fallen in his days. Their lands now lay divided between countless little kingdoms, fiefdoms, duchies, principalities, and khanates. So many languages and cultures! Europe was a mess. Everyone vying for their own little slice of territory, with no regard for the souls they trampled in their unyielding thirst for power.

He slipped his hand off the tree. Would it still be standing a thousand years from now? Would he?

"How long, O Lord, will You have me walk this earth? How long till I may at last rest at home in Your presence? Until the cities be wasted without inhabitant, and the houses without man, and the land be utterly desolate?" A wave of despair threatened to engulf him, and he pressed out a sob.

*It's my fault.*

His ears still rang with the clash of steel, the cries of those now dead, butchered where they stood by the heartless cruelty of those soldiers. In his nostrils hung the stench of blood and death, and he wondered if he'd ever smell anything sweet again.

He'd seen countless butcheries in the centuries of his long walk. The weight of man's cruelty and sin brought his spirit to the ground and kept it there more resolutely than a thousand anchors. But none of it had prepared him for the blasphemous assault they'd just endured.

Help, Defend, Heal. Indeed! The Teutonic butchers who'd assailed their monastery showed no interest in helping, defending, nor healing. In fact, when Nicholas had upbraided them for their treatment of the pagans they'd captured, they'd accused him of standing against God, and burned the monastery to the ground.

*And they believe they're doing God's work.* He turned and spat, the taste of blood still in his mouth. More than one of the so-called knights had tried to run him through. Their swords lay broken for the effort. Witchcraft, they called it. That's when they'd set fire to the monastery, to burn him and his disciples for sorcery.

He'd come to Lithuania because the Gospel had made so few inroads here. That, and the Lord had told him to go north. The pagans resisted every attempt at conversion. They clung to the old ways more stubbornly than ivy clings to rock. And yet, he still managed to win some converts and construct the monastery. His hope had been that these disciples would soon take the good news—the true Gospel, as he called it—to their former cities and win them over that way. The Lithuanians resisted conversion because they saw it for what it was: subjugation to a foreign power. Sadly, that's all the Church had become. Emperor Constantine's peace had withered, and the Church that once suffered persecution now inflicted it instead.

And not just upon the pagans. Upon their own brothers as well.

Such irony. He himself had once boxed Arius's ears for heresy. Now his Church freely murdered those who disagreed, like they had against the Cathars in the Albigensian Crusade. Over twenty thousand people—men, women, and children alike—perished at the massacre of Béziers in France, seven thousand in the Church of St. Mary Magdelene alone. As Arnaud-Amaury, the Cistercian abbot-commander said, *"Caedite eos. Novit enim Dominus qui sunt eius."*

Kill them all. The Lord will recognize His own.

Such a far cry from the Spirit of Christ Who warned Peter to put away his sword, for all who live by it will die by it.

None of those men seemed the least fazed by His warning. And why should they? In truth, they were no more Christian than the pagans they sought to subjugate. Even the Cathars, for all their doctrinal faults, lived better lives than the average Christian these days.

"Lord," he prayed aloud, "preserve us a remnant, I beg Thee."

He sucked in a heavy breath, and started after his men, who'd stopped some ways up the path, awaiting his arrival.

"Father," one of them said as he drew near, "what is it?"

"The span of years weighs heavy upon me this night. I would rather leave this place than continue to see such dark days as these."

Another murmured, "What would we do without you?"

"That," he rested his hand on the monk's shoulder, "is why I stay."

"You stay because Christ commands it," said a wizened voice. Brother Grigory, he knew. One of his first converts in this land. He hadn't known the old man had survived the battle.

He spared him a half smile. "And that."

Grigory grunted. "And what else does the Lord command for us this night? Since He has seen fit to decree suffering for His servants, do you think He might see fit to decree shelter for those that survived?"

Nicholas frowned. Bitterness filled the man's voice. And who could blame him? He had every right to be bitter, especially when the wound they'd endured was yet so raw.

"There is a small cave nearby," he said. "We will shelter there for now."

He led them forward, ignoring Grigory's grumbling and the stifled sobs of some of the younger brothers until at last they came to the caves he'd mentioned. They weren't much: barely tall enough for them to stand up in, and hardly deep. But it was shelter, nonetheless. He gave orders for wood for a fire and food, if they could find any. Then, exhausted, he sat down beside the root of a tree and leaned his head against the sandstone wall.

Grigory shuffled over and sat down beside him. "Do you despair?" he asked. Nicholas glanced toward the other monks, to see if any were listening.

"No," he muttered, "but neither do I hope."

"Hmm. How is that not despair?"

"I haven't given up. But neither do I know how to keep fighting. Nor even what I'm fighting for."

"Fighting." Grigory held up his thumb and forefinger about an inch apart. "I was this close to picking up a weapon."

"You would be dead."

He nodded. "Probably. I'm still not so certain we shouldn't."

"No, Grigory. Not against armored knights. 'The weapons of our warfare are not carnal, but mighty through God.' It is through prayer and the ministry of the Word that we shall be victorious."

"Prayers did not stop swords or arrows this night."

"Nor did I say they would. We must persevere in doing good. Not in returning evil for evil, or blow for blow."

"So do you intend to rebuild?"

"Not as such." Nicholas sighed and ran a hand through his hair. "If we go back to what they burned down, they will only return and do it again. We'll find no shelter in the bosom of the Church, not so long as she wears a breastplate of iron and carries a sword."

"Go east? Seek shelter from the Orthodox?"

He shook his head. "It is more than a hundred miles to the lands under the influence of the east, and the way is fraught with peril."

"But we could make it," Grigory insisted. "And you yourself have said you owe no greater loyalty to the west than you do to the east."

"Constantinople and Rome both have my heart, though it is rent in twain. But I have respected the division in communion. No one present has been trained according to any of the eastern rites. They would not recognize you as anything but heretics."

"We're heretics here as well, according to those knights."

"I am aware."

"Then what do you propose we do?"

"We stay and fight for this land. For its people. Not with sword or shield. But with charity and forbearance. We'll shelter among the pagans, if they'll have us."

Grigory snorted. "The pagans themselves are just as likely to kill us as the Teutonics."

"I think not. I think they are just waiting for someone— anyone—to show them true Christian compassion, and to teach them the ways of Christ apart from any subjugation to the will of

Rome or her Bishop."

"An independent communion?" Grigory turned and stared at him. The firelight showed the shock and fear in his eyes. "Are you mad?"

"We'll be independent, but no one need know it. We keep our heads down and remain quiet. Non-confrontational. Our numbers will grow. In time, when we are discovered, we will be so many they will have no recourse but to treat with us on more equal footing. And we shall give them no cause to cry heresy. Our only goal shall be reaching the lost sheep of Lithuania. Nothing else."

Grigory clamped his jaw shut and closed his eyes. "Well then. Wake me when you're no longer dreaming. And if we survive the night, maybe we'll see this dream of yours come to pass. But for what it's worth, I still say we should go east."

# Twenty-Two

In the weeks that followed they continued their journey on foot, farther and farther into the wild. They lived off the land, taking turns hunting, fishing, or grazing for what they could find until by early spring, they came to a village with no name nor any indication that it knew anything of Christ. The villagers regarded them with suspicion, but when they explained they were fleeing the knights, they allowed them to stay.

The brothers cut trees and built up a common house for shelter, and bartered for seed to plant fields. Lacking cows or horses, they corralled a herd of deer from the forest and harnessed them to the plows. The does that had recently given birth they used for milking, much like the locals themselves. But for that, Nicholas insisted they keep their interactions with the villagers to a minimum, not wanting them to think they were in service to the Church.

While Grigory oversaw the re-establishment of the order and their communal work, Nicholas himself went into the village frequently, to visit with the village elders and act as emissary on their behalf. By Autumn, they'd harvested their crops and traded the goods for casks of wine and other stores to see them through the winter. The brothers themselves built up a reputation in the village as solitary men of integrity and hard work, whose produce showed a careful, attentive hand. This cemented Nicholas's standing in the meetings of elders.

It was at one such meeting in early winter that the subject of the faith at last came up. Darius, a gruff shoemaker, sat beside the fire with a mug of beer in his hand. "You are not the only ones fleeing from those knights," he said to Nicholas.

Nicholas stroked his beard. "It has been a year for us, but I do not doubt it."

"I've heard that an entire village was forced to flee. Those that did not were killed or put in chains. The homes were set ablaze. All in the name of their crossed God."

The others around the fire nodded, muttering angrily. "And at winter, too. 'Tis a shame indeed."

"What became of those who fled?" Nicholas asked.

Darius grimaced. "They are not far from here. Like you, they've sought shelter near us. This keeps up, it'll draw the knights to our village. You and your sons have been fine neighbors, Nicholas, but I'd sooner see you gone than t'see the banner of the cross waving at our doorstep."

Gvidas the baker belched loudly and said, "I say, if any of those bearing the cross come by, we ought to welcome them in."

The others scowled at him, and even Nicholas could not resist a frown.

"Welcome them," he continued, "give them three pints of mead, and then strangle them in their sleep."

"Hear hear!" the other cheered.

Nicholas pushed back his chair and stood. The others glanced his way. "Where're you off to?" Darius challenged.

"I'm going to see to those villagers you mentioned," he replied. "They may need aid."

"What is that to you?"

"I intend to give it, as much as I and my sons are able."

Gvidas sneered. "How is that your business?"

"How is it not yours?" he returned. "They lie at your doorstep. Hungry, destitute, and bereft. Care for them now. Help them get back on their feet, and they will be loyal neighbors forever. Spurn or ignore them now, and they would more easily turn against you."

Gvidas slammed his mug down. Mead sloshed on to the table. He wiped his mouth with the back of his hand. "These villagers were routed by those bearing the cross. Do you really think they would take the side of those who harmed them against those who have not?"

"I think," Nicholas spoke in measured tones, "if the Teutonic Knights had come bearing bread instead of swords, that a great many more would be wearing the cross today. *'Helfen, Wehren, Heilen.'* That is their motto. Help. Defend. Heal. How poorly they live up to it."

There was a general murmur of agreement around the room.

"I suspect," Nicholas continued, "their loyalty to the cross is the same as their loyalty to their motto—that is to say, nonexistent. How could it be otherwise?"

"You seem to know a lot about them, stranger," Gvidas said.

"I know a good deal more about the cross they wear than I do about them, and what I can tell you is this: they are no servants of the One Who gave His life to save mankind from his sins—not while they continue to sin in His name. With their lips they profess the Savior. But with their actions they deny Him. And it is by their actions alone that we must judge who they are and what they do, not by what they claim to be."

The elders studied him quietly, and Nicholas suspected he'd given himself away. But it was bound to happen anyway, and better now that he could draw a contrast between his followers and the Teutonic Knights.

"What about you?" Darius asked. "What do you claim to be?"

Nicholas smiled thinly. "Observe what I have done and what I do, and you will know." With that, he bowed gracefully, and left the room.

Once outside, he glanced upward at the full moon shining in the azure vault of the heavens. Only a few stars glistened beside it. The rest were obscured by its silver brilliance. He took in a deep breath and started off toward the far side of the village, where Darius had said the refugees were encamped. As he moved along, he became conscious that some of the men from the tavern were following. His heart quickened a pace. Should he have told them outright that he was, himself, a follower of Christ? Given the abuses heaped upon these people by the Teutonic Knights and others professing Christ while denying Him with their actions, to do so would be signing the death warrant of his unsuspecting men.

Then again, none of the men in this village were fools. It was entirely possible they'd already come to that conclusion, and meant him harm because of it. If so, he'd have little way to warn his followers of what to expect. Especially if they attacked him now.

Even so, he walked at a steady pace, and the men behind him kept even as well. Surely, he reasoned, if they meant to attack they'd have done it by now. Was it possible they only wished to see how he'd treat those who fled the knights of the cross?

He pursed his lips, still not slowing his pace. If that were the case, then the only right and proper course of action would be to continue along to the refugee camp even as he'd already planned.

*Walk with me, Lord,* he prayed, *but most especially watch over those brothers of mine who know not what has transpired between me and these men this evening. Keep them safe, I beg You!*

He didn't have to go far outside the village to find the encampment. Those living there made no attempt to hide their presence or their numbers. As he entered the camp and moved among them, a good number of people glanced his way with hollowed eyes, showing signs of hunger. Others stank of disease.

A few men, but mostly women and children along with the aged sheltered in numerous tents, with watch fires burning before them to keep them warm and to light the darkness. They stared up at him from gaunt faces. Some had wounds still untended from the battle. *They have nothing!* he realized. *How will they ever survive?*

He dared not pray for them nor make the sign of blessing upon them, at least, not just yet, anyway. Instead, he moved his lips silently, bringing each family in turn before the throne room of God and making intercession for them.

At the far edge of camp, he encountered the idol. Supplicants bowed before it, offering what meager scraps of food they possessed to a scrap of wood, leaving otherwise edible food to be consumed by ants. Nicholas bit his lip and turned away.

When he'd seen enough, he left the camp behind and hurried back through the village toward his own encampment. There, he knew, his brothers waited with food growing in their well-tended garden, with plenty of firewood stacked against the wall from the hard work of his disciples, and with casks of beer and wine from their careful trade with the very same villagers who now turned a blind eye upon their neighbors.

He no longer saw his shadows—those men who'd followed him from the tavern and watched as he'd inspected the refugee camp. If they remained, they were keeping their distance.

As he neared the gate, a monk named Abraham called out a challenge. "Who goes there? Be you friend or foe?"

"It is I, Nicholas," he replied without slowing his stride. "Wake the brothers," he added as he passed him, "and have them assemble in the common room. We've work to do this night, and I'll not see the sun rise without it done."

"Yes father," Abraham answered, and scurried off.

Nicholas made straight for their meeting place. He threw open the doors and fell to his face before the altar with its cross in the back.

"Oh God," he prayed, "please grant me wisdom and favor that I might aid these wretched souls I found this night!"

He stayed there in prayer as the recent memories of the refugee camp flowed through his mind. Then, at last, he heard the voice.

*This is what I have called you to.*

He opened his eyes, feeling the dirt floor beneath his fingers. A fragment of scripture ebbed at the edges of his mind. From the epistle of James. *Pure religion and undefiled before God, even the Father, is this, to visit the fatherless, and widows in their adversity, and to keep himself unspotted of the world.* "What shall I do?" he whispered.

A noise behind him caused him to turn. The monks filed in, led by Grigory, consternation etched onto their faces.

"There is an encampment on the other side of the village. Peasants fleeing the cruelty of the knights who burned our monastery. They are pagan. Diseased. Wounded. Hungry. Utterly destitute."

"What would you have us do?" Grigory asked.

He looked at their faces. "We're going to help them."

They spent the whole night, gathering what they could and loading it into the sleigh they used for bringing goods to market: baskets of bread, bags of onions, potatoes, carrots, salted meat, and casks of wine—their entire stores, more or less. When at last the sleigh was full and could hold no more, Nicholas called a halt to their efforts.

"Hitch up the deer. We'll use them to draw the sleigh."

"We'll need more than our usual pair," Abraham pointed out. "The sleigh is much too heavy for just two."

"Use them all," Nicholas instructed. "I want speed as well as stealth."

"Why is that?" Abraham asked.

"Because I do not wish to be seen," he answered, "'Let your giving be in secret, and the Lord Who sees in secret will reward you.'" He raised his voice, "We will not let the left hand know what the right hand is doing."

"Aye," Grigory agreed. "That'll keep them from coming to us and seeking more of what we have, too."

Nicholas scowled, but Grigory set his jaw firmly. "Do not ask an apology. You know as well as I that those who give are oft easy targets for those who take. And we know not what manner of people might be receiving these gifts. If'n we have to turn beggars away from our doorstep, they're just as like to turn on us as easily as they once turned to us."

"Let us not prejudge the responses of people we've yet to meet, let alone assist."

"I am simply agreeing with your wisdom and our Lord's. 'The horseleech hath two daughters which cry, "Give, give."'"

"And yet we ought to support the weak, and to remember the words of the Lord Jesus, how that He said, 'It is a blessed thing to give, rather than to receive.'" With that, he climbed up into the driver's seat and took the reins from Grigory. To the rest of the men he said, "You have shown yourselves to be selfless and generous, as good Christians ought. Do not fret now for what we shall eat or drink, for our heavenly Father knows well our need. He shall provide again for us an abundance, that we may continue to be charitable toward all."

With that, he snapped the reins, and the sleigh lurched into motion. In moments, he was flying through the trees, trusting the deer to keep him on an even path. Still, the sleigh bumped over the roots and rocks of the uneven ground, leaving muddied leaves in its wake. Above the canopy of trees, the sky brightened and the air felt crisp with the first blush of dawn. He cracked the reins harder, urging the deer faster.

At this hour, it was unlikely any were awake. Or so he hoped. The only sounds were the running of the deer over the ground and the slice of the wooden rails through the snow.

In moments the sleigh flew through the center of the village, flashing past the tavern where he'd been informed of the widows and orphans earlier that day. He saw at least one person come out as he drove by, but he had no time to wave and even less desire.

He made the turn at the end of the village thoroughfare, feeling the sleigh slip sideways before righting itself and zigzagging down the path. He cracked the reins again. In moments he was once more in the woods, drawing abreast of the refugee camp.

A few fires still smoldered, with lazy trails of smoke rising through their ashes to flavor the morning air. He spotted no one moving about, though. Quickly, he clambered out of the sleigh and dropped to the ground. The deer panted, steam rising from their muzzles and flanks. He'd driven them hard. "Worry not, lads," he muttered to them. "The way back'll be easier without all this to carry."

In the back of the sleigh, the brothers had tied up everything within several large sacks. He pulled them out and hefted one

over his shoulder, grunting beneath the weight. Trudging toward the first tent, he dropped it near the entrance, then returned.

By the time he'd unloaded all the sacks, curious eyes peeked out at him from the nearest camps. He caught them looking at him, but when they saw his face, they ducked back quickly into the folds of their tents, as if frightened by his strange demeanor and far stranger actions. Wordlessly, he climbed back aboard the sleigh, picked up the reins, and gave them a quick snap.

As he left the encampment behind, he hazarded a glance over his shoulder. People were hastening from their tents, some pawing through the sacks and crying joy to their neighbors while others stood silently, extending their hands toward him in fond farewells.

By the time he returned to their tiny lodge, he was beaming broadly. His heart soared with the giving, the looks on the faces of the people he'd barely glimpsed as he'd driven away etched in his memory.

"Brothers and sons!" he cried as he thundered into the lodge. "Such a glorious thing we have done!"

The brothers turned to him, their faces sullen and worried. He furrowed his brow, unable to comprehend their response. Then they parted, and revealed the villagers behind them,

swords strapped to their belts and grim expressions above their folded arms.

"What is this?" he asked.

Darius shifted his feet. "I should like to ask you the same, bishop."

# Twenty-Three

Nicholas's eyes flickered to their swords. *Not again*, he prayed. *Lord, I beg Thee!*

He turned to the younger monk who quailed beside Gvidas. "Michael, tend to the deer."

Michael took a step forward, but Gvidas's arm caught him by the shoulder. Nicholas stared at the villagers evenly. "If you wish, send someone with him. But the deer have had a long ride. They must be unhitched and fed."

Gvidas caught the eye of one of the other armed men, and gave him a quick nod, and then released the hapless Michael. Nicholas gave the monk a reassuring smile as they headed out the door.

"So," he said when they were gone, "has anyone offered you tea? Mulled wine, perhaps?"

"We do not come to drink with you, Christian."

"And yet you are welcome just the same. Why are you here?"

"We should ask you the same thing," Darius growled.

Nicholas cocked his head. "You know why we are here. We came fleeing armed men who fell upon us like brigands, entered our home unbidden and threatened us with their... swords." He took a step toward one of the chairs beside the table and dragged it out, then sat upon it. "They murdered our friends and burned our home with fire. And so we fled."

"And yet you are a Christian."

"I do not deny it. We all are."

"Why didn't you tell us when you first arrived?" Gvidas spat.

"Because those who attacked us also wear the cross—though they do not live by its tenets. I did not wish to confuse the matter. I wanted you instead to judge us by our actions. Not our words."

"You're here to convert us!"

"In all the year I've spent with you, have you heard me preach a single sermon?"

The villagers exchanged glances. Nicholas continued unfazed. "I've given plenty, and every one of them has been through what I have done. We've been good neighbors. Even friends with some of you. We've been honest in our dealings. Excellent in our work. Fair-minded and true in every way save one: we did not tell you that we truly serve the same God Whom those crossed knights serve falsely. I should think it obvious why."

Darius shifted his feet again and pushed a sigh toward the ceiling. "What is it about your God that compels men to take up the sword?"

"Nothing," he replied. "It does not require my God to make men take up swords against their neighbors, Darius. Men need no encouragement for that. Unless," he added as an afterthought, "it is this: that the light of truth and kindness shames those who do not live in it. This might lead one to take up a sword against us. The Teutonic Knights tried to force us into taking up arms and joining their mad crusade against the Muhammedans. We refused. For this, they attacked. I believe we shamed their cause."

Darius shot Gvidas a look. The baker wilted under it. The cobbler cleared his throat. "Do we have your assurance that you will not take up arms against us?"

Nicholas burst out laughing, earning disapproving scowls from the villagers.

"Forgive me," he said. "There are few swords on any of this land, but they all belong to you."

"And what if these knights come hither?" Gvidas returned. "Will you take their side against us?"

"Have you heard nothing I've said? We take no side against any man. The mandate from our Lord is both to love our neighbors as ourselves, and to love our enemies."

Gvidas snorted. "Why would I love my enemies?"

Nicholas smiled thinly. "To deny them power over you."

"And what of us?" Darius asked. "Are we your enemies?"

Nicholas leaned back and folded his hands. "I suppose that's up to you. As for me, my house and my sons and brothers here, we will love you regardless."

Darius nodded. "Well, then. I suppose we're done here." He jerked his head toward the door, and the armed men quietly departed. Gvidas came last. He paused by Nicholas's shoulder.

"You're quite mad. Aren't you?"

Nicholas shook his head. "No. Not in the least."

The baker snorted, shook his head, and followed the others out. When they had gone, Grigory shut the door behind them and latched it. He opened it again a second later and let Michael back in, and then closed it once more.

"That was close," he said. Turning, he regarded Nicholas from across the room. "Too close."

"They left peacefully. We've no more to fear from them."

"I don't believe that."

"Believe what you will, Grig," he snapped.

The elder pursed his lips into a tight frown, then grunted. "I suppose some mulled wine sounds good right about now. Abe, could you stir up the fire?"

Abe nodded. "Yes, brother."

"We have so little of it left. But tonight seems the time regardless."

Nicholas dropped his head into his hands. "What else would you have me do?" he asked aloud. "For better or worse this is our home. And they are our neighbors. We must learn to live with them."

Grigory came to the table and pulled out a chair, sitting across from the bishop. "There are other villages."

"And we shall run into the same problem again."

"We could keep going north."

Nicholas hesitated, conscious that all eyes were on the two of them and all ears attentive to what they said. "It is not time yet. Certainly not right after that. If we made any move to leave now, they would take it as a sign we were lying to them, and I'll not risk Christ's reputation by anything on our part. Enough damage has been done already on that account. Besides, the Lord has revealed to me how we are to serve this land and these people."

Grigory licked his lips and glanced toward the fire where Abraham was warming the wine. Disappointed that it wasn't ready yet, he asked, "And how is that?"

"By doing more of what we did tonight. Grig, you should've seen their faces!"

"I thought it was supposed to be in secret."

"And it was. But they rather discovered me as I was leaving."

He grunted. "So they might not know it was you."

"I don't know. What I can tell you is that it was wonderful. And more of that is what we all need most. Us and them."

"With what?" Grigory sneered. "We have nothing left!"

"The Lord will provide a way. I'm sure of it."

He raised his eyebrows doubtfully, then shrugged as Abraham set a cup of mulled wine before him. He put a second cup down before Nicholas.

"Thank you, Abe."

Quickly, he put a hand over Grigory's cup, causing the old

man to look up in consternation. "Half a moment. Everyone, take a cup. Michael, pass out that bread."

Michael reached into the cupboard near the fireplace and withdrew a basket of bread. "It didn't rise properly," he said.

"I know. It's perfect."

As they passed the bread along, tearing off chunks, Nicholas said, "On the night when Jesus was betrayed, He took the bread and gave thanks, then passed it amongst His disciples and said, 'Take and eat. This is my body, which is broken for you. Do this in remembrance of Me.' And then afterward, He took the cup and passed it to His disciples and said, 'This cup is My blood of the New Covenant, which is poured out for you. All of you drink this in remembrance of Me. For as often as you eat this bread and drink this cup, you proclaim the Lord's death until He comes.'"

They shared the meal, and crossed themselves afterward. "Amen," Grigory said. Then he leaned across the table. "New communion indeed."

Nicholas grinned and set his cup down. "So: I want to hear your thoughts. Your ideas. Your fears."

"Well, I fear those men coming back," Michael put in.

Nicholas patted his hand. "As do I. But if we do our task aright, if we do not grow weary in the work of charity, I believe it will light a fire in the hearts of all, and that will keep the wolves at bay."

Abraham studied his cup. "These lands are full of the poor

and needy. We cannot hope to feed nor provide for them all."

"Nor should we," Grigory added. "To do so would breed lethargy, complacency, and even resentment. The Lord has ordained and sanctified work. As it is said, 'if a man shall not work, neither let him eat.'"

"I do not mean to reward idleness," Nicholas agreed. "And the Lord Himself said, 'The poor you shall always have with you.' If I may speak to what I think is the heart of Abraham's question, it is this: how do we decide who shall receive the gifts?"

"The children," Daniel said. He was a soft spoken monk who'd once had a family of his own, before they died of consumption. When the others glanced his way he added, "They've done nothing to deserve the fate which has befallen them, and parents are oft aggrieved they cannot do more for them."

Grigory made a noise in his throat. "We're back to rewarding idleness, then."

"Not at all," Daniel protested. "Children oft work as hard as they are able. It may not be as much as a man, but it is honest work nonetheless. And besides, if you win the hearts of the children, you win the hearts of the parents as well. And you secure for yourself a pleasant place in the mind of the next generation."

Michael put in, "That's provided they know it is you who've done it. If we remain anonymous, how can we win hearts?"

"And yet it must be done in secret," Nicholas insisted.

Grigory shook his head. "It's already late for that. At least as far as those people you aided this morning are concerned."

"True. Let us hope the Lord receives the glory nevertheless."

"What of these peasants you aided last night?" Grigory asked. "D'you think they give glory to God for what we've done?"

"Someone should ask," Michael suggested.

Nicholas sighed. "If I showed my face there, they shall know it is me."

"Begging pardon, Father," Michael protested, "but I did not at all mean you. I will go. None of them know me. I daresay I remember enough of the old ways that I shan't stand out at all."

"Very well. Go then. Find out if God receives glory for what we've done. As for the rest of us—it's been a long night. If you've yet to catch some sleep, now may be a good time."

"Now?" Grigory took on a scandalized expression. "In the middle of the morning? What about prayers and chores?"

"I think just this once, given the night we've all had, we can delay for an hour or so."

He snorted. "So long as it does not become a habit."

Nicholas shook his head and patted his arm, then rose from the table to find his sleeping mat.

By the time Michael returned it was near noon. Some of the

brothers busied themselves quietly with chores. Nicholas himself had slept little, though he did close his eyes and try to rest. However, after an hour of listening to Grigory snoring, he'd given up and now sat by the fire staring into the embers. That's where he sat when Michael came back.

The younger monk entered with his hands clasped before him and an unreadable expression on his face. He sat down beside Nicholas and warmed his hands before the fire.

"Are you going to keep me in suspense?" Nicholas chided.

He opened then closed his mouth, and then said, "I'm trying to figure out the best approach."

"The truth will do fine, I should think."

"Of course. And there are several, I think. Both good and bad." He leaned back and tucked his hands beneath his armpits. "The good news, I suppose, is that they don't know it's you that gave the gifts. You wanted it done in secret and it is a secret indeed. Our wonderful villagers were there—the baker and cobbler. Giving them an earful about us. Actually, it was mostly the baker who was talking. The cobbler stayed back with his hand on his sword, trying to look important, I think."

"What was Gvidas saying?"

"That we cannot be trusted. That we are liars, serving the same God as the crossed knights who burned their village. He just about had them stirred up enough to march on this place and send us all to our just reward, I should think. The cobbler talked them down, though. Said we'd made peace and promised to keep out of it if'n the knights should come here."

"They made no mention that we ourselves had been attacked?" he asked. Michael shook his head. Nicholas rolled his eyes. "No. Of course they didn't."

"The real kick in the pants—pardon me—was when the cobbler said they could ransom us to the knights, if it came to that."

Nicholas snorted. "He has to know that would never work."

"He may. I had the feeling he was trying to find a way to keep them from coming over here and attacking us anyway. They're all pretty worked up about it."

"I can imagine. So, were you able to learn anything about the gifts? How they responded?"

"Oh yeah. They responded all right. Pure gratitude. Seems until our friends from the village arrived, they were all morning just pouring out their gratitude to the little statue of their snake goddess they got set up in the middle of camp. Whole base of the statue was just overflowing with tiny little offerings—every bit of it from our own stores. Did we really grow our own food and prepare our cakes so they could rot at the foot of a snake lady? 'Cause that's what's happening."

Nicholas frowned. Michael kept his face turned to the fire, dark eyes reflecting the flames. *He looks angry*, the bishop realized. He blew out a long breath. "Well then. It seems we need a way to... direct their affections... while still preserving our anonymity."

"They said you were a fey."

"Fey?"

Now the man faced him. "Yes. One of the little people. A faerie. Elf. Sprite. What we know of as demons. That's who they think gave the gifts. So why not just tell them? Why all this sneaking around? They already think us deceptive, and they deceive themselves about the gifts."

"Michael, giving in secret—and protecting that secret—is hardly the same thing as deception. No more than preserving the sanctity of the confessional."

"In the confessional, it is only what is confessed that is protected. The fact of the confession—and who does it—is no secret."

"I know. But this is different. We cannot have them know that we are their benefactors. Grig is right in this. For all his faults, he is right. Should they learn that the gifts come from us, we would be inundated with the destitute, and some of them—resenting that we cannot possibly meet their every want—will grow resentful. Even violent."

"So what do we do?"

He folded his hands. "We must pray that God give us an answer."

# Twenty-Four

The answer came in a way so startlingly obvious it caused Nicholas to chuckle. He'd gone into town a week later to barter for supplies with what little they had left when he overheard some of the villagers discussing him.

"Here comes one of them now," the man whispered. "Bet he's their brishop."

"It's *bishop*, y'fool, and he ain't one at all," said his comrade.

"How would you know?"

"'Cause their bishops always dress themselves up in fancy robes. Scarlet, like little kings with strange, pointy crowns on their heads. They don't go 'round like common folk."

"So what is he, then?"

"Beats me."

"Hush. He approaches."

Nicholas did approach, and bade them both a good morning, then passed by without further word. Behind his back he heard, "Friendly-like. Ain't nothin' king-ish about him."

He couldn't help the grin that spread over his face. *This just might work*, he thought. After his shopping, he hurried back to the monastery. Coming inside, he approached Michael and

Grigory. "I have a solution."

"Does it involve telling them who we are?" the older man asked.

"After a fashion." He put his hand on Grigory's shoulder. "But not in way that implicates us. None of the villagers know I am a bishop."

Grigory and Michael exchanged glances before shrugging.

"That's how they will not know it is we who assist them."

Michael sat on the edge of the table. "You're going to go out dressed as a bishop."

"Yes. In full, scarlet robes. Unmistakable."

"They're just as likely to shoot you," Grigory pointed out.

Nicholas cracked a grin. "So?"

The man opened his mouth, then closed it again. "Good point."

"All right then," Michael agreed, "but what shall we give them? We're out of supplies. And we certainly cannot afford to give away our produce."

"Aye," Grigory agreed, "especially if'n it's gonna wind up food at an idol's feet."

"Agreed," Nicholas smiled. "There is another solution. Daniel, could you come here please?"

The man lumbered over, broom still in hand. "Yes, father?"

"You've a heart for the children, yes? If we could not give them food, what would you suggest?"

He thought a moment, then said, "Play things."

"Toys?"

Grigory snorted and folded his arms. "Idleness."

"Not in the way you think," Daniel objected. "Play is how children learn. They practice being adults."

"Better practice'd be spent doing something useful," Grigory observed.

"Learning is useful."

Nicholas stroked his beard. "Well, it's a better idea than what I came up with."

"Which was?" Michael asked.

"Clothing. But I couldn't figure out how we were going to get the sizes right. Do you have any skill making toys?" he asked Daniel.

The man nodded. "Some. I've been known to carve a block of wood or two in my day."

"Excellent. I'm putting you in charge of this, then. Put together a list. A variety. Things we can manufacture quickly and in quantity."

"There goes my arthritis," Grigory complained.

Daniel nodded. "I can do that. So we're to be elves, then?"

"Excuse me?"

"Michael told me that's who they think gave them the gifts. I assume we're still doing this in secret. It might take them a while to figure out it ain't elves."

"If ever," Grigory groused.

"If ever," Nicholas agreed. "But if they're going to charge our good works to elves, then we're going to put those elves in service to Christ."

"One thing," Daniel said. "My essential task is been cleaning. You want I should do both?"

Nicholas took the broom from his hand and handed it to Grigory. The old man looked stunned. "So your arthritis won't suffer," Nicholas said.

Scowling, Grigory took the broom in hand and sauntered off toward the fireplace to continue sweeping.

"When d'you want these done by?" Daniel asked.

"Our next holy day is Christ's Mass. Let's have things ready by the eve before. Maybe the sight of the mad bishop giving away toys will draw some in to the church to thank him in person. Won't that be a lark?!"

By the time the holiday rolled around, they had more toys than could fit in the sleigh. The problem had become evident about a month beforehand, when Daniel pointed it out to him. Nicholas assured him that he should continue, and that if God could feed five thousand on a child's lunch of five loaves and two fish, then He could arrange a way that too many toys could still fit into one sleigh.

In the end, the answer came clearly. And it required a map of the whole country. They gathered around the table in the common room the day before, studying the map.

"Two man teams," Nicholas said, "will go on ahead of me. Station yourselves here," he pointed at the map, "here, here and here."

"That's a lot of territory to cover in one night," Daniel observed.

"These all mark the places where the Teutonic Knights have ravaged the land," Grigory pointed out. "Which of them would you like to leave unblessed?"

Nicholas smiled to himself. It was good to see the old man come around, even if he was still bitter and cranky about it.

"I'm not saying it can't be done," Daniel objected, "just that it's a lot."

"I'll have to travel at speed," Nicholas said. "I'll go from sundown to sun up. A little over fourteen hours."

"We should need fresh teams as well," Michael added. "Fourteen hours is a long time to pull at speed."

Nicholas grunted. "We've got nearly twenty four head of deer in our pen. We'll break them up into three groups of eight, harnessed and ready at these stopping points." He again pointed to the map. "After I come through, we'll switch out teams and reload the sleigh."

Grigory grunted. "It'd be better if we had three sleighs. Then we could simply switch you out. Or better yet, three of you. Then we could get it all done at once and call it a night."

Nicholas patted his shoulder. "Next time, perhaps, when we're less likely to be shot at." He heaved a breath. "All right then. We're as ready as we can be. Tomorrow morning we'll start. For now, let us rest and pray that God is honored by our efforts."

"And that none of us get shot," Grigory finished.

"Amen."

Morning on the day before Christmas broke with a light snowfall covering the ground. The monks opened their day with prayer and breakfast, and then packed food for themselves and grain for the reindeer before loading the sleigh. The route Nicholas had mapped out for them followed a circuit, and required they first go in groups of four with a full load of hand-crafted play things drawn by a team of ten deer to each of the designated stopping points. There they left two monks at each location to watch over eight of the deer and the toys, and sent two deer and two monks back. Even planning it out this way still took hours of preparation—as well as several more hours of anxious anticipation as the monks awaited the sleigh's return.

Nicholas spent most of this time in prayer, begging God for the protection of the deer, the toys, and especially of his brothers now camped out in the wild. By late afternoon the last of the teams returned, having gone the longest distance to the midpoint of the circle and returning via the other side, they confirmed that all men and animals were ready and waiting.

Nicholas's prayer changed from one of entreaty to one of thanksgiving. As afternoon wore on to dusk and the sun neared the horizon, he opened the chest by his bed and withdrew his old bishop's robes. Straightening, he fitted them over the bulk of his furs. Grigory assisted him with a belt.

"This get up makes me look fat," he complained.

Grig chuckled. "You're going to be out in the cold a long time. Immortal you may be, but you're not impervious to the chill. It'll at least keep you warm."

"Do you think what we're doing is wise?"

"No. In fact, I think yer all struck with a touch of moon madness, truth be told. A rational man would say the same, I reckon. He might even go so far as to say this plan is not only likely to fail miserably at what you hope to accomplish, but will also cost us more dearly than you can possibly imagine. A wise man would call it foolish, and beg you to reconsider," but then he straightened and met Nicholas's eye, "but the foolishness of God is wiser than the wisdom of men, and as maddening as it's been to follow you down this course, you've nonetheless led us straight and true, and I am eager to be proven wrong."

He then turned around and withdrew something from deep within the cupboard, then held it out to Nicholas. It was a knitted hat with a furred brim, done up in scarlet to match Nicholas's robe. "I've given up hopin' ever since the knights burned our monastery. And maybe it's made me a tad bitter. More'n I like to be, anyways. You make me want to believe again."

Nicholas took the hat from him. "Thank you, Grig."

"It'll keep yer head warm, at least."

Nicholas put the hat on, fitting it over his ears. "How do I look?"

"Ridiculous."

They burst out laughing, then the bishop drew his old friend into a hearty embrace. "Keep watch for us in prayer."

"Always," Grig returned as they parted. "And the home fires will be kept burning till everyone returns safe and sound. Then we shall feast and celebrate Christ's Mass in our own fashion."

"Sounds wonderful."

Grigory tipped his head sideways. "Go, and God speed."

# Twenty-Five

Nicholas came outside the monastery, where the few remaining monks waited for him as he climbed into the sleigh. He made a show of checking the presents in the back before assuring himself that all was well. Then he settled into the driver's seat and took the reins.

He paused, looking over the faces of his men. "A long time ago, I had a toy ship my father had given me. When my father and mother passed, in anger, I threw that ship away, thinking I was done with childish things. In truth, it was one of the most selfish, angry, and immature things I've ever done, for in that act, I forgot how our Lord chooses to see us, and how He wishes us to see ourselves. It is good that we remain as children, that we retain our sense of wonder and awe at the world and the God Who made it. My brothers, this ministry we do has restored that to me, and I am grateful.

"What we do this night may never be done again, and even quickly forgotten by those we hope to serve. There is every real chance our friends are already in peril. I go to see each of them returned safely to us, and to deliver these treasures which have no value to bandits or thieves, but which might be precious to

315

the youngest amongst our neighbors.

"I enjoin you to remember the words of Christ, when His followers asked of Him, 'Who is the greatest in the kingdom of heaven?' that He took a child and set him down among them and said, 'Verily I say unto you, except ye be converted, and become as little children, ye shall not enter into the kingdom of heaven. Whosoever therefore shall humble himself as this little child, the same is the greatest in the kingdom of heaven. And whosoever shall receive one such little child in my Name, receiveth me.' And He also said, 'As ye have done it unto one of the least of these my brethren, ye have done it to Me.'

"This is the heart of our ministry from this time forth, whether the world long remembers us or never knows our names. We will serve the least of these, as if we were serving Christ Himself.

"You will not see me again until Christ's Mass, where we will celebrate that happy occasion when God gave us His gift of a Son. Pray for us continually, and keep watch with Grigory until we all return. Good night."

"You look a jester in that hat," Michael said. A ripple of laughter rose from the group.

"God be with you," he replied.

The answer came from them all. "And also with you."

With that, he cracked the reins, and the sleigh surged into motion.

Huffing steam, antlers bobbing as their hooves pounded over the snowy trail, Nicholas felt the wind lashing his face. The sleigh raced along the path, kicking up plumes of the light powder that blanketed the heavier icepack beneath. It had been almost a thousand years since he first discovered snow in the regions around the Black Sea. Now he couldn't imagine living in a country without it. Something about the frozen precipitation transformed the land. Places in the woods that once might have seemed dark and foreboding took on a peaceful hue, as the white drifts reflected back the light of the moon and stars. And in the daytime it was even better. The sun light broke through the clouds and lit the ice in the trees, making even the dourest hovel seem a castle embossed with gold.

At this moment, the snowpack reflected the light from the lanterns glowing on either side of his sleigh, and gave him a sense at least of the way ahead. The first village he meant to visit was itself newly built, being populated by more peasants fleeing the same knights who continued to ravage the countryside. It angered him still, that these men visited brutality upon the weak in the name of Christ, but he also knew the best way to insure against that was to help these people discover the real Christ—to know His salvation apart from the cruelty of those wicked imposters.

He cracked the reins again and turned the sleigh, driving the deer to the left a bit. They passed down a mild slope and he felt the carriage lurch beneath him. His hat slipped over his brow and he had to put the reins into one hand so he could push it back up again. Up ahead he could make out the smoke in the village as it curled from the tops of the rough hewn hovels. He drove the sleigh into the center of the community and pulled up sharply, drawing them to a stop.

For a moment, there was no sound but the creaking of the sleigh and the stamping feet of the deer in their harnesses. Nicholas secured the reins and stood.

"That's far enough, you!"

He turned abruptly, startled by the appearance of a bedraggled man in fur aiming a loaded crossbow at him. The man wore a studded helm on his head and a leather jerkin over his chest. The look in his eyes suggested he meant to use the weapon no matter how Nicholas answered.

The bishop smiled anyway. "Good evening! And may God find you well."

"What you want here?"

"Nothing. I do not come to take nor to receive, but to give. Tell me, good sir, do you have children?"

"I'm asking the questions around here! Don't you see what I've got at you?"

"You may point your arrows any way you like, and ask whatever questions you will, but I'm afraid I've not time to answer. I'm on a very tight schedule, you see."

Abruptly, he turned and hefted one of the sacks from behind him, then dropped it on the ground between himself and his accoster. The man's finger tensed on the crossbow trigger.

Just then, a woman came out of the hovel behind the bowman. "Sven?" she asked.

"Go in the house, woman!"

"What is going on?" she persisted.

"Presents, madam," Nicholas answered, "for your bairn. And all those in the village here."

The couple stared at him, perplexed, but slowly, the man lowered the crossbow.

"We know how much you have suffered," Nicholas went on. "Your children especially have seen too much of the heartache of war. Perhaps these simple tokens will help them forget for a time."

"Why?" they asked, almost in unison.

He retook his seat and lifted his reins. "Because tomorrow is Christmas. And it is a time for peace, joy, and knowing God's good will toward men."

"Who are you?" the man asked.

"Happy Christmas!" he bellowed, and snapped the reins. As the sleigh disappeared he heard the couple talking.

"Who did he say he was?"

"Something about Christmas. He looks like a bishop."

"A father?"

Then their voices were lost to the woods.

The next two villages were much the same, though the threats didn't always come from a frosty man with a crossbow. But at every turn he was met with suspicion and fear, followed quickly by bewildered confusion. By the time he reached the first checkpoint, he seriously questioned whether or not they were making any difference in the lives of these people at all.

"How goes it?" the monks eagerly inquired.

As they worked, he stretched his back. "I am threatened at every village I come to," he told them honestly, "and I can't say their affections are any warmer to me when I leave—though I don't suppose I should expect much in the scant minutes I'm there."

"How do they seem when you leave?" the monks asked.

"Confused, mostly."

"Confused is better than hostile."

"Yes. That it is."

With the team of deer changed out and the sleigh reloaded, he climbed back aboard and snapped the reins once more.

The night wore on. The darkness deepened as he passed by the lee side of a hill, where the moon in her course lay hidden in shadow, and it was here that he got his first real taste of danger. It came not from confused or hostile peasants armed with bows, daggers or farming implements, but from a pack of four legged predators surging down from the hill and closing in on his path. He could hear their snarling, and the deer suddenly broke hard to the side, dragging him off the trail and into the woods. He gave a sudden cry as the sleigh banged against a tree before righting itself and flying along. But one of the lamps lay snuffed out in the snow behind him.

The wolf pack, howling, charged ahead, intent on running down the deer. Nicholas gave up the reins and leaned to the side, snatching up the broken branches of pine saplings as they flew by. Quickly, he wrapped them together, twisting the wood till he had a makeshift torch. Then he snagged the one remaining lantern from the side and brought it into the carriage out of the wind. "Lord, I need Your light now!" he prayed, and thrust the tip of the pine into the fire. It flared quickly, sending curling smoke and heat flashing upward. He held it out and up, seeing it churning with fire, then he turned in his seat and flung it behind. The flaming brand spun through the air and landed at the feet of the pack just as they neared it. The wolves yelped and leaped to one side. Nicholas gave a shout of triumph, then turned and reached for the reins.

They slipped below his grasp, falling to the ground between the last two deer. The team raced ahead, out of his control. He gasped and lunged for the reins. They bounced just beneath his reach. Looking up, his eyes widened.

Ahead, ·the trees cleared before a sudden gap. The ground seemed to drop away before a massive cliff. The reindeer surged forward, too frightened by the wolves' pursuit to realize their danger. *Oh no!*

He dove forward, straining for the reins. If he could just get them in time...

There! His fingers closed around them and he straightened.

Too late, the team plunged ahead.

And he was airborne. He felt his body lift in the sleigh as the ground dropped beneath them. For a moment, he felt nothing but air, and then the sleigh rebounded against the hard-pack snow of the downslope with a bone-jarring impact. Some of the deer stumbled, and the sleigh careened sideways, threatening to overturn. He pitched outward. He hit the ground feet first, still gripping the edge of the sleigh. His boots slid in the snow.

For a moment, he balanced between two fates. Either the sleigh would tip over on top of him, or fall back and dragging him with it. He blinked.

And suddenly he was no longer there. No longer sliding down the hillside. No longer wearing his bishop's robe. No longer anywhere he recognized. He lay on a sandy beach beside the warm seas of the Mediterranean. He felt the sun on his face, the water gently washing against his ankles. He sat up, utterly bewildered. That's when he saw a child playing in the surf, his laughter mingled with the rush of the waves. He sat up, and a hand caressed his back.

"Were you going to sleep all day?"

The musical voice made his heart skip a beat. He turned, and Johanna sat beside him, her smile radiant in the morning sun.

She laughed, and then gently stroked his cheek.

"How is this possible?" He took her hand in his, startled by the smoothness of her touch.

She shrugged. "A choice."

"Choice?"

"Yes. You always can choose. No one makes you stay, Nicholas. We are here for you. Always."

"We?"

She tipped her head toward the child playing in the water. "Our son. Would you like to meet him?"

His heart leaped. "Yes!"

She stood and held out her hand. Nicholas scrambled to his feet, and followed her down into the water. The boy splashed over to them and leaped into Nicholas's arms. He wrapped Nicholas in a tight embrace, then pulled back and looked at his eyes.

Nicholas stared at him in amazement. "You look so much like

your mother."

"Hello, father," the boy returned. "Are you going to stay this time?"

Nicholas hesitated, and then looked over the lad's shoulder and saw a massive storm cloud billowing toward them. The thunderhead roiled faster, dark as the night and swirling with snow.

"I can't," he whispered.

The boy met his gaze, smiled again, and climbed down to play once more in the ocean. Johanna touched his elbow. "It is all right," she said. "We'll be waiting for you. Always."

The storm washed over him, lashing his face with ice and snow. And just as suddenly, he tipped backward into the sleigh as it continued careening down the slope. His hat fell over his eyes. He pushed it up, and saw they were at the bottom. The deer scrambled to their feet. Looking left, he spied the village not a mile off. Smoke curled from the tops of the huts as they stood grouped together in the shadow of the hillside. He found the reins and gave them a quick snap. The reindeer tugged the sleigh into motion, pulling toward the village.

## Twenty-Six

"Was that the time you supposedly flew?" I asked.

He nodded. "Seems some hunter witnessed it, and the rumors spread from there after I'd gone into the village. I made the rest of the deliveries that night, and every Christmas Eve thereafter for a generation. It took a while for the effort to have its intended effect. But Brother Daniel was right. We won the hearts of that generation, and by the time they had children of their own, there was no going back. The idols were put away, broken and forgotten for the useless hunks of wood and stone that they always were. And the land became Christian—quite apart from the swords of the crusaders. It wasn't long before it became necessary to move again."

"Why?"

"We were found out, and as Grigory had feared, we became the targets of those who preferred idleness to work. In a way, it's not at all unlike what happened to our Lord after He divided the loaves and fishes. He travelled with His disciples to the other side of the Sea of Galilee, and large crowds chased Him down around the sea so they could get another free lunch. They were prepared to make Him king by force—a view quite contrary to His actual mission.

"Like Him, I also found it necessary to escape to somewhere more private, into lands where I was not known, so that the true pursuits of our monastic life would not be obscured by the nature of our ministry to the poor. I took some of my brothers north with me into Finland, where we settled in the Lapland Province, on a fell known as Korvatunturi, or Ear Fell, because of its shape. All I knew was that it was largely uninhabited, and it gave me a secure place to build a solid monastery, where we could continue our traditions. I had, as you may recall, been charged to go to the far north, and this was as far north as I'd thought to go.

"We stayed there a long time. Kept goats for their milk and meat. Ironically, somehow I became conflated with the goats. I think it was the beard. Joulupukki, they called me. Outside, the world changed. Protestantism further split the Western Church, and the holy lands—including the country of my birth and youth—were finally given up as lost to the Mohammedans." He stopped a moment and shook his head.

"Times were difficult, as they always had been, but I had friends now—people in distant countries, in fact—who knew my secret. Always before, you see, I had kept them close beside me, and so our ministry was limited by what I and those immediately with me could accomplish together."

"Why did that change?" I asked.

"Necessity, I suppose. And peace. There existed now a network of small brotherhoods that extended all the way from Korvatunturi to the Black Sea, with men who'd taken oaths never to reveal the truth about who I was. And, of course, they did anyway."

I laughed, and he joined me with a chuckle of his own. "It did not matter. Most people, upon hearing the stories, dismissed them as so much legend. Those who did know helped us with the ministry, and for a while they even dressed the part. After a while I called a halt to the practice, though."

"Why's that?"

"It had become distracting to the purpose of our ministry. Always we meant to draw people to Christ. But soon I found that we had inadvertently begun drawing people to ourselves—to the myth we had created: Father Christmas—or Papa Noel, depending on language—and, of course, Sinterklaas."

"Santa."

"Yes. The myth endured nevertheless. It took on a life of its own. In England the Royalists—those who opposed the Puritans—used Father Christmas in their polemics against the excesses of that order.

"In time, I once more found it necessary to relocate—largely for the same reasons. This time, however, I was aided by the invention of the compass, which led me here."

"Magnetic north."

"Yes. And effectively, I can go no further. The pole itself is in the Arctic Ocean. Magnetic north has since moved on. It's somewhere in Canada now, I believe. And that will change one day, too."

"What will you do if you have to move again?" I asked.

But he fell silent, then, his attention drawn by the ragged breath of Oleg from the bed. I put my pen down and rubbed my eyes. It was getting late. Already this interview had gone on for hours longer than I'd anticipated, though with the story he'd shared, it could easily have taken several weeks, if not longer. I didn't begrudge him the details he'd skipped over. Centuries, if he was to be believed. It'd be hard enough to encapsulate a life story into a single tale, let alone the generations he said he'd lived.

I looked up, watching him kneeling at the bedside, his hands clasped in prayer. I felt my heart skip a beat. Had Oleg died? He'd seemed so lively just moments—well, hours—ago. The Abbot appeared to be in prayer. I cleared my throat, uncertain how to ask.

"He hasn't passed, if that's what concerns you," Nicholas said. "At least, not yet anyway."

I blinked. "Well, that's good."

"It is neither good, nor bad. It is simply delay."

"That's not good?"

He straightened and returned to his seat. "You tell me. We

spend a good deal of our lives waiting. Nothing more. How many hours have you spent waiting in traffic? Waiting at an airport? A doctor's office? A single moment can encapsulate a lifetime. The fate of nations has often hinged upon a moment's hesitation or thoughtlessly plunging into action."

"You speak like time is precious."

"Isn't it?"

After what he'd told me about his vision in the sleigh, I could see his point. "I suppose so. For me, that makes sense. Even for Oleg. Our time is short compared to yours."

"Have you never noticed how time speeds up the older you get? A young couple falls in love and marries. They bring children into the world. They blink, and those children are gone, swept off to college, career, or marriage and children of their own. Before that couple yet realizes it, they are grandparents, and they have no idea how they got so old. Especially so quickly."

I nodded.

He leaned forward, elbows on his knees. "Now magnify that a thousandfold, and you will have some idea just how precious time is to me."

I shifted in my seat, eager to change the subject. As much death as I had seen, I had no desire to keep revisiting the subject. I'd once been interviewing a soldier when a stray bullet knocked him out. At the time, I'd thought he'd just been killed in front of me. While I felt relief the man had survived, I couldn't shake the horror of it, and had to come home. Spent a week inside a bottle till Marshall talked me out of it.

"So I take it the point of these last stories was to convince me not to go the whole 'Santa' angle? Telling people this place is 'Santa's workshop,'" I made quotes with my fingers, "would practically guarantee you'd get inundated, right? I'm sure the U.S. Mail alone would bury you, if they got ahold of your address and forwarded every child's letter along."

He interlaced his fingers and propped his chin on them. "Santa belongs to the world. Nicholas of Myra belongs to Christ."

I tapped my pen against my forehead. "And yet... everything. Everything in the Santa myth has a root in your history." I ticked them off on my fingers. "The red suit was a bishop's robe. 'He sees you when you're sleeping and knows when you're awake.' That's from your heightened sensitivity. The north pole. We're here. Or at least we were, till it moved on to Canada. The sleigh. Drawn by reindeer. The gifts. Given to children. Made by elves!" I stopped, thought a moment, and laughed out loud. "That's brother Don's apron, isn't it? 'I'm an elf.' That's what it said. The elves are really just your brother monks."

"They've been called that for centuries, and still find it very amusing," he said.

"I'm sure."

"As I told you: many of the traditions associated with that legend have their origins in benign facts. It's just been blown out of proportion."

"I want to respect your wishes. And his," I tipped my pen toward Oleg, "How do I tell this story? What angle do I come from?"

He opened his mouth, but we were interrupted by a sudden gasp from the bed. Nicholas dashed to his side and took his hand. Oleg opened his eyes wide, and then a ragged breath escaped from his mouth, and his body sank down into the bed, staring sightlessly at the ceiling.

"Oleg," Nicholas murmured. "Greet Johanna and my son. Tell them I think of them often, even still." With that, he reached up his hand and closed the man's eyes.

I wiped a tear from my eyes. I hadn't really known Oleg at all, but I still felt sad at his passing. "I'm sorry, Nicholas."

"Don't be. I shall miss him dearly, but he won't miss me. Time does not pass in eternity. One day he'll turn around, and I shall be there with him, and it will seem like we've never been apart." He sighed. "I look forward to that day."

"Do you think it ever will come for you?"

He rose and ushered me toward the door. "Everything comes to an end eventually. This world and all that is in it shall one day burn with fire, and we will all appear before the judgment seat of God. Even I. Even," he opened the door and we stepped into the hall, "even if I should walk this earth for another thousand years."

"Such a long time."

"I've been around for seventeen centuries, Brett. I've learned patience."

"In your vision, your wife said you could come home at any time."

"So I could."

"So why stay?"

He clasped his hands behind his back as we walked. "Saint Paul once faced this question. In his letter to the church at Philippi, he talked about the desire to go and be with the Lord, and yet the urgency of his ministry among believers compelled him to stay, for it was more necessary for their sakes. I suppose that's why I stay. For them," he gestured down the hall, "my followers. My ministry."

"Surely it could go on without you."

"So it could. And the myth will endure no matter what I do, nor what steps should be taken to correct it. Yet I find joy in what we do. Especially now. We are secure, here, in our anonymity. The world will not believe any longer that I actually exist. The myth has accomplished that much, at least. I like giving, Brett. True, I face loss as I always have, but for the first time in my long history, we actually have an opportunity to serve the whole world. It is my view from the top, and it is spectacular."

We'd reached the foyer where Brother Don had first welcomed me inside, and there Nicholas offered me his hand.

"Thank you," he said, "for listening to my story. It is late, you are welcome to stay, of course."

I opened my mouth to accept his offer, then thought better of it. "No, that's all right. I have a hotel room back in Hammerfast. Marshall will want an update, as well."

"And what will you tell him?"

I shook my head. "I have no idea."

The journey back to "civilization" took less time than it had to find the monastery. I had a room waiting at a Thon hotel in town. The modern lines and accoutrements felt oddly foreign when I checked in. The room with its oversized bed, the table, dresser, and the chairs all seemed wrong, even though they looked just like every other motel or hotel room I'd stayed in all over the world.

I set my bag on the bed and my notes on the desk, then withdrew my laptop computer and fired it up. After connecting to the WiFi, I opened my Skype account.

And did nothing.

I sat there and stared at the screen. My finger hovered above the button that would connect the call. I should call. Marshall would be waiting. Expecting to hear from me.

But what would he hear? What could I possibly tell him about this wild-goose chase of a story he'd sent me on?

As a journalist, I have a duty to the truth.

But what was the truth?

Undecided, I closed the lid to the laptop, turned down the lights, the bed, and slipped beneath the covers.

As tired as I was, it was a long time before I fell asleep.

The next morning I fared no better, and all the long flight home, the laptop stayed closed in front of me. Normally, I'd have had most of the story written by now, ready to bring to Marshall for the few finishing touches a good editor could provide.

But I was utterly at a loss.

When the plane descended into LaGuardia, I felt a twisting in my gut. It was the same feeling I got when I had to fly into war zones, but without the glib anticipation of a waiting story. It felt like New York and my home no longer belonged to me.

I wondered if I'd ever belong anywhere again.

*What is the truth? What do I believe?*

That's when I realized, for the first time in my self-assured, self-aggrandizing life, I had no answers. How could I, when I had just spent the previous day recording the life story of a man who'd spent the past seventeen centuries doing nothing more than giving of himself in service to others? Which was more impossible to believe, that a man could endure that long on earth, or that anyone could be so selfless?

New York was decorated for Christmas, and a dank chill brooded over the city. I'd just come from a region far colder, but somehow it didn't affect me the way the city did. In Norway, the cold came with the smell of spices, of cinnamon and mint and pine. Here it was exhaust fumes and sewer vents. Crowds passed by me on the streets. None of us met each other's eyes in classic New York fashion. I passed by a homeless person on the street, and then stopped, my heart thudding in my chest.

What would Nicholas do?

I took the money out of my wallet and tucked it into my pocket, and then took off my coat and handed it to him. "Here," I said. "Merry Christmas."

"Uh, thanks, Buddy," the bum replied. "Merry Christmas to you, too."

I shoved my hands in the front pockets of my jeans and trudged the rest of the way to the office. The kindness had warmed me, but only a little bit.

*What do I believe? What is the truth?*

The questions continued to swirl in my mind even as I waited outside of Marshall's office. When he finally opened the door and called me inside, I had no answers.

"Well?"

I collapsed into the seat before his desk and threw up my hands. "I don't know what to write."

He'd sat on the edge of the desk, and now stared at me over his glasses. He raised an eyebrow, and then scratched his forehead. "You wanna tell me what that's supposed to mean?"

"Means I don't know how to tell this story."

"You're a reporter, ain'tcha? You report the facts."

"Well, I don't know what they are."

"Then what the hell you been doing up there? You telling me I spend all that money on international flights and a hotel room, and my star reporter comes back with bupkiss?"

I shook my head. "No."

"Then what?"

"I got too much, that's what."

"Too much." Miles had an annoying habit of repeating me back to myself. He took his seat and rested his elbows on the desk. "So, we talking about a series of articles?"

"The Abbot at the monastery—he's not who you think he is."

"So who is he?"

"He is Nicholas of Myra."

"Myra? Where's that at?"

And now things got dicey.

# Twenty-Seven

"It used to be on the southern coast of Turkey."

"Used to be?"

"Seventeen centuries ago."

"Wha—?"

"The man you sent me to interview told me his life story. And he has been alive for seventeen hundred years. Yeah," I pointed at his slack jaw, "that look? Right there? That's where I'm at."

Marshall stared at me, then leaned back in his chair. He glanced out his window at the city below, as if trying to ensure he was still on planet earth. "So he's crazy."

"No."

"But he thinks he's been alive for seventeen hundred years."

"He says he's immortal. He was killed in prison by the Romans and raised to life again by Jesus. And he's been walking around ever since."

He started laughing, shaking his head. "Wow. I guess they don't always work out, do they?"

"No."

"Yeah, there's no way we could print that. Owners are gonna be disappointed."

"I suppose."

He rose and sauntered over to the cappuccino machine, offering me a cup. I nodded. "For what it's worth," I said, "he didn't want his story told anyway."

"Really? Not going for his fifteen minutes, huh?" He measured out the espresso.

"He's already got it."

"How's that?"

"Nicholas of Myra is known the world over. Recognized by both the Orthodox and Catholic communions as a saint. Even the Protestants call him such."

He straightened with the milk still in hand. "*Saint* Nicholas?"

I nodded.

He finished the cappuccinos and brought mine over to me. "As in Santa Claus?"

"He really hates that term."

He chuckled as he took his seat. "I'll bet."

"The thing is, he had an actual explanation for just about every part of the legend. The sleigh, reindeer, red suit, elves. You name it." Briefly, I filled him in on what I'd learned.

When I finished he'd folded his hands together and propped his elbows on the desk, resting his chin on his fingers. "Wow."

"You know, if it weren't for the whole undead thing, I'd find every explanation he gave entirely plausible."

"You almost sound like you believe him."

"He was probably the most gentle, devout, and sincere person I've ever met. I think the only thing that troubled him was that we would publish his story, and then there'd be nowhere left for him to go. Tourists and the curious would overrun their monastery and effectively shut down their ministry."

"Right. 'Cause of course everyone would believe what we wrote." He took his pen from his ear and tapped it on his desk. "You know what? Screw it. Write the article. We'll title it, 'I'm not Santa Claus: An Exclusive Interview With Saint Nicholas' and we won't give away the location or the name of the monastery. Just that it was, at one time, magnetic north. That should be general enough. The rest of it? We tell his tale. His way."

"You think people will actually believe it?"

He shrugged. "So what? It's Christmas. It's a fresh take. It'll get people thinking about the... spiritual aspects of the holiday. People love bashing commercialism anyway. Especially while shopping. And it's bound to sell a few pape's. Thing is, people won't *believe* believe it, but they'll want to believe it. And that's downright magical."

I nodded slowly. "I think I could do that."

"Then what are you sitting around for? Go! Write!"

I wrote up the story as Marshall instructed, and he was right.

*I'm Not Santa: An Exclusive Interview with Saint Nicholas* sold so many copies of the newspaper that week that we went into extra editions. On the web it became our most linked to and downloaded article. We had pingbacks from all over the world. Marshall was so excited he even pitched hiring back some employees to the new owners.

I was back on top, and I should have felt fantastic.

But I didn't.

Instead, I felt lower than the bums on the street that I kept giving money to, like I'd betrayed a trust that was given to me, told a secret that was never meant to be shared.

All manner of justifications played through my mind, everything from *I'm a reporter and this is my job* to *it was Oleg's last wish and I'm honoring his memory*.

But I couldn't shake the feeling that I'd sold out a friend.

And so that's how I found myself on Christmas Eve sitting in a bar on the lower east side, nursing a gin and tonic. I'd just put down my glass when two half-drunk ladies—a blonde and her brunette friend—turned to me on their stools. The blonde asked, "Hey, aren't you that reporter who made up that story 'bout Santa Claus?"

I grimaced. "If you read the article, you'll recall it was titled, *I'm Not Santa Claus.*"

"Right," she nodded.

The brunette came to her rescue. "I just wanted to say that

was a really neat story."

The two of them bobbed their heads, looking for a moment like they had springs for necks.

"Well, thank you." I tipped my glass to them.

"It was like, really deep, you know?" the blonde continued. "Spiritual without being...?" She turned to her friend.

"Religious."

"Sure," I replied.

"I'm a deeply spiritual person myself," the brunette offered.

I threw back the rest of my drink and stood. "I should go." I gave them a wink. "Don't wanna wind up on Santa's naughty list. It was nice talking to you."

Sure, I probably could've gone home with them both—or at least to a private room somewhere. But it was bad enough I'd shared Nicholas's secret for the sake of a story. Using it to get laid by a pair of half-drunk cougars just seemed a bit too low to fall.

As I exited the bar into the frozen night air, I felt a presence leave behind me. I barely had time to turn my head when a familiar voice said, "For the record, I don't keep a naughty list."

I spun, and the man in the overcoat beside me startled me. The face was unfamiliar, but the eyes gave him away. He'd shaved, I realized.

"Abbot Nicholas?"

"Nick is fine, Brett."

"What are you doing here?" I could barely suppress a grin.

"Looking for you, believe it or not."

I wanted to know why, but instead I asked, "How did you find me?"

He said, "I searched the skies for the darkest cloud in the city, and it was centered over you." When I didn't answer, he clapped my shoulder and started walking with me. "I spoke to your editor, hoping to reach you. He told me where to find you. Interesting fellow. Kept staring at me."

"Well. He knows the whole story," I answered, "not just the stuff we put in the article." He nodded, but I furrowed my brow. "Wait a second, what are you doing here? You didn't fly all this way just to see me, did you?"

"Not precisely. I came to see the owners of the *Uptown Free Press*."

"The *owners*?"

"Yes. Personal friends of mine."

I grimaced. *Should've known.* "That's a conflict of interest."

"It is, which is why it was vital that neither you nor Marshall knew of the connection."

"Still—!"

"Brett," he faced me, "we're not discussing an exposé on mayoral scandals or political machinations. It was a human-interest story for Christmas. Nothing more. And it did what it was intended to do."

"What was that?"

"Save your paper, of course. Eventually, they hope to bring back the jobs they had to phase out in the restructuring. And, naturally, there is the desire to reform the city that is their driving ambition."

I snorted.

"Don't scoff," he reprimanded. "Your recent article is proof that the city is receptive to positive stories."

"Yeah, but it's also Christmas. People expect sappy things this time of year."

"Sappy."

I stopped and stuttered, "I-I didn't mean—"

"Sappy. Is that what you think of my life?"

"No."

"But that's what you think of positive stories. Stories of triumph. Heroism. Hope. This is sappy."

I fidgeted. Something about Nicholas always made me uncomfortable. "I suppose not."

"Brett, if you have learned anything from my story, I would hope it is this, that true goodness is not easy nor simplistic, nor is it weak in the face of evil." He turned and we started walking again. "This is not my first trip to the city. I have been here many times—not as far back as its founding, of course, but still when it was young. I visited Thomas Nast after he drew those ridiculous depictions of me. He took almost as much convincing as you. My point is that I have observed both the influence of this city grow, as well as its concomitant cynicism. For many years I've yearned to find a way to reach down and touch its heart."

"Might as well caress a stone," I snorted.

"Hmm. Are you familiar with Ezekiel?"

I wracked my brain a moment, wondering if he was asking about a monk whose name I'd simply forgotten. Then I guessed he must've meant the Old Testament prophet. "Guy who saw the UFO?"

"Wheels."

"Right."

"I take it 'No.' There's a passage in Ezekiel where the Lord speaks through His prophet to His people. And He says, 'I will give you a new heart and put a new spirit in you; and I will remove your heart of stone and give you a heart of flesh.' That is my prayer for this city. It is also my prayer for you."

I felt that same nervous flutter again. "For me?"

"Of course. How could I not be praying for you? Do you think I don't know what my story has done to you?"

"Done to me? What do you mean?"

He half-smiled. "I have turned your world upside down. That is why instead of celebrating this Christmas Eve and rejoicing in the most successful article of your career you are here at a bar taking a drink and trying to dull the pain in your heart. The thing is you do believe me. You know my story is true and you believe it. And that terrifies you, because if my story is true, as you know it is, then so is the story of the One Who inspires and drives me—and to Him you must give an account. You must believe in Christ. That He is the Son of God. That He lived a sinless life, died in your place, was buried, and in three days rose again from the dead—and that one day He is coming to judge the living and the dead. You must believe on Him, because the eternal destiny of your soul hangs in the balance."

I stared at him, then, feeling as if the city and the skies above held their breath, waiting for me to say something. The questions I'd been asking myself earlier that week came flooding back with a vengeance. *What do I believe? What is the truth?*

And then it hit me. It was not a question of evidence, as if it had ever been. The evidence was all around. Staring me in the face. And he was right. It wasn't Nicholas that I had to give an answer to. It was God.

And I had a choice to make.

The End

# Author's Note

## Concerning Cloud Factories

Every parent who tells their children about Santa Claus must, at some point or another, confront the fact that their previously trusting and adorable children have turned into hard-nosed skeptics. In my case, this occurred just prior to the teen years, which in our family happened approximately seven years ago, which is also when the seeds of this novel were sown.

Prior to this time, I delighted in the way my children believed almost anything I told them. As a story-teller, I took particular glee in weaving strands of fact together, pointing to the most nebulous threads in evidence as proof that whatever tale I happened to be crafting in the moment was true. Among my favorite stories were the "cloud-factories." We encountered these frequently while driving along the highway, when my curious kids would point to some factory or industrial complex puffing out billowing plumes of white vapor and demand to know what that particular factory made. Thinking quickly, I answered, "Clouds."

"Clouds?" they wondered.

"Yes clouds. Those are cloud factories. See the clouds they're making? That's what they do."

"But Da-ad! Doesn't *God* make the clouds?" my oldest queried. Ah, the Divine trump card, and played so quickly, too!

"Of course He does," I answered. "But these factories are built so man could help God. It's not that He needs our help, but He wants us to join Him in what He does. That's why we have cloud-factories."

Oh. *Cloud-factories.* That explained everything.

My children exposed similar vulnerabilities when it came to getting them a treat from the local fast food joint—though this time my wife was the culprit. "Okay kids, now we're going to get a special treat. We're going to get some *tap* water!"

"Yay! *Tap* water!"

They bought that one for years.

I digress. About seven years ago, they began asking skeptical questions about Santa Claus. He couldn't possibly be real, could he?

My heart fell. They were too young to be so skeptical! I wasn't ready for them to stop believing. I needed their belief. That's where the magic was. If they stopped believing, then all the wondrous enchantment of childhood would evaporate too soon, leaving the damp autumn of the teenage years as a warning that the harsh winter of the empty nest was just over the horizon.

"Of course Santa is real," I answered. I knew something about Saint Nicholas, having written a Christmas sermon some years ago where I pointed out that the real Nicholas believed in the

Christ Child given on Christmas Day, and would not want to stand as a substitute for Him.

"But how could he be real?"

Reluctantly, I began to share with them the origins of Nicholas of Myra, pointing out that he was a bishop who loved the Lord. And as they continued to press in about the details, I would reply "That's what the legend says," as a way to evade queries about elves or delivering toys to millions in a magical sleigh overnight.

"But how could he still be alive?"

And that's when I brought up Christ's words to Martha at the tomb of her brother Lazarus. Of course Nicholas was still alive. He believed in Christ, and all who believe in Jesus and give their lives to Him are alive with Him even now, as the Scriptures say.

And from there, it was a short jump in my fertile imagination to the story you have just now read.

## Blending Fact and Fantasy

In developing *Nicholas*, I wanted to merge the story of the actual St. Nicholas with the legend of Santa Claus as we've come to know and love him here in the United States. Toward that end, I am indebted to the Saint Nicholas Center, at stnicholascenter.org. Most of the research I conducted for the origins of Nicholas was done through this site.

There is very little actual information available about the real

Saint Nicholas. Much of what has come down to us conflates Nicholas of Myra with Nicholas of Zion, another saint who followed after the original by about three hundred years. But given that these combinations are historical, I determined to keep them as far as this story is concerned. The names of Nicholas's parents come from this latter legend.

The legend of the man with three daughters is one of the oldest stories, and is said to be the origin of "stockings hung by the chimney with care." I retained it toward that end, though the names are made up. Nicholas is also supposed to have gone to Jerusalem on a pilgrimage, where he received his calling. The legend of him raising a man back to life is also quite old and original to Nicholas of Myra.

During the time of Nicholas' ministry as a bishop, it was not unheard of for bishops and priests to marry, though not common. I decided to make Johanna Nicholas's wife to answer the question of "Mrs. Claus." Such a marriage might have raised eyebrows back in the day, but there were no injunctions against it. I endeavored to express those concerns in the context of their brief romance.

The account of Nicholas in prison is real. He was imprisoned under Diocletian and Galerius, though he did not die as he did in my story. This was a plot device I employed to explain his longevity. When Nicholas came out he was hailed as a "Confessor" because he refused to recant his faith.

The story of Nicholas at the Council of Nicaea—especially the part where he boxes Arius's ears—is also true, and one of my personal favorites.

The other legends in Nicholas's life: calming a storm, providing grain during a famine, rescuing the three prisoners, the story of the three generals and many others are original to Nicholas as well, and I have endeavored to retain the names given to the other actors in these stories as well.

It is after he left and went north to the Black Sea in this tale that my own imagination took over—and quite honestly, this was a part of the biggest struggle I had, because there was so much I had to leave out. Truly, he was an amazing man, and someone I look forward to meeting in the resurrection. I hope you do, too.

Merry Christmas,
Michael J. Scott, 2015

# About the Author

Michael J. Scott is passionate about the Bible, the Declaration of Independence, and the United States Constitution. He is a lover of freedom and the rights of men, and is more interested in being truthful with a bias toward action than in being nice, but that does not mean he is unkind.

He writes fiction that doesn't shy away from hard questions or dicey situations. He treats his characters like real people with real flaws who sometimes do wrong and stupid things—especially when they're trying to do the right thing.

His interests range from the erosion of the American family, socio-political unrest in the U.S. that threatens to break into civil war, UFO's, adventures in Biblical and Christian archaeology, dystopias, sword and sorcery fantasy, to getting inside the mind of a serial killer.

# Other Works by Michael J. Scott

If you want more by Michael J. Scott, check out these other novels and series, available in print and online at Amazon.com and other retailers.

### Jefferson's Road:
*(These are political thrillers about the downfall of America and the beginnings of a second Civil War.)*

The Spirit of Resistance
Patriots and Tyrants
The Tree of Liberty
God And Country
A More Perfect Union – coming soon
We the People – coming soon

### Janelle Becker Books:
*(These are psychothrillers about a Special Agent with the FBI's Behavioral Analysis Unit who specializes in religious-based crimes.)*

The Coppersmith
Topheth
Puzzle – coming soon

### Jonathan Munro Adventures:
*(This is a Christian Action Adventure series with a focus on archaeology and ancient languages.)*

The Lost Scrolls
The Elixir of Life
The Music of the Spheres – coming soon

### New World Order:
*(A Young Adult Dystopian series about escaping an oppressive bureaucratic system of death.)*

<u>Turning</u>
Anarchy – coming soon

## The Dragon's Eye Cycle:
*(A "Sword and Sorcery" fantasy series about an ex-Sheriff who relies on forensics to investigate murders rather than relying on magick.)*

<u>Eye of Darkness</u>
The Blood-Eaters' Coven – coming soon

## Spilled Milk
*(An anti-hero thriller about father-turned- domestic terrorist who battles government corruption. Badly.)*

<u>Spilled Milk</u>
<u>A Glass Half-Empty</u>
A Glass Half-Full – coming soon

<u>Descent</u>
*(A tale about alien abductions and government cover-up.)*

The Wizard of the Sky Pirates – coming soon
*(A teen story about—yup, you guessed it —wizards and sky pirates.)*

## The Issachar Initiative
(A series about a secretive agency that assists the government in addressing world events that have apocalyptic overtones.)

<u>Rock of Ages</u> – coming soon


Connect with Michael J. Scott online at:

Facebook
Twitter: @AuthorMichaelJS
MichaelJScottBooks.com

355

Made in the USA
Middletown, DE
01 September 2019